NOVEL

Vaughan Rapatahana

Novel published by Rangitawa Publishing, Feilding,
New Zealand 2018.

ISBN 978-0-9951046-6-2

www.rangitawapublishing.com
rangitawa@xtra.co.nz

Cover design and all art work Pauline Canlas Wu

Disclaimer.

This is a work of fiction. Names, characters, organisations,
places, events, locales, and incidents are either the products of
the author's imagination or used in a fictitious manner. Any
resemblance to actual persons, living or dead, or actual events
is purely coincidental.

Dedication.

For Blake.

Me tangi, ka pā ko te mate i te marama – let us weep, for his is
not the death of the moon.

LOCATION KEY:		
1. Aotearoa New Zealand		
2. Hong Kong Special Administrative Region		
3. Republic of Philippines		
4. Philippine Sea		
5. Peoples' Republic of China (aka Mainland China)		
6. Marianas		
7. Okinawa		
8. Laos		

Afterword: Marianas

"Christ Jesus – it cannot be him," was her first reaction when she snapped to a sit after her dream. "No," she shook her head. "That's impossible."

As she lay back, basking in the surreal sun baking down on the sparse, mingled tribe of Japanese and Chinese sunbathers bedded on Tumon Beach in Guam, Ruby then began to think of the past few months and the events which had led to her coming over to Agana and staying there. She was thankful that finally she not only had some peace and quiet, but also a measure of safety and security, staying as she was now with her extended family and working for them part-time in their bakery store.

She long since had had enough of Filipino men, lazy *lelaki* as she used to call them – that or *tambays* as in 'standbys'. She had consciously - after several unhappy encounters with her fellow countrymen, where she had been expected to be mother, breadwinner, housewife, sex slave - made a more conscious effort to live alone for a while, with her two children in Hong Kong.

Actually, she further reflected, she had had enough of most men by that stage anyway, especially after that quite disastrous marriage with that Chinese cook, turned even more sour.

Later, as the sun continued to trawl the sky, she reflected that *putih or* Western men and Filipina often made for a pretty stable relationship - more especially if the *putih* wasn't originally from the Philippines to start with. For Ruby, *putih* didn't necessarily mean they had to display seriously white skin, nor did they have to be fabulously wealthy – although that would have been nice – but, more, they tended to treat women better all around. Didn't view them as some sort of disposable appendage or accessory. Well, not so much.

So she had drifted into slightly less distraught relationships with a couple of *putih*; one claiming to have a Kenyan father somewhere. All of whom had indeed looked after her far better, but who also had a fair number of externally derived pressures and problems of their own. These exigencies had made any long-term serious relationship with them untenable.

Then again – and here she looked out across the wonderful warm waves pelting down onto the near-golden sand – there was no guarantee of any such thing as a perfect man anyway. Anytime. Anywhere.

Her last male friend was probably as close as she was ever going to come to finding anything approaching perfection. She wondered what he was doing now and if the jungles had gobbled him up just as he said he wanted them to do. What was it that he said about how he was usually treated by everyone? Something about being an 'escapegoat'. That he was going to 'fade away into the sunset', or something similar. Ruby smiled fondly, rolled over and now fully bared her back to the blasts from above.

In so doing she glanced up again and saw what looked like the naked black upper torso of that American doctor she had once lived with: his back to her, but with a distinctive tribal tattoo emblazoned across his left shoulder. Yet, she had been assured by the photo in his obituary in the *Northern Pacific Daily News* last month, that it could not be him. It was impossible, of course, but she squinted anyway, just as the man paddled in the low range waves and the Koreans rafted on their huge inflatable fish slightly beyond him.

"Christ Jesus"' she mulled again, just as she was sinking once more into a full-on doze, "These Americanos are everywhere. Just can't seem to get rid of them. Even if they're dead."

And when she stirred and scanned the beach, perhaps thirty minutes later, all she could sight were a small hoard of sun-screened, sun-glassed Taiwanese tourists following a tour guide, struggling under a huge flag twenty sizes bigger than him, with that curious Five Eyes Tours logo emblazoned all over it. They seemed to be heading to a parade of coaches, parked on the scrubby carpark underneath a haughty hotel.

Ruby lay back down into a full-on sleep; this time the extinguished man-ghosts of her past receding into the distance almost as soon as she closed her eyes.

Peace at last.

Part One: Aotearoa New Zealand

1.
It was stuck again.

His life never seemed to get out of first gear; always jammed somewhere in between stasis and impetus.

And the knife reflected his overall paralysis.

It was stuck again. He tried to rip it back out by twisting and turning and poking and prodding, but all to no avail. The flesh proved unwilling to play along.

Sweat bellowed along his brow. What if someone came in here now? Unlikely, true, but what if? He garnered more energy and ripped away, hoping like hell that this time he could free his blade and get the fuck out of there. Blood was now not only pumping out of the fissure, it was pounding around his temples in ever-increasing waves.

Suddenly he was free and fell backward onto the hard wooden cold floor. The knife cascaded further away, well beyond his reach, and he scrambled blindly around in ever-increasing spasms to grasp it. Speaking of tight fits – he was having them now.

He just had to stop this stabbing shit. Could get him into trouble, eh.

Outside there were not many people left in the plant. It was still broad daylight, but apart from a late shift of grey men with frosty faces, down in the freezer chambers, there was no one else much around. A few errant clerks and office crew who worked normal hours and a watchman out near the front gate, but everyone else had buggered off already. With their pilfered cuts of meat wrapped in stolen greaseproof paper sheets, ready to raffle them down at the Arms and Masters pub, or to take home for a *kai* that night.

He, however, had other things to do. He could just about feel the newly honed thin heft of his borrowed blade through his leathers, which he'd put on after showering all the blubbery fat and clotting spouts of dead crimson off himself, soon after leaving the cooling floor with the stiff dull white cadavers rammed in rows; left there as dumb sentries.

He had to get some measure of *utu*, eh, after that greasy little prick Trevor King had smashed the padlock on his locker, splintered half the fucking door, and ripped off his week's pay. It had been stashed in a gummy brown envelope, deep in the knife pouch, hanging on its cheap chain from the nail he'd coerced into the back wall. A pouch stashed well beneath his overalls and high above his lumbering thick-soled boots, that had always been too bloody big for him since he started there all those years ago.

He utu reka, nē rā.

He spat bilious into the dandelion scurf on his way to the train. The pace of his synapses blurting out quicker than the scuff of his jandals, as he sought out the platform.

The lumbering train shunted in - late, as per usual – and he clambered on board and stuffed himself into one of its ancient caste-iron seats. Almost as if they had been made sometime in the last century. The carriage smelled rank, as though a league of pissheads had practised there recently. So, he tried to ram up the reluctant window to let in some aura of air.

Not much luck there either, for the wafts that slinked in through the miniscule gap he had succeeded in prying, were merely the smells of the dead animals he had just left. And stabbed.

Norton slumped further into the upright rigidity the seat beckoned and tried to snooze until he reached his far suburban stop, way down the line. Images of blood and sputum and more blood ranged liberally through his forebrain, as he continued his ruminations regarding revenge.

Part Two: Hong Kong

2.

Godfrey Woo didn't feel so good these past few days. He'd had a hell of a headache ever since his last few bets had been eaten up at the Hong Kong Jockey Club and his latest mistress, Kwok Li, up in Shenzhen, had threatened to finally leave him unless he brought her over to Kowloon very soon. He hadn't wanted to try and go back to his Filipino wife and their two kids out in the North West New Territories, because he had so many bills – financial and emotional – and his ledger would never balance ever again. That was no option either. His elderly mother and his two stone-faced sisters hated him, he knew. Everything had turned to shit for Godfrey and deep, deep down within he knew he had done it all to himself.

The triads were also after him for his many unpaid bills at huge interest rates. They were mean bastards. Especially Ho Fat Kit, who was a known killer with the chopper. Woo could only keep on hiding and running and escaping.

Woo ran his sweaty fingers through his thinning hair; plastered black strands spread across from one side to the other over his big balding dome. Kwok Li had always said he looked a lot like Mao Tse-Tung. Godfrey Woo wasn't in the mood to think about that though. He hadn't smiled for months either.

He farted out the congee he'd scrambled down that morning at the cheap kitchenette and stumbled on down the alley to the scrappy motor parts shop, where he also scrambled out a living taking engines apart. Luckily, he did have some skill as a mechanic. It was about the only thing going for him these days.

His teeth ached too. He spat out a wad of sputum past their yellowing decay and wiped the remnant of the spit from his stubbly chin. He hadn't shaved for days.

Someone was waiting at the doors of the shop.

Woo couldn't quite discern from this distance who it might be – but they – whoever they were – seemed particularly small and short. Someone was actually more than one – more like three - and Woo thought he could just make out their tattoos from here, or maybe his eyes just hurt too much these days too.

He knew what that meant.

He started to run then. Real fast. As though his life depended on it – which, of course, it did. You didn't muck around with the Wo Sha Ni triad.

The dull side of the chopper blade – fortunately for him – just glanced his left shoulder, but had been thrown with such force that this would soon welter up into an ugly purple bruise. It didn't slow Godfrey Woo one iota, or even two – in fact it only made him run even faster. Fortunately he was a tall man with legs like tent centre poles, and he managed to avoid being captured and chopped. For now, at least.

He knew that only one man in Hong Kong could hurl a chopper that distance, that strongly and that savagely – Ho Fat Kit - and Woo sure as hell wasn't going to wait around to be sliced up by him.

It meant, however, he couldn't go back to the car bits and pieces shop ever again. Another door closed for good.

Woo sweated so much, he was almost a liquid pool on the pavement. And now his knees hurt worse than ever and his shins were completely out of tune with the rest of his body, which wasn't exactly thrumming with any sweet melody either.

What to do next? He couldn't even ring Kwok Li anymore either, because he still owed his stepson money. Even though her kid was only aged about six, Godfrey had already filched all of the savings put aside for him, promising he would, "pay you back soon."

Woo spat again, chewing his own lips like a ravenous dog.

What to do next?

Part Three: Philippines

3.

Romeo saw the *putih* approaching the Burger Machine cart from a long way away.
He swilled down another quaff of Fundador brandy straight and sneered at Louis –
"*Sino*?"

Louis didn't reply, as he was ogling a young woman on the other side of the
highway and was evading the cars and *jeepneys* with his eyes, scanning to see if
he could in fact spy her again.

"Who does he think he is, the fuck?" Romeo took offence that the Westerner
seemed to be happy, walking hand-in-hand with a local girl, smiling – and this is
what really annoyed Romeo – he wasn't wearing any shirt or even a singlet to
cover his multicoloured tattoos.

The *putih* and his woman friend strolled across the road with a certain nonchalance
and approached the burger cart from the other side. Behind them the cars and
bikes and trucks were scuttling past in one continuous sigh.

They had started to order, and Romeo was sure the *putih* was talking in Tagalog –
which only served to piss him off even more: he didn't really know why.

"Hey – you - put your shirt on here!" he snarled, surprising himself with his own
anger. His drunken tongue had started to curl under his lips, and he had to make a
real effort to force out his suffocating words. "What do you think you are doing?"

Upstairs, the sun had neglected to tell night to stay away and day was quickly
disintegrating into twilight. The man only smiled and ignored Romeo as he ordered
two double cheeseburgers and waited with his girlfriend. She also seemed
uninterested in the sprawling verbiage sprouting from the other side of the cart.

Romeo tried to escape his high stool but stumbled and had to wrench his hands
back on the metal counter to stop himself from cascading into the gravel

surrounds. Louis was smiling, but Romeo wasn't too sure as at what.

By now, the *putih* had already grabbed the food and was walking off back down into the *barangay*, after waiting patiently for the traffic to desist just a bit, so as to manage to avoid getting hit. It looked like his girlfriend had told him to walk fast and to say nothing.

She must have had sort of a second sight, because as they were nearly at the other side – over there by the broken cement paving – an empty bottle of Fundador smashed violently into the wall directly in front of them, missing the *putih* by about six inches.

Then it was night and Romeo couldn't really see them no more. Besides, Louis was castigating him, "What will we drink now, man?"

Romeo turned his bloodshot eyes to his *kaibigan* and merely spat, "Wash nomaw lef anyway."

The *putih* had strolled back down J. Pintella lane, deep into the *barangay,* munching on the cheese and beef burgers and holding his Filipino girlfriend's hand like a winning lucky dip lottery ticket.

Ruby wasn't particularly worried about what had just happened.

She knew the Doctor was a crazy old bastard, and she knew he still had the service revolver hidden out back in her Mother's outside toilet.

He didn't take any shit whatsoever – not from her, not from anyone. Especially not from her drunken cousin Romeo, who should have known better and who would wake up tomorrow with a headache to die for.

Doctor Cross frequently came back to Pampanga and not just because he had invested so much into the house there.

He came back to relax and soak up the continuous sun and to relax a bit more.

Here he did not have to bother about anything much and didn't have to dress up or splatter small-talk bullshit with workmates.

Here he could be himself, whoever that was.

Here he could shoot into the air at weekends for no clear reason and sleep all damned day if he felt like it.

And his mother-in-law always fed them good too.

Except for tonight, when he had had a craving for Burger Machine burgers.

He pushed open the gate door to let them both back inside the enclosure, when the sound came.

It started off low and steadily grew real loud, until both of them found themselves staring at each other.

Just as they both opened their mouths to ask, what the hell it was, it stopped.

Doctor shrugged as if to say, 'fuck it, let's just go inside to the aircon', and indeed had already turned the front door handle, when the noise shot back at them. Louder and more urgent than before.

The door didn't need him to open it because Mrs Tuazon had arrived in the front yard with a handful of dry clothes ready to fold traipsing behind her, and a mouth wide-open, querulous. Her daughter and she exchanged big-eyed glances at each other, while the noise slowly spiralled back down into a dull thumping whisper.

"What is that?" It could only be the Doctor talking, because mother and daughter already knew. Especially because the dark had by now finally invited itself in, uninvited. There was no moon and only a couple of reluctant streetlamps flickering their sorrows further down the lane.

"Better we go inside, now," said Ruby, 'I'll tell you in there.'

4/1

Makere woke up with a brutal headache. Too much wine the night before, made worse by the fact she had ended up drinking alone, if you didn't count the ever-babbling television locked onto the Māori TV channel. Her young daughters had gone back to their own flat around midnight, by which time she was pretty plastered anyway.

'Night, mum,' she seemed to recall them saying, "We kicked out your cat already, eh, ha ha ha."

She must have put herself to bed sometime later, but she hadn't done a very good job with herself. Still in her work clothes. Hadn't showered. Had only eaten the junk food one of the girls had brought home from their stint at Burger King.

Later, in the shower, she remembered that the three of them had got stuck into their husband-father, big time. It had gotten so heated there for a while, that she had caught herself defending her ex. Which now surprised her, as the force of the water blast whacked out her dopiness.

"Oh, c'mon girls," she now recalled stating, "Norton wasn't always that bad, eh. He did love you and he always tried his best to care for you."

As she dried herself in front of the cracked bathroom mirror, Makere daydreamed a bit too. It was a pity for them all, that Norton had somehow, somewhere got waylaid. Drifted into a sort of gully. Lost his own plot, she mused. He didn't seem to have the zing he used to have and never seemed especially motivated to do much except go to work, come home, sleep. He never now read a newspaper, let alone any books.

"You're not the man, you used to be," she remembered saying to him – on more than one occasion - before he had finally moved out a few months before.

The mobile phone was ringing its nuts off. She neutered it, by picking it up and saying, "*Kia ora.*"

Seemed there was to be another *Tino Rangatiratanga hui* the next weekend. At least that was what her half-brother, Trevor was mumbling at her.

"Yeah, yeah," I'll be there, she replied, while the clock was winking down at her and telling her she better get to work soon, eh.

She nearly killed the cat as she sped out the back door into the carport. It must have been waiting for its breakfast or a chat or something.

Pity, wasn't going to get any of either right then.

Makere was running late.

And Trevor had wanted to know about the guns too.

The funny thing was that they found Trevor King's body stuffed into a slaughterhouse locker a couple of days later – and it was, of course - because of the smell that was so obscene that it overran even the usual foul stench of death and decay in the Meatworks. Long after the mutton chain had ceased for the afternoon. He had an idiotic grin on his face, which was strange, because he must have died in agony with that bloody sharp boning knife leaving a crevasse where his throat had been. And Trevor King hardly ever smiled – unless it was because he had scored some money underhand. From a Pākehā, preferably.

Norton didn't hear about all this 'til much later. Because on going to his ex's home that night, after a bit of a session at the Arms and Masters pub, he had been questioned about other things, after Makere had called the cops because he threatened to 'whack the shit out of her' for spending his non-existent money at the local wholesalers. That's what oh-so-easy-to-get credit cards can do to you, eh. She had kept her own copies after their split-up.

He never had any intention to whack her either, and in fact never had, although he'd come damnably close a few times, but it was the tone of his voice and the tautness of his posture that scared her more than a little this time around. And when he got all argumentative with the fresh-faced constables, they had decided to take him away for a while, just to settle things down a bit. So really, he shouldn't have smashed the younger one on the back of the head. Meant he was thrown into a cell and would not be going anywhere for a few days now.

Fuck – how he hated these bloody cells. They all smelled heinously of urine, like someone had been pissing there every night for 100 years. The walls were a wallpaper of graffiti scratched into the actual concrete somehow, almost as if some poor bastards had had to scribble themselves into existence. Norton knew that throwing a man in there was meant to break him, flatten him, expunge him. Shit – the smell alone did that enough anyway.

Over in the corner, cockroaches were sneering at him big time.

If he could have slept somehow he would have, but these places weren't exactly designed to develop sweet dreams in.

He heard about the murder a bit later on when some rotund Detective Sergeant came into the adjoining interview room and asked him, if he knew Trevor King?

"Yeah"

"When did you last see him…?"

"Cuppla days ago, why?"

"They found him stuck in a meat locker at the Works this afternoon. Dead as. Been like that a fair while too."

Norton went into a paroxysm of laughter. The thought of an overweight Trevor King being stuck into a smallish locker at the Works was just too much, maaaaan.

"How did he die?"

"We thought you might have an idea actually…"

Norton shut up real quick then.

He knew he'd probably be pinned with a charge for something he hadn't done, because that had happened previously – though he had to admit he'd thought about killing King a few times.

"Mr. Norton. I asked you if you might know something about how Trevor King – who we know you used to work with on the mutton chain – got stuffed into a locker in the same locker-room you shared?" The fat D preened his hair a bit before coughing violently. "Any ideas, Mr. Norton? We also hear that you and Mr. King were not exactly the best of friends…"

Norton couldn't help but guffaw. "I dunno, but he sure as hell is stuffed now all right eh."

Fatso wasn't so happy with this riposte and sneered like a jackal, his teeth sharp against the crappy light ploughing the ceiling of the stinky and skanky cell chambers.

'Whoops,' flickered Norton's brain streetlights, 'I think he's playing the bad cop. *He poaka mōmona, nē rā.*

Indeed Fatso soon whacked Norton across the kidneys with a rolled-up *New Zealand Star* – which really hurt more than any other newspaper in the land, it being so bloody thick and deadly in the wrong hands.

Norton went down like the proverbial ton of bricks.

He woke up a bit later with some other cop shining a torch deep into his eye abyss. He knew he was back in that bloody cell as soon as he realized what his nostrils were telling him. His back was really complaining and throbbing, and irritating him to the point that he was going to kill Fatso when he finally got out of there. Didn't matter that the street code was 'Never kill a Pig, man'. His head hurt bad too, after that mighty smash the policeman had also administered to it.

'Bugger it' he thought – 'that fat prick just gotta die.' Norton started to compose further ways of killing, as his brain slowly slunk back into sleep, when he slumped down into the thin stained squab that was to be his bed that day anyway. At least until Monaghan came and got him out of this urinal set in stone.

Monaghan had been a schoolmate of Norton's hundreds of years before – or at least it seemed that long ago. He was also a pretty good lawyer, who had helped out Norton a few times in the past.

Plus they had both served some time overseas together. But that was just another whole big story.

Monaghan merely shook his head.

It wasn't going to be so easy this time.

The cops had seemed pretty resolved that they, 'had their man'; that Norton had killed Trevor King – somehow – and that even bail would be a difficult option, let alone getting off the charge.

"Are you going to charge my client?" He asked the rather rotund detective with the ruddy face, who was squinting at some paperwork under the naked neon lights in the station. "As you know, he cannot be held without charge for more than 24 hours."

The fat detective just squinted some more. Finally, he placed the paperwork on the desk and sneered, "He's free to go – at this stage. My advice is that he remain in town and be prepared to come back in at any time."

With that, he shifted sideways into an alcove and began peering out through the twisted slats of the dirty Venetian blinds, which shrouded the station like unwanted dinner guests.

Monaghan went down to the cells and passed on the news to Norton, who smiled a bit as he slowly got up off the thin, low-slung bed.

As they went their separate ways outside, Monaghan had to ask, "Is there anything that you want to tell me about any of this? Is there anything I need to know?"

Norton looked at him bluntly and said – just as straight-up, "Nothing." He then seemed to relent a bit as he added, "I know nothing about this shit – man, I was in the pub, eh." With that he just walked away into the cascading shadows, leaving Monaghan staring after him for a bit, before he too went out of sight around the next corner.

The fat detective was still scanning from the high window, rubbing the side of his spread nose with a sweaty finger or two.

5/2.

Godfrey Woo was hiding in the cubicle of his half-brother, who didn't even know he was there. It was only about 20 square feet and partitioned off from several other makeshift rooms in this subdivided poor man's hell-hole. A veritable cage home spinney deep in what was supposed to be one of the richest places on Earth, Hong Kong.

It smelled of stale shit and dead fish and rotten cabbage all around the skinny bed that folded out from the wall and was held only by a rusty chain. Woo lay under there a long time, because he wanted to ensure his trackers couldn't find him – and because he also knew his brother wouldn't be back until the small hours of night, as he worked on a shift basis and always grabbed any extra hours that might be asked of him.

Woo had once borrowed the key to the cubicle and had it copied. His brother Kah Kay did not know this. That was how Woo worked – via subterfuge and cunning and cowardice. Only, it all seemed to be catching up with him more and more these last few weeks.

Woo belched into the torpidity and picked his nose, while he wondered where he could sidle off to this time. Places to escape to were becoming thin on the ground – a bit like the hairs on his increasingly exposed scalp.

And he was hungry – again. He started to bite his nicotine-orange fingernails as a sort of sop to his stomach, because he had no cigarettes left, or maybe he had dropped the last couple of butts when he ran away earlier.

It wasn't until he heard somebody banging on the thin particleboard partition walls and the sound of rats scuttling, that he woke up fully and scratched his scrotum and knew he had to keep on moving.

Right now.

6/3.

Ruby was combing her long hair out back, where the clay ran into the scattered shingle pieces. Her mother was squeezing out the laundry and getting ready to hang more clothes on the taut line stretched across the yard. The sun was not benevolent, in fact it was downright nasty that morning, as it twisted and fretted the sky until it attained complete mastery.

"*Kailan balik?*" her mother was asking, as she stretched a little to peg up the Doctor's pants.

"*Hindi ko alam,*" answered Ruby, not really caring too much when they would leave Pampanga and go back to Hong Kong. Life with the Doctor was O.K. at times, given their age gap and the fact that he was *putih*. At least he paid all the bills, and more. There was money to buy food, a luxury Ruby had not always had when growing up in Pampanga, as she remembered sometimes eating only rice with a bit of soy sauce for her dinner. Cross also never seemed to be in any particular hurry to do anything – he always seemed to have a sense of presence.

Ruby's mother rarely talked at the best of times, and said no more then.

She hadn't said much the night before either, when Cross had pushed Ruby for more information about the weird noise at the front gate.

Cross heard his mother-in-law and his de facto wife talking real fast in Kapampangan, which he couldn't speak.

All Ruby had said was something about *asuwang.*

Doctor Cross had gone to bed early that afternoon after drinking too many sweet bottles of Tanduay Ice. The last thing he had remembered seeing outside the locked gate before they had come inside the house, into some semblance of coolness, was a pack of black dogs sniffing around on the other side of their lane. Then he was snoring.

It was now quite late, yet the heat had only got more intense.

Ruby went into the living room and sat down, waiting for him to wake.

She did wonder, however, when he might go back to Manila, "for a few days to catch up on some business", as he had tended to do more and more of late.

7/1.

Back in South Auckland, Norton had a hell of a lot of explaining to do to his ex-wife, Makere, because he'd been away from her home for a few days and was only now out on bail. Through Monaghan's efforts on his behalf.

Not just because he'd threatened to whack her the last time he saw her.

Not just because he'd hit out at a fresh-faced police constable, who looked about fourteen.

Not just because he had been supposed to go to her house then to, 'finally pick up all of your shit' either - and still hadn't.

No – not because of all this. But, because he'd been splashed all over the front page of the newspapers, in stories about Trevor King. Norton' name and photos of him leaving the cop shop were everywhere - on newspaper sandwich boards, on newspaper boys' sandwich chomping lips, on the tongues of all the chatty stay-at-home-because–they-were-so-fucking-lazy neighbours. Indeed, everywhere – as though there was a vast polyglottal conspiracy organized to connate Norton's name with King's death.

And it didn't help that Trevor King and Norton's ex-wife were brother and sister – or at least that they had the same father – a disreputable old rogue with *ngutu* lips and swayback hair who only came to see Makere when he smelled money growing. Maaan, he could sniff it out from miles away too.

So, Makere berated Norton for quite some time before she even let him come inside. While outside, the Warehouse lacy curtains were all too obvious in their chorus of open-mouthed staring, pulled aside as they were, at the neighbour's dirty windows.

Makere felt like saying, 'fuck off,' to her ex-husband, but realized he had at least made sure their teenage kids had some pingers to buy groceries and had at least rung her once from the cell block, during his absence. And he had still to actually ever hit her with more than a *kihi* or two when he had felt amorous after too much alcohol. She didn't really think her husband of twenty-five years would have killed her brother. She didn't think he could kill anyone, actually. Mind you, she didn't know much about his years before they met.

Still, he may have changed a lot in the several months they had been living apart, eh.

It meant that things were a bit more than strained at the little house down the long shifty driveway. Makere and Norton sort of spent a fair bit of time side-stepping any issue of who had killed Trevor King and a fair bit of time feinting here and there about anything too serious whatsoever. But, Makere's bottom line was this, something she had to repeat several times, "please take all of your crap out of my house. Now!"

Yet they would both have to go to the *tangi*. Together too. Had to be seen together and had to attend. No excuses. All the *kuia* back home didn't know that they had split up.

Norton had to go into the Works and explain all this and apply for some leave of absence. Lucky for him – again – they let him go, with his job still intact.

Hey – he had been a pretty exemplary knife-hand for years there and hadn't caused much, if any, bother. Not as much as that fat little prick, Trevor King, anyway.

So bereaved ex-husband and his ex-wife got into their car together, still pretty quiet like, and set off for the *urupā* way down south.

Makere only really said one thing at the start of their journey, "You just watch your mouth down there, eh. Some of those fellas don't need any excuses to deal to you."

Norton steered the car down the replica creek-bed driveway and stared at her. He didn't say anything for a long time either. Only, "I hope the kids are O.K. with Nana going around. They should have come with us actually."

Nana Norton didn't mind checking on her *mokopuna* sometimes – not every bloody time though. They were good kids, but she was getting old these days and liked to be by herself. Still, what could she do – her son was a suspect in the murder of his brother-in-law, the brother of her own daughter-in-law.

And Makere was a relative anyway; Nana Norton's mother and Makere's grandmother were first cousins.

So maybe Norton had killed his own blood. A particularly bad thing to do.

They drove on in silence and then the rain started to *hōhā* them and to tongue-lash their journey for a while.

It was only after the squall lifted that Norton swore that he could see a police car right behind them. Following them, "right up our bloody arse, "as he muttered to no one in particular.

Norton was pretty sure it was the fat cop sitting in the passenger's seat too.

Makere just slunk lower into her seat and pulled the blanket tight round her shoulders. 'Fuck, what a mess this is turning into,' was the only thought she could muster, before she shot off to sleep. It was a long drive.

She had a funny dream about being put into a sack - and woke up wide-eyed when the top was being pulled tight around the top of her head. She glanced across at her ex-husband, who might as well have been an alien these days. He was off in some dream, by the look of him. Driving the car like he was a robot.

They parked up in the muddy field next to the other huge monoliths, twenty years out of date and using twenty times the amount of petrol than Japanese cars. No one left their vehicles in straight lines in pre-designated places there. A few stray dogs lurked around, pleading with their eyes for just a few scraps to wolf down.

The rain had lifted itself into a light drizzle and some pale imitation sun was bleating through the patrolling clouds. Familiar faces met up with them as they slouched toward the *whare moe* and Makere was recipient of bulk *hongi me kihi*. Norton got a few handshakes and a lot of hard stares. That was all.

They went over to see Trevor King laying outside on the verandah and, as Makere bent to kiss her brother, Norton shot a couple of glances at those standing around, to spot who was glaring at him. He recognized one or two who had come down from the Works and one or two others who were gang-patched comrades, who'd done a few jobs with Trevor King. Then there were *ngā kuia* sitting by the coffin, who were the ones to really worry about.

Still, *tangi* weren't the place to fight, eh. Bad *tapu*. Everyone knew this, so no aggro was going to go down on that day or two anyway.

Later, they all ate together and there was some semblance of civility between Norton and his ex-wife and Norton and his relatives. And her's.

Still, he couldn't help sensing undercurrents, an undertow. Like there was a plot to the story but no one could quite sus it out just yet. They all knew they had a role or two to play, but no one had gotten round to giving anyone a script, eh. Who was the bad guy? Who was the killer? Who was the sheriff? Who was the author and what were they on about anyway?

When he was about to fall asleep, much later – after a bit of chitchat with those who didn't know him, or who did but didn't care - Norton rolled over to see how Makere was. She was laying on her back on a mattress nearly a metre away from his, staring at the roof and the *tiki* were staring right back down at her.

"You didn't kill my brother, did you, Norton?"

"What do you think? Fuck, I didn't much like him, but I didn't touch him. You know me."

It didn't matter what he said anyway, because Makere was already asleep, dreaming to some purpose.

In the middle of the night, Makere woke up sharp. Same dream. Someone was doing bad things to her. She didn't quite pick the person, but knew it was a male. And white. *He pākehā, nē rā.*

He seemed somehow familiar too.

8/3.

Ruby heard her mother out in the kitchen and got up to join her. She had a quick glance at the Doctor, who was sound asleep and snoring his way through the early dawn.

She quickly closed the door and went to see her mother, who was already cooking food for the entire upcoming day.

Mother rarely slept beyond five in the morning. She seemed to get by without too much sleep anyway. Acquilina liked to keep busy.

They talked of Ruby's brother who had been living overseas for many years and whether he would ever come back to Pampanga. They talked also about other family members and their problems and peculiarities.

Ruby's mother mentioned that Romeo had been arrested quite recently for arson. Seems he had gotten sodden on rum and set fire to a small *sari-sari* store, owned by someone he had had bad dealings with in the past. Lucky for Romeo he hadn't done any real damage, as the fire had died down very quickly. Still, he had to stay in jail for a month. Seemed to have made him even more crazy. And made him drink even more – if that were even possible.

Ruby reflected that Romeo had actually once been quite a good student at their local elementary school just down the main highway. He just started to go awry once his father moved off overseas to earn more money to send back home, but then never came back to his family to live. Romeo later learned that he had a few half-siblings, while the money dried up, and then his own mother had died.

"Only in the Philippines, eh Ma?" she said, "only in the Philippines." Though her mother rarely spoke English and had to leave school very young, so as to earn money for her impoverished family, she certainly understood what that meant.

The sun was in full force by now and sending its armed guards to search every crevice in their small kitchen. The fans did their best to fight them with their skinny blades, but this just wasn't enough to prevent heat winning the day. All the doors and windows were open for some semblance of breeze, but it was always too damned hot there, especially in this hollow where their home lay. They just couldn't afford to consistently run the puny air conditioner, even with the Doctor's wallet contributing.

Ruby wondered how her mother could stand this every day, all day. 'Stoic.' That was the word the Doctor had used. Yes, stoic. Pretty much summed up the situation in Pampanga. If you weren't stoic, you died. Or went mad. Or went overseas, if you could.

9/2.

Godfrey Woo didn't really want to end up sucking other men's cocks in dirty toilets, but in the end that was all he could do to survive. He hadn't deliberately gone to the old wooden building in Sham Shui Po with sex in mind, but when the *gaylo* had followed him into the cubicle where he had gone to sleep in desperation of finding anywhere else to reside, and when the *gaylo* had offered him $500 for a blow job, well Woo didn't hesitate too long. He just couldn't afford not to.

And he was permanently hungry.

So it started. He found himself now able to recognize who wanted what and for how long. He actually became quite proficient in his craft. His trade. Call it what you will. He rationalized to himself that he was, 'no homo'.

After a while, he began planning just how much he would make and where and when. He was now living in a doss-house, where an old woman with severe facial scars dealt up something that could never be called food, but which filled the gnawing and gaping hole in his gut. He needed urgent dental work on his rotten and rotting teeth, but beggars could not be choosers. Just as his mother had always chanted at him endlessly when he had complained to her about always eating a plateful of rice and nothing else. Or about only having the one pair of short trousers that didn't have big holes around his arse. Or when he complained about having to go to the temple, light the incense and pray. Something he had long since stopped doing.

The main thing was that he remained well-hidden, deep in Kowloon somewhere. He mused that one day he would get out of all this mess, this deep debt stuff.

He just didn't know when.

Or how.

And it hadn't always been like this. He once had a lovely Filipino wife, two good-looking kids, a thriving business, a quite spacious apartment in Kwun Tong.

But he had fucked up. Big time. Firstly, the rampant gambling, then the mistresses. And more gambling to pay for them. A cycle that grew larger and larger in diameter, which he could not escape. Or so he rationalized. Woo knew deep within, however, he was lying to himself. To everyone around him. The circle could be broken.

He just wasn't sure how.

10/1.

Monaghan shrugged. He had seen and heard it all before anyway. Nothing much was new to him anymore and it would have to be something seismic to even gain his somewhat jaded attention nowadays. The detective sergeant was rattling on about, 'how they had enough evidence to charge Monaghan's client with the murder of Trevor King and that now was the chance for both lawyer and client to get together and plead guilty so as to save the taxpayer a lot of money.'

Monaghan knew that this was mere police procedure, bullshit intended to get some momentum into a case that had stalled somewhat because the cops just did not have enough evidence to charge anybody. Let alone his client Norton, who – as far as he knew – was still down country somewhere, grieving the very man he was supposed to have somehow stuffed into a locker room cabinet. After first slicing his throat with a butcher's knife. And then disposing of the selfsame blade elsewhere.

Monaghan and Fatso just played the game – both knew the rules here. The lawyer said the usual spiel in response to the usual drivel. The detective left the lawyer's office soon after, without obtaining any semblance of sanction, and the lawyer soon also left the office in search of something to eat. It was about lunchtime after all and Monaghan was getting sick of all this stylized crap.

He suddenly wished – right then and there – that he was back in Viet Nam doing something knife-edge dangerous or at least smoking ganga so good that his eyes would feel like they were bleeding into themselves. That had been the last time he had felt something like a man was supposed to feel like, or at least what his own father had said a man was. Everything since had been a watered-down pastiche.

He rubbed his disappearing hair and ordered the food, smiling at the same time at the last occasion he and Norton had been together as equals and not as a legal provider-legal supplicant duo.

Shit – that had been over thirty years ago…Monaghan went on with his technicolour daydream. The food went cold while waiting for him.

11/3.

Joey Rodriguez was a tricycle driver in Pampanga. He hated his job, but had no choice. Shit, at least he had a job – of sorts, for it meant snoozing much of the day away, every day, while waiting for a customer or two. If he was lucky.

Right now, he was about sixth in line at the top of the street by the broken-down traffic lights and he was laying half-in, half-out of his tricycle, semi-asleep waiting, just waiting. He hadn't had much business that day at all and he knew Maria would give him her screechy-voice-look if he came back to the hut with only a few *pesos*. She would thrust Ocean at him and say, 'Whach she gonna have to eat, you fat lump?' in her peculiar lisping throaty voice, which came out weird because of her broken front teeth. 'Whenya gonna get a real job and bea real man fur ya vamily?'

Joey was just starting to get into deep-snooze mode when someone banged on the tricycle frame. It was that *putih* from over the other side of the *barangay*, whom Joey had spied a couple of times before.

Joey smiled, like he always smiled around *putih*. He jumped into his bike seat better and started to pedal, even although the white guy – who, come to think of it, wasn't actually very white – wasn't completely in the carriage yet. And still hadn't even told him their destination.

Joey soon learned that he had to pedal to the far side of their *barangay* - and fuck it was hot. But hey – he kept smiling. Maybe he could take some sweets home for his little daughter after all.

The *putih* had on real dark sunglasses – the ones that menace you if you even look at them. He carried himself sort-of staunch too. And he had a few tattoos on his upper arms and back – not the sort you usually saw around there either. They were some tribal design, although Joey wouldn't have ever said that. To him, they were just crazy squiggles.

When they got outside the high-walled two-storey house, Doctor Cross – for it was him all right – threw Joey far more than the 30 pesos he had expected.

And as the Doctor lumbered over to the closed iron gates and was speaking on his mobile, the grin on Joey's young face just got a bit bigger. Maybe Maria might give him some hanky-panky tonight too. About time.

Joey did a sign of the cross on his white singlet, and wiping his hands on his shorts straight after, turned his tricycle right into the path of the bully sun, still beating down on everyone. He rode off, as behind him a couple of fat black dogs barked and the gate swung open.

Cross was looking for Ruby, who had gone to visit her cousin here a few hours before. He had gotten bored back in the family home, where his mother-in-law was watching *Eat Bulaga* on the T.V. hovering in the bedroom - and he'd had enough sleep recently to last him for a long while.

Except he couldn't find Ruby and her cousin or even the daughters in the house. In fact it didn't much look like anyone had been around there. Everything was tidy. Ordered. Placed.

Then he heard voices out back in the large yard, which itself stooped into an even larger mangrove swamp.

Ruby and Grace were feeding bloody chickens. And in the other corner there were about six big cockerels staring at him with their hideous eyes spooning over their sharp beaks, as if to say to him – 'What the fuck do you want here?' All the birds were chained up to the yard. Cross knew that they were Grace's main way of income and could earn her and her two kids big money, if they won well in the cockpit arena down the road away.

Ruby looked up. "Hello darling," she smiled and waved.

Grace stopped chucking scraps at the squalling chickens and also smiled.

They went inside to the cooler air and ate lunch.

It was later – after eating – when Doctor Cross first heard that one of Grace's two young daughters were missing.

Seemed she had gone to study in the big city and was boarding there. She had been supposed to return to Pampanga the day before, so as to begin preparations for her role in the big religious parade on the weekend – but there had been no sign of her.

And her mobile telephone rang dead.

Grace said she would just, "I will wait a bit longer." And that was that.

They ate lunch, while some of the cockerels got the time of day completely wrong and tried to greet the dawn.

12/1.

Norton heard about Makere's death early the next morning. It was the wailing and sirens that first got him going.

He had assumed she had gotten up from the *whare moe* before him and gone for a walk outside or to go and help in the kitchen, as she was wont to do. He had rolled over and half-raised himself to see her, but he only sprained his fingertips on the bare wood floor. Everyone else had either still been snoring or – a few - had already risen and gone to ablutions, and to assist in the kitchen.

He sat up pretty damned quickly when the yelling outside came closer and closer. All the other former sleepers were also well awake by now, staring pretty blearily at each other, and muttering.

The front doors of the *whare* were pushed inward and the sunshine hit them all at once. Sheila Raumoko ran over to him, crying. "Makere is dead, Makere is dead."

And it was true. Norton sprinted past the lollygaggers at the door, across the dew-wet long grass and straight into the *urupā*, one hundred metres away.

There was a group standing and crouching around Makere – or her body anyway. She wasn't near any graves, but up against the shrubs and scrub infiltrating the sidelines of the burial ground. Jim Pelorus was kneeling down next to her, but as soon as Norton got close enough, the local policeman stood up. Norton could see that his ex-wife, his wife of twenty-five years, had gone. Her eyes were staring well past him at some far horizon, and there was a bit of a smile on her taut lips. Her long hair was still unbrushed and she still had her nightie under her jeans and t-shirt.

Norton touched her face but it wasn't even warm. He snatched her hand but her fingers were reluctant to clasp his. Seemed she was still pissed off with him.

Before he knew it himself Norton was bawling his eyes out. Man he lost it all big-time. His *hūpē* spilled into his mouth, but he just didn't give a shit. It was his ex-wife lying there. Dead. Makere was dead.

And he had absolutely no idea how it had happened – let alone when. Or how.

Which is exactly what he told Jim Pelorus and the other Māori detective guy who'd soon arrived up from town.

They were sitting outside the kitchen, drinking overwrought tea from big chipped mugs, tempered by lashings of sweetened condensed milk.

Other cops had kept nosey-parkers at bay and there was a surreal silence about the entire *marae* now.

Two dead. Brother and sister.

It was going to be a gangbuster of a *tangi*.

And Norton was likely going to be in even deeper shit than he was already. Up well over his shoulders now and still rising. Thick, mucky stuff you can't just wipe away.

Especially when they saw the stab wound in Makere's back. Right through to her heart.

Looked like someone had skewered her with a huge butcher's knife.

Norton did not know what to say to his two daughters - their two daughters - at the best of times, for he had become increasingly estranged from them both. He had absolutely no idea what to say now.

In fact he was dreading even picking up the phone.

13/3.

Doctor Cross didn't much like his own countrymen, especially the fat white middle-aged male ones. Which of course would have included a lot of his own ethnic make-up, if he had rationalized a bit away from his own father's African heritage.

He felt they were all so self-centred, opinionated, blind to other cultural realities and so damnably certain that their country was so far the best one on the planet that nothing else mattered. He was embarrassed to call himself one of them at times; most times in fact. Except when it came to their money.

The odd thing though was that so many of the locals in Pampanga lusted to be like them. The shopping malls all sold his country's wares – especially the fast food obesities. The TV channels all ran bulk programmes where the singing was all in his language, by artists who merely mimicked his countries' singers and who blindly rattled back lyrics about swinging on the back porch in Arkansas. The movie theatres were sold out on the opening days of any new Hollywood blockbuster. Half the population – it seemed to him anyway – had cousins in his country somewhere – whether legal or illegal entrants there.

Cross didn't envisage ever returning home to live. 'Fuck the family', he sometimes thought. He was suffering culture shock from his very own culture these days and cringed when he spotted a walk-short-wearing fellow countryman from his homeland smiling at him with a big toothy grin, on the few times he and Ruby went down to the local SM mall.

He noticed that all of these fellow countrymen were hand-in-hand with a local *babae maganda* – which would probably account for why they were even in the country to start with. And all of them must have been at least twenty years older than their lovely companion. Some even had the woman's toddlers along for the ride. And their aunties. And cousins.

Ruby's mother never wanted to go anywhere with him and Ruby. And at least – he justified - Ruby was only ten years younger than him

Sort of made him feel better, especially since he also knew the rudiments of the local language, Tagalog, these days.

Yeah – he didn't much like his fellow countrymen at all and didn't even rate himself in their category any more. The irony was however, that he still lived off their taxes.

And he still worked somewhat undercover, for a nation, that – despite his many misgivings about so many of its citizens – he firmly believed was the most powerful in the world. It certainly paid very well too, thank you.

Cross compartmentalized himself very well. So well, that he set aside his own reflections about this ability. Even when he looked into a mirror, he somehow dodged himself.

Time for lunch. He wondered what they would eat today. What had Ruby's mother prepared this time?

14/1.

Norton sank further into the long grass surrounding the *urupā*. He lay there a long time ruminating on what next to do.

His ex-wife had been buried alongside her brother the day before and he had been allowed to go to the *tangi* by the local police, with a caution that he report to their police station down in Ruatoria every second day until, 'we are ready to charge an individual.'

In other words, they didn't have enough evidence to point the finger at anyone just yet. In other words also he was a marked man, the prime suspect, and every other cliché in their well-thumbed book of them. There was evidently no way he would escape the police reckoning of him as a double-murderer, and he knew his country's notorious set-up-by-the-D's history all too well. If the cops couldn't pinpoint him specifically with watertight evidence, they would invariably and inevitably manufacture some. Especially when it involved a tattooed Māori male with a less than pristine past record.

Norton was doomed. Unless they found another stooge, which was unlikely, given his very strong links to Makere and Trevor King, he knew he was facing jail big time. His daughters had not actually accused him of murdering their mother, but their eyes were evil enough when they looked toward him at the *tangi*. There would be no empathy from them or that side of their *whānau*. Fortunately for him, they stayed on the other side of the small town.

He was staying at his cuzzie Hemara's place for the time being – no questions asked by Hemara, who believed in his cousin's innocence, mainly because he, Hemara, had grown up with Norton. They'd both been *whāngai* to their Grandma years before

Others of course – mostly everyone in the small village, because small town talk spread like wildfire in the same hackneyed fashion – believed he had somehow murdered their *whanaunga*, his wife, Makere. The residents still saw them as a couple, as most didn't have any inkling that in fact, they had been living separate lives for nearly a year already.

It was just that no one could quite work out how and when he had managed to do it, eh. The word was that, 'He would have had to have been ultra-fast and ultra-stealthy to have scarpered out of the *whare moe* just as dawn was breaking and knifed his wife near where she had knelt at her own parents' gravesite, and then crept back in and feigned sleeping, without a track of blood or dirt on him anywhere. And where was the knife?'

He was getting tired of all their small town banality rattling around in his own skull, so for the past few days he had lain low and watched a heck of a lot of television; not that there was much choice of channels up on the Coast. He couldn't or wouldn't go to the local drinking spot, the RSA, as there was no chance he would be left alone, especially if the beer began to flow fast. Bound to be a punch-up. With him involved somewhere.

So, he just lay there, musing, in the tepid autumn sun, chewing on a bit of paspalum stalk, thinking, thinking, thinking. He hadn't heard any more news about his other supposed victim back up North – Trevor King - but he had made one call to Monaghan about this latest bit of bother. Monaghan – pressed for time – had just told him to, "lie low, brother, lie low. Let the dust settle." Easy for him to say; he was nowhere nearby.

And he couldn't get out of the skinny country either, as far as he knew, because the cops had asked him for his passport, for 'reasons of security', whatever the hell that meant. Yet the thought of fleeing all this hassle certainly ran several laps through his brain more than a few times. He did not fancy any more cell time.

So Norton just sprawled there and waited.

15/2.

Godfrey Woo had rather swiftly begun to disintegrate from being a tall, quite-well built man to a stooped, wrinkled, rapidly balding, skinny man with rotten teeth and suppurating sores caused by too much oral contact with the all-too-often private parts of the vast array of strangers he now accosted in public toilets. Or they accosted him, as his fame started to go before him.

Woo had finally begun to self-reflect. His Filipino former wife would now certainly never recognize him – even if she would want to – and nor would his mother and sisters, who just didn't want to know him since he had deserted his family, bankrupted his own partners and his own businesses, all to scoot off to Macau to gamble, gamble, gamble. And more latterly – and finally – to flit back and forth to Shenzhen, to defacto his ugly mistress and to father another little bastard; all the time promising her that, 'yes, I will soon bring you to Hong Kong to live.'

But even Kwok Li hadn't wanted to see him again after he asked her for money. And their snotty little fat kid had just looked away when his father hadn't given him any gift when he had returned that last time. They wouldn't want to even glance at him nowadays.

Woo could almost feel his flesh being flenched from his frame and when he sometimes looked into the cracked and dowdy mirror in the shared toilet-bathroom, the creature looking back at him seemed like some CG extra in a double B-grade horror movie.

Still, at least he had the semblance of a bed. Food. Some clothes. He could shave his cracked face.

And no triad had yet rediscovered him – and given the way he now looked – he doubted they would even recognize him anyway. He cracked a tooth-rotten grin at this animal self, seeping back from the reflection.

Time to go to work again.

Although the rain was pouring heavily and everyone he saw on the drenched streets was hustling an umbrella or two, Woo wasn't too worried. He had learned already that *gaylo* came out to play on such days; true *gaylo*, play-*gaylo*, wanna-be *gaylo*, *gaylo*-on-trial, *gaylo*-in-denial, bi-*gaylo*, *gaylo*-on-pills, *gaylo* who didn't know they were *gaylo* – the entire gamut headed for the safe cubicles to escape the rain, alleviate their pain.

For Woo this all meant money. And his heart was made of the stuff. Hard cold currency was his only god. Just like his own late father apparently – at least that is what his mother said. "Bugger Buddha," Woo said out loud. "Never did nothing for me."

Later, the rain was still fair pissing down. Streams of water drooled their way through his hair, plastering his greying locks even more firmly to his balding pate. He had no umbrella and soon his holed sneakers were drowning themselves in the instant puddles everywhere he trod.

The back of his neck was also soon swamped and he could feel the moisture sneak right down his long back.

Now he could barely see at all, as the drops became so dense as to reduce his visibility to near nil.

There was little traffic on the roads, for a Number 8 gale warning had been issued by the Metropolitan Weather Authority and people had been advised to stay indoors. And not to drive. The occasional greedy taxi swam past him in the turmoil, but that was all.

He felt his way to his doss-house doors and floated in, drenching the security man, who stared at him angrily from behind his saturated desk.

Woo stomped squelching up the stairs to his narrow 30 square feet room and slumped onto the sole hard wooden chair, which just fit itself inside by the door. He struggled to remove his lifeless footwear and grabbed the towel that had died possibly five years earlier. He could feel shreds of toweling penetrate his scalp as he dried it.

Still, at least he would not need to have a shower that day or two and therefore argue with the other tenants about the water. Which had never been anything like hot since he had moved in all those days ago.

He took off his remaining clothing and belched. At least also he had recently eaten, given that it was a sort of thin congee with some semblance of fish in its entrails.

He crawled into his bed, a tiny far-too-short mattress, and covered himself with the thin-faced blanket, which he had stolen from the laundry downstairs.

He couldn't sleep very well usually, but on this day the water torrent outside lulled him into some sort of snooze.

Until today, he had long since given up thinking too much about why he was in this deep shit of a life, because – deep down anyway – he knew full well why. His sleeplessness on most other nights was caused instead by his having no money, no food, no no no nothing. It was not caused by guilt or shame.

Something had to give.

16/3.

Despite the relative comfort caressing the practical side of her life, Ruby had started to get sick of the doctor a bit more and more of late.

It wasn't just because he seemed to have grown weary in bed.

Or because he had grown more and more dependent on her mother to feed him day in, day out.

More, because he had gotten boring for her. He kept on saying basically the same things and doing very little about them.

It no longer mattered that he continued to pay just about all of the bills. It didn't really seem important anymore that they had no major worries.

Or that he sometimes just disappeared to, 'do some business' back in Manila – for a few days, every so often.

No – none of this stuff mattered.

She had just fallen out of love with him. If – she reflected more honestly to herself - she had ever been in love.

It happens all the time. To Ruby, it had happened more than once.

She wasn't going to show any signs of her disillusionment though. She was happy enough to be back home in Philippines – at least for a while, although she did miss her adult kids – sometimes, anyway. She liked being with her mother, even if she – her mother – was suffering more and more these days from a mixture of age-related ailments.

But – increasingly – she was thinking that she wouldn't miss Cross, if he went back to his home country. Or anywhere else for that matter.

The doctor came into their kitchen just then and smiled at her.

"What are you thinking about, my darling?" he asked.

"Aww, nothing really. How about us going down to the mall this afternoon, for a change?"

"Sure, why not..."

But, as they got ready to go out, Ruby noticed he had put his gun into its holster under his shirt.

Quite why he often did this still puzzled her, even after all this time together.

They climbed into the *jeepney* and squashed themselves in against the crowd inside, as best they could.

He had also put on his sunglasses. Maybe just for some sort of effect – she didn't know. Probably the same reason why he always seemed to show off one of his tattoos. Or two. By rolling up his shirt sleeves to display them. Which he was doing right then.

She sighed inwardly and they sidled off over the potholes of the main road taking them to SM Mall.

A bit further down the same road Romeo was drunk once more and sitting semi-sprawled on a stool outside a Burger Machine after his early release from jail.

He yelled something incoherent as the *jeepney* stumbled past, and as a couple of sunburned dogs splattered their piss on the wall next door.

High up above the sun turned itself up to HIGH. Then HIGHER.

As they thrummed along, Doctor Cross was thinking that he had better communicate with his bosses soon. Been a while already and he wasn't sure anymore just what was going down. He hadn't heard anything from them for some time. He hummed to himself as they manipulated the bumps into some sense of style.

Ruby's mother was happy now too. No one there. No need to cook for a while. Or to wash more clothes that didn't really need to be washed.

She lay on her bed, by the big twirling fan the Doctor had bought her, and switched on *Eat Bulaga.*

Within five minutes she was sound asleep and didn't hear the Doctor's mobile phone ringing. & ringing. & ringing again just to make sure.

17/1.

A few days later Sergeant Jim Pelorus came around to Hemara's place for, "a bit of a chat, eh," as he put it, rather icily. Seemed that they couldn't charge Norton just yet as they needed to collect a bit more information, so he could go out of the district all right, but they would need to keep his passport for a while. "Just to be on the safe side," Pelorus had added.

As Pelorus left the back porch, just after he laced up his boots, he looked right at Norton and said, "We know you killed her. We know you killed her brother. It's just a matter of time...eh."

Hemara said later, that the best thing for Norton to do was to get out of the country. Bugger the passport. Hemara knew a guy who worked on a fishing boat up in the Bay of Plenty and who would be able to fix up a way to ship Norton out pronto. For a bit of smoke and some pingers.

When Norton asked where the hell he would go to, Hemara just said that Manny would get him back to his place somewhere in the Philippines. No one could get at him there and – anyway – there was no extradition treaty between the two countries. Shit – it was hard enough even getting into Aotearoa if you were a Filipino. "Imagine, then," said Hemi, "how hard it would be to grab a Kiwi back from the Philippines!"

Funny, thought Norton later, it was pretty easy for a New Zealander to get into the Philippines. White man's privilege, he supposed. He smiled, for he was sure as hell no Pākehā.

Hemara and Norton spent the night in Te Araroa down at the RSA. Getting blotto actually. No one really seemed to be on guard about Norton being there, but he could sense a coolness about their attitude towards him. He was Māori, but so what? Māori didn't always like other Māori. There was no rule saying one had to share the pork bones with another. Then he thought about him and Trevor King as an example. He didn't like that arsehole one little bit. But then, he quickly went all morose, because he had once really loved King's sister.

Once. Now he felt grief, but wasn't grieving.

When Cody Delamare asked him if he had, 'killed his wife' — Cody's first cousin — and when Norton said 'No', everyone just left it at that. Went on with playing pool and drinking. And laughing even more.

Didn't mean to say they believed him either. Just that some things were best left alone for a bit.

Time would tell.

Just before Hemara said, "Cuz, let's go home. *Mahi āpōpō,*" Norton had been thinking about jumping on the fishing boat in Mount Maunganui and then crewing to Manila somewhere. He laughed silently to himself.

He had been there before in a previous life.

When he and Monaghan had been fighting for truth, justice and the American way. As Kiwi soldiers in Viet Nam.

Then after the manifest war and during the long unreported interplay afterwards, that no one much ever knew about. In the later 1970s a small Kiwi contingent had been assigned to look after Nam allies who were too valuable to leave behind and who had managed to crawl to Cambodia or Laos. Norton and Monaghan and a few Americanos had been conveyed there to 'escape' them. No expenses spared. No mercies to be shown to any impediments. America had wanted to retain their services, just like they had for several supposedly valuable Nazis after World War Two.

Bullshit. It had all been bullshit.

"C'mon man. Let's get outta here. Time to go." That was Hemara, who had his arm around some *wahine* Norton had never seen before. One with an electric-engraved *moko* draped all over her chin.

Outside the rain was piddling itself all over the roads.

Norton shook himself and shook away his sadness about Makere, as best he could. He was more angry than down. Pissed off about being accused of killing her and her half-brother, Trevor King. Irate that someone else had murdered them both and that no one seemed to be even considering this. And knowing pretty much for certain that he would be the scapegoat, especially with his known skill of wielding a butcher's knife.

Made him think back to all the times he had been picked up by cops just for being. Being Māori that is. He fumed a little more

He was also hurt that his own daughters wouldn't even talk to him without rage in their eyes. There would not be much, if any, support from them either. Did not make him feel especially welcome to hang around in Aotearoa at all.

He wouldn't forget all this shit in a hurry.

And he also couldn't forget what Hemi Hemara had also relayed to him - when Hemi was semi-sodden in beer – earlier in the evening. Something to the effect, that, "I saw your mate, Monaghan, down in Ruatoria last week. I never did like that bastard." To which Norton had merely shrugged and filed away to brood on later.

Which meant now.

18/2.

Woo knew what to do when he saw the men dressed in unfashionable black suits and hair that was far too black to be black, striding toward him that dusk.

They were holding cigarettes ubiquitously, as if in a pre-arranged pantomime routine – flicking the ash consistently, all as if synchronized.

But this was no high school play. This was no dress rehearsal.

The mean men from the Mainland were looking to harm somebody and Woo sensed it might well be him.

He merged into the shadows, pretending he was a wall, feigning brickwork.

Up above the pale-wan moon was but a thin echo of Wu's thumping heartbeat. He was extremely scared.

It was the never knowing when they might find him, might maim him. Might kill him. This insecurity did bad things indeed to a man's blood circuitry system.

One of them spat out a large sputter of sputum, which – presumably coincidentally – landed just east of Godfrey's left foot.

Then they moved on. Trailing bitter smoke fresh from their cheap cigarettes and signifying nothing.

Woo waited for some considerable time. He couldn't sweat anymore: he was sweated out. He was sure his blood had turned into white lymph.

Later, when he was home, Woo rubbed his own scalp for far too long as he sat there in the gloom of his room, hoping he would not again see those three goons – for that is what they were.

He took to carrying a knife of his own. A long-bladed skinning knife that he stole one morning from a butcher at Ho Man Tin wet market. It was menacingly sharp and he kept it tied to his inner forearm by tape, with the blade encased in an old leather re-fashioned spectacle case one of his clients had left in one of the toilets.

Woo had, in fact, learned to handle knives many years before when he was overseas, working as a cook in the Middle East. He was rather good at it actually, although no one would ever have guessed this by looking at him nowadays.

Meanwhile he lay lower that was possible for anyone.

It was almost as if he did not exist.

About two days later, at pretty much the same time, Woo did see the Mainlanders again. He couldn't be sure it was exactly the same guys, but they had their peculiar smell of over-smoking lingering about them as they passed. A permeating permanence that was like dog's piss in its territoriality.

Again, he stood dead still, as if riveted to the wall, appreciating the warm whispers of his knife against his palpitating skin-cells. Waiting for the men to move on and beyond.

Except they didn't. One of them, pausing to spit, glanced more closely at the wall than would seem normal.

Woo slunk into the very fibre of the bricks. He could feel his skin morphing into the mortise. Segueing his sweat into the minute chasms of stone.

The man muttered something in Mandarin, something Wu could not pick up, for his own ears had melted into the mortar.

The man's colleagues just laughed a little and then they all moved on.

Woo knew that they were looking for him. Because the one word he did hear was 'cocksucker.'

Seems the triads knew more than he thought they did.

He would – yet again – have to alter his modus operandi somehow and, inevitably, somewhere else.

He had to move away from this Kowloon basin.

He couldn't even begin to think about going to Mainland China.

Macau was an impossibility, after his mountain of debts there forebode even considering it.

He had no money to travel far afield either.

He couldn't be seen heading up deeper into the New Territories – too many people might see him there and report that they had too.

He didn't have much choice, but to head out to Lamma Island. Yet he knew it would all be a matter of time. Especially going there, as it now really limited his options about remaining unnoticed. Lamma was an island, after all.

19/1.

James Clement Monaghan had a cruel dark loooong look at himself in the mirror. He liked to think of himself as cruel and dark, although – to most others – he always seemed cool, unflappable. A nice guy, well-presented and fastidiously groomed. And white.

Little did they know, eh.

Monaghan was a double agent par excellence. He was particularly well-paid, even for a top legal brain, but he was far from effusive with his earnings.

For, Monaghan acted for reasons deeper than mere money. He liked to think of himself as one of the few remaining heroes – for most were long-since dead. He had been instilled certain long-standing and rather conservative values by his American mother, who basically had brought him up by herself, as his father was always overseas dealing to insurgents. Which was all hugely ironic as his father was not American, but an Irish-Armenian exile. Who had anglicized his family name and moved his entire young family to New Zealand when he was posted there by his government.

Monaghan acted in certain ways because he believed he was the upholder of all that was good in the World – that meant the United States of America. If this entailed dealing with messy and dim moral situations, his ultimate mission was to see that his form of good prevailed. Money was just a nice side-suite to his moral mission.

Today, however, Monaghan was a bit twitchy – somewhat unusual for him, given his years of intermittent overseas undercover activity and his proven abilities to cope with extraordinary scenarios.

His colleagues in Asia had been warning him for quite some time that the situation there was getting complicated and dangerous. Something to do with software secrets being spilled - and spyware. That maybe he would soon be directed to take a quick break from his less important legal cases in New Zealand and head off over there for a look for himself. And to act. He was deemed a master agent, after all. He picked up the telephone once more. He would pre-empt the call he knew he'd soon be receiving.

JC Monaghan was, quite simply, one of the best in his business.

20/3.

Cross was living up to his name. He was upset, tired and frustrated. Quite angry in fact.

The promised telephone call had not come through, as far as he knew. He was – then – still in the dark about what was going to happen as regards the project he had been assigned to, in Pampanga. Quite some time ago now.

He had reported back frequently enough that – at least as far as he knew – there was nothing to worry about in his zone of interest and that the few instigators had been more fuelled by too many San Miguel beers than any actual fundamentalist zeal. Indeed, he hadn't actually met any sympathizers for NPA or MILF or even many for the current administration either. People seemed more interested in going to the mall or church or to the next cockfight. Or back overseas, where they could earn far more *peso*.

He had asked Ruby's mother if anyone had telephoned the house recently, but *Apu* had just smiled at him vaguely, even after her daughter's translation to her. There were only cell phones with patchy coverage there anyway and no such thing as a land line in her home. Never had been in fact.

Cross paced up and down outside in the broiling heat for a bit, until he realized he was too damned hot to be doing it, and came inside and sat by the fan for a while.

Later, he just went back to sleep and waited. Again.

Ruby wasn't around at the time. She was busy helping her cousin Grace file a missing daughter report at the local police barracks down the road, a short tricycle ride away. The student daughter, Euris, had still not been located or made any communication with her mother, who was now a bit frantic. It had been quite a few days already.

Down at the barracks Captain Pedro Almodevar asked the same routine questions, such as. "When was the last time Grace had heard from her daughter?" And then

"Had they been fighting about something? How old was the girl?"

"18 already," replied Grace.

"Old enough to be able to do what she liked", replied Pedro. "Did she have a boyfriend? She might have eloped…happens all the time. What's his name?" Pedro sighed. "How much money did she have?" he continued.

"Rustico Tuazon and I'm unsure about money," mused Grace, "but I always gave her enough to get by."

"Who were her friends, what was she studying?"

"Sociology and art history."

"Sociology majors are usually socialists anyway."

And so on, until Ruby stepped into the dialogue and asked, "What exactly will the Police do…?"

"We will file this of course and wait another three days. Regulations state that we do not act on missing person's cases until at least five days after the initial report," Pedro quoted, wiping his sweaty forehead with the back of his hand.

"But if you want my opinion – off the record of course – she's probably decided to run off with the boy you mentioned, especially because he's known to us."

"What do you mean known to us?" gasped Grace.

"He's a known stirrer and political agitator."

Ruby was getting sick of the whole episode already: "So, what are you going to do about all this, Officer? Are you going to go looking for him at least?"

"No need, Ma'am," spat back Pedro Almodevar. "We know exactly where he is…But I can't tell you any more right now. If your daughter comes into the picture we will let you know."

Pedro escorted the two cousins outside and re-introduced them to the searing sun. Said Ruby to her cousin, "*Bola bola*. If they know where Rustico is, and they haven't seen her, how can they say she has run off with him?"

Grace had already called out a tricycle driver and was shaking her head angrily. "I will ring her father this afternoon and tell him about this. He still has contacts in Pasay. He can help track down his own daughter. Damned *Pulis* are *basura*…Rustico is an agitator. Pah! He would have to be one of the laziest men I have ever met. *Bola bola* all right."

They were driven in silence to Grace's home. The only sound was the cackle of the fighting cocks and a few men down the lane whistling at their dogs. Ruby had long since decided to go back to her own house anyway, "Let me know if you hear anything, cousin. I'm sure that she will be O.K… she's a good girl, she's no fool, not going to get mixed up in all that politics stuff."

Grace was already tapping the digits onto her mobile. She wasn't really listening.

Ruby walked herself home down the back way to her mother's home, worrying about Euris. She was now thinking a lot more seriously about getting out of the Philippines and going back to see her own kids in Hong Kong. It had been far too long since she had even talked to them over the computer. Especially since her mother's home had no internet connection and Ruby was no fan of walking hot down to the internet café, which was actually a tight overheated room on the corner intersection.

Besides, she was now even more sick and tired of the Doctor, who – more recently at least – seemed to do nothing more than sleep. He didn't even talk good anymore. If he spoke to her at all.

21/1.
Norton sat down quickly.

The news sure came thick and fast these days.

Now, it seemed his long-time friend, his ex-Special Services comrade, his current
lawyer, Monaghan, wasn't going to be able to help him at all. Something about,
"urgent business," his secretary had parlayed to him down the phone.

"What do you mean?" thundered an annoyed Norton.

"I am not really able to say more, sir. Sorry," was her trained reply.

"Well, where is he, then?" Norton continued.

"Sir, all I know is that he is soon to travel overseas and has had to convey his
apologies. Thank you sir." She put down the phone.

Norton was left irate at his feeling of impotence, and pissed off with the sweet yet
firm tone of what he later clicked onto was Monaghan's Filipino secretary.

Monaghan had referred his erstwhile buddy to some other guy, whom Norton had
never heard of – some other Pākehā dude in a big office in downtown Main Street
in the capital city. Who probably would insist on cash up front and who would no
doubt wear a grotesque rainbow tie.

"Fuck that shit," muttered Norton, who hated going to the capital at the best of
times.

He mentioned all this to his cousin later the next day, after Hemi Hemara had come
back from his dive for *kina* off Matakaoa.

"Man, I told you, you don't need no lawyer. Firstly, no one has charged you with
nothing. Second, you said you didn't do nothing. Third, like I already said, get out

of the country for a while and lay low, before they set you up big time. Soon all blow over, if you know what I mean." Hemi was sucking on a doobie the size of Mount Hikurangi and his eyes seemed to have grown exponentially with each and every inhalation.

When Norton pointed out – yet again – that, "the cops have got my passport, bro", Hemi just repeated, "Go up the Coast and jump on a boat. Like I said, I know a fellow who will fix anything for a few hundred bucks. And some good smoking dope".

Which is why Norton was now looking back at his homeland from the outskirts of Tauranga harbour, as the dingy little dinghy slunk him offshore to the dirty looking only-slightly-bigger boat lurking on the horizon. It was spewing piles of black smoke into the palatial sky. He clutched his canvas tote bag close to his body and shut his eyes, wondering if it was the right thing to have done. Despite what his cousin had said and despite what Hemara had later organised with these Filipino fishermen to get him out of Aotearoa for a while, for Norton it all seemed like an admission of his guilt in – somehow – engineering the murders of his ex-wife and her half-brother in a very short period of time. Another part of him had told him he should have stayed to prove he had not been involved. This despite his intuition telling him that he was soon going to be charged with the crime anyway, by a police force who needed a conviction.

He was riven.

And his anxiety was all meshed up with very real feelings of loss for Makere and guilt that he had not been a better mate for her. Norton was probably running away from himself as much as anything else: and he knew it.

But it was now – of course – too late to go back to shore and have to wait and be followed around and to report to the cop shop every other day and to see his own visage still lambasted all over the Sunday papers, with the big red headlines basically calling him a mass killer.

Which, ironically he had indeed been several years before in a vastly different place under vastly different rules. There had been no rules there at all actually.

More, he was also extremely peeved because he couldn't comprehend why the cops had not tracked down the killers. "I mean," as he had spat out to Hemara one afternoon, "Just how easy is it to creep into an *urupā* and slaughter someone and then get clean away? Bullshit *e hoa*. Bloody bullshit." For Norton, someone was covering up these murders somehow and rather than fight what he knew from experience was a greater and whiter foe, flight was, after all, the one option left for him.

He stopped brooding when he heard a voice behind him.

Eric Canlas shook the tawny-coloured and multi-tattooed guy's hand. "You are at the boat, sir," said Eric, an experienced merchant mariner who had spent over twenty years plying the world's rampant oceans and whom Hemi's mate, Manny, had contacted days earlier. "Time to get on board and get away."

Norton threw up about one hundred times over the next day, until his guts were starting to vomit themselves – or so it seemed. It wasn't so much the swell, but more, the filthy retching wretch that was the bilious diesel fumes spilling all over the boat. He couldn't even look at the thin gray piddle that Eric served up to him, "compliments of the chef, sir," with his ready and genial smile written like graffiti all over his boyish face. Made him want to just puke a bit more – if he could have.

All he could muster was, "How long will it take to get to Manila?"

"Manila? Manila?" laughed Canlas. "We aren't going to Manila. We are going to Puerto Princessa. Nowhere near Manila actually, sir."

Later, much later, when Norton had gained some measure of balance and had endeavoured to eat the dry bread and butter and hashed-up chicken *calderata*, he learned that this was no ordinary fishing boat. When he casually lifted up the lapsing canvas tarpaulin off one of the containers lurching on deck, he could see that the cargo was listed as Munitions. Because it said exactly that in sketched on black letters for all of the world to see: *'Property of New Zealand Army.'*

His head began to swim even more murkily. "Fuck," he mused out loud, "What is going on with these guys?"

His incubus just seemed to be getting deeper and swifter and even more inescapable.

22/3.

Dr. Cross had become preternaturally restless. He usually had moped around on Sundays, eating, belching – sometimes fucking Ruby under the slow ceiling fan in her mother's bedroom. Today though, from reasonably early onwards for him, he was pacing around a fair bit – not itself an easy option in the heatwave collection stored throughout the *barangay* and beyond.

His movements were making even Ruby sweat, and she was pretty used to the tepidity that rumbled like a permanently voracious dragon throughout the entire country. She had to ask him more than once, "What is the matter with you today?" but never quite received a sensible answer from him. He was fiddling incessantly with his cellphone, as if the finger dances he spun on its tablet typeface would somehow breathe life into it. He took off his shades several times and soon after shoved them back on his worried-looking face, after rubbing his eyes vigorously each time. Ruby gave up counting after six.

Later, after her mother had served up a huge feed of barbecued pork and deep fried banana fritters, Dr. Cross was only slightly less twitchy. He didn't retire to the middle, unused bedroom for his usual afternoon nap though. He was now writing something down in his scratchy longhand, which Ruby could never decipher. He was also drinking the Red Horse lager that she had bought a few days earlier, at the *sari-sari* store run by her aunt down the lane. She had actually anticipated drinking them herself, but what the hell? At least the alcohol content seemed to slow her partner down more and he became steadily less restless the longer the day spun itself on, always high-blue-skied and bright-yellow-sunny.

"Dah-ling," he stuttered – it came out later this selfsame blue afternoon – "Why don't we go up to Manila tomorrow for a couple of days? We could stay with your sister couldn't we?" This last was more of a command than an idea.

Ruby shrugged. If anything else, she could *chika chika* with her sister for a day or two after her work and maybe – the idea grew like a tsunami in her mind – she could try and discover what had had happened to her niece – Grace's daughter, Euris.

"*Walang problema kaibigan*" was all she could muster in reply. At the very least it would be some sort of a break. Besides, she knew the machinations of her doctor mate all too well. He would be up to something shady in Manila.

23/2.

The sun never desisted and merely melted anything that resisted. So he sweated a bit more until there could be no further possibility of him actually having any sweat left in his increasingly gaunt frame.

He swept back the few remaining hairs on his sharp-angled fontanel and burped copiously on the remnants of his noodle soup breakfast, scored from Ah Wong's $6 noodle shop out the back of Lamma's back beach.

Godfrey Woo scoured the horizon, out beyond the broken fishing boats and the broken men crewing them. All seemed to be in order. No police launches. No big fast luxury launches either, swept off the coasts of the Mainland and sent to find him. Not yet anyway.

Some pliant gulls let him past as he loped on up the reluctant trail away from the harbour.

There were hardly any folk around anywhere, probably as it was already far too hot to remain outside, unless you really had to. Woo scuttled, rather like the sand crabs that were everywhere, toward his thin shack up on the hillside. It was a tarpaulin monstrosity, which lurched sideways even as he approached it - the wind acting as a force to launch it almost into its maiden voyage.

Inside, under the heavy blue mass, Woo snuggled down as best he could to do what he did best – to slumber for an inordinate time, until hunger or a desire to defecate overcame him. This – or someone finding him and dealing to him big-time – were the only things that were going to wake him that day, at least. He lay backwards on the corrugated cardboard mattress he had scored from outside the only big grocery store on that part of the island, and was soon asleep. Dreaming about his two children from his marriage all those years ago; for reasons he couldn't quite fathom, seeing as he hadn't seen them for some time after he deserted them. In his dream they were both crying, but he couldn't quite figure out why. Something to do with a missing toy.

Woo would have had no idea about what his kids were doing out in the New Territories, not so far away from where he was right then. One of them had already graduated from Police College. This son, however, had never become a policeman, although he still pedaled a bicycle. Woo would have been even more surprised to learn that his ex-wife, Ruby, wasn't anywhere near them at all, but was intending to come back to Hong Kong to see their young adult children, sooner rather than later. Truth is stranger than fiction after all.

Woo slept on, while the wheels of the weirdness that is daily life, just churned on a bit more.

Despite him.

Part Four: Philippine Sea

24.

Two or three days' sailing later, one of the crew – an amiable Thai called Sid –
asked Norton if he was, "one of those rebels?"

Norton didn't really understand what the Thai guy was on about, so had to ask him
to explain himself.

Sid said that when the crew had berthed in Mount Maunganui for the three weeks
layover, to pick up the cargo full of small containers, he had read a couple of
newspaper headlines and had also seen the news a couple of times. '"All about the
insurgency somewhere in the North island: Māori rebels with guns were in training
for an armed re-takeover of their land," as Sid recounted all this, except not quite
as grammatically watertight

Norton had to explain that just because he was Māori himself, it didn't necessarily
mean he was a rebel.

The truth was that he did empathize quite strongly with the cause: the Treaty of
Waitangi had been sanctified by the British Crown, but they had historically never
stringently adhered to it and there were multifarious grievances still at play - for all
iwi Māori. He didn't say any of this last part to the Thai guy, though, but grew rather
quiet as he thought a bit more about recent developments in his life.

His late wife, Makere, he knew, had much stronger connections to the rebels than
him and had been quite outspoken about any Māori cause. She had actually
become rather a poster girl, of what she claimed was the impending revolution in
the country and she had attended some, "sorta camps, you know" – in her words -
down in the remote Urewera country.

"Insurgency," Norton repeated, for he rather liked Sid's word. It made him smile,
albeit wanly, when he associated it with Makere.

Norton fell to musing a bit more – and later on – when his brain reconnoitered itself more deeply – he dimly recalled Trevor King taunting him - Norton – as being a honky for not standing up to the Pākehā management at the Works. As well as for not coming with the bros up to Te Tii to protest on Waitangi Day the previous year. Especially since Māori had had so much of their territory taken by the British and it had never been sufficiently returned. Los Anglos. Their prime grievance still remained the loss of huge amounts of land, as connived by these Pākehā colonialists. No land had meant complete spiritual impoverishment, for they then had nothing to connect themselves to, be rooted in. In many ways, many Māori were a lost people; *he tāngata ngaro*.

This all provided something for him to think about for the rest of the increasingly stormy voyage; though not when he was pressed to service the loosened rope lashings around the containers, as the big waves threatened to cast them off the deck and well overboard on a couple of occasions. He couldn't quite get his head around any potential big picture, but some brushstrokes were clutching the canvas of his mind now. He thought briefly also about Makere's killer or killers and then thought again more intensely…when the waves later became mere whelps.

And a few more scenes infiltrated inside the frame when Canlas shared with him the fact that, "back home, there's lotsa rebel groups eh. NPA, MILF, MNLF, Abu Sayyaf - Philippine Police Force…ha ha ha!"

They were now sitting on old canvas chairs from another era and were resting themselves in the resurgent sun. Canlas had been going on about how good it was to actually be out of the Philippines, "What with all the political *basura* going on there all the time, my friend."

When Norton asked him to explain, Canlas had repeated himself, after first explaining that, "*Basura* equates to rubbish…there are too many rebel groups and too much infighting all the time. Even within groups of supposed allies."

Later on, Norton reflected in his hammock on the front deck, just before he sunk into slumber, that Eric Canlas may well have been describing his own homeland of late, namely Aotearoa. "Insurgency. Yeah – good to be out of there too," was his last cogent thought that night, before sleep snapped him on the crest of its latest wave.

25/3.

The next day Ruby called her second cousin, Fred, and asked if he could drive
them up to Manila tomorrow.

No problem for Fred, who was always looking for work. He had once been an avid
National People's Army guerilla, but after the government amnesty a few years
before, he had surrendered his gun, gotten a jalopy and become a taxi driver –
without a licence or registration. But his cheeky smile always seemed to escape
him from the law. That, plus a few *pesos* of course.

At the next morning sunrise, Fred was already parked outside – about 90 minutes
too early. He would snooze there, just waiting. Ruby supposed Fred did this so as
not to be upstaged by some other driver whenever she asked him to drive her
anywhere – which to her knowledge had never actually happened.

Dr. Cross was moaning about the hour, but Ruby – again – told him about the
humungous traffic drawl as they would approach Manila and that it would be quite
a long day already. Fred had on his car CD player and it was the usual antiquated
Americano music drifting around inside the vehicle – '*My Way*' as originally sung by
about seven different crooners, who all sounded the same. Even Cross soon got
sick of the pap, and he had grown up with such lift muzak. After all, his countrymen
had invented it - and they had also ensured that small arms were littered around
the Philippines more than the actual litter on the streets. Every man and his dog
and even his dog's brother seemed to have a gun somewhere. Fred, of course,
had a gun – a small Luger, which he kept under his driver's side seat, just in case.

They got near to Pasay City after their swift start, then ran into a considerable
period of stasis where birds flying outside got further faster than them. Ruby knew
her sister would still be working for the Koreans and because they were hard
masters, that she – her sister – wouldn't be home until quite late.

God, it was hot and humid inside the guts of Manila.

The aircon was up and running, but Cross was perspiring worse than a leaky tap valve and his T-shirt was wetter than a wave. He wanted to piss real bad too, but there was just nowhere to go to and no way of even getting out of the van. Hemmed in ludicrously. Moving slower than any snail he'd ever seen.

Ruby was fast asleep, snoring gently into the mist streaming down through the aircon apertures, oblivious to her partner's frustration. He didn't want to use the mobile phone with all these ears around either.

Ruby wasn't so asleep actually. She was sort of feigning – her doze fluctuating between deep slumber and an airy fluttering. Her mind was percolating about Euris and what may or may not have happened to her – if anything. Just as her mind seismographed everywhere, so did the potential Manila avenues down which Euris may have traveled, slowly pass by just outside.

POSSIBILTIES:	DOUBTFULS
Maybe she had gone overseas or offshore with a new boyfriend, with the funds to finance this?	Yet, as far as Ruby knew, Euris had no such wealthy companion.
Maybe she had just decided to not contact her mother, Grace, for reasons unbeknown?	But Euris and Grace were pretty much like Siamese twins. A highly unlikely possibility.
Maybe she was in jail? Or had been kidnapped?	Whatever for? And anyway the Police/kidnappers or police-kidnappers, would have made some effort to let the family know by now, surely?
Maybe she was in hospital?	Perhaps more likely, but surely the hospital would have tried to contact her family? Eventually.

Ruby didn't want to think about more nefarious options, such as Euris being held by a psycho, locked in a basement. Ruby being sold into prostitution down in Tondo. Or even into Indochina. Ruby being forced into gun running for the MILF against her will. It all happened. Only in the Philippines.

Euris being dead somewhere, buried in a shallow grave by someone who had needed to expunge her real bad.

Ruby didn't even want to think that last one, but it kept knocking on the door of her brain, incessantly and annoyingly.

Later, after finally attaining Pasay City, Manila, Ruby let herself and Dr. Cross in, after slipping Fred one thousand pesos.

Straight away, inside, she noticed that Cross was on his mobile, avidly ignoring her and the GMA game show blaring across the room from the wide-screen T.V. she had automatically switched on, on their arrival. He was outside on the verandah, semi-closing the sliding glass door, so she could only make out bits and pieces of his strangled conversation – words about 'deadlines' and 'quickly close it' and some name that sounded like Mondaugen or something. Then her eye caught Lovie Poe on the screen and she turned away from the door. Lovie was cute. Way cuter than Cross.

Then followed the news flash item.

The very sad thing is that Ruby's most feared possibility was possibly true, because right then, Mike Enriquez was announcing the fact very clearly on GMA's 24-hours news update. Euris wasn't yet named as the dead young woman found semi-buried out on Pangasinan beach, but that was likely to follow.

Later, Ruby and her sister Ivy hugged each other, bawling, when they saw the grainy black and white photos taken of the body and flashed onto the television screen in typical Philippine fashion. If they were to believe what they saw, it was Euris - and she was gone.

By then, in the aircon-on-steroids bedroom of Ruby's sister's apartment in Pasay City, Dr. Cross' brain had already crumbled into crud soon after his reaching the room lintel. He was dead to the world, snoring obliviously to the tremendous grief the two sisters were bawling, out in the living room.

It was almost as if he didn't care.

26/2.

Ho Fat Kit was scanning the entire perimeter with his pair of binoculars, his hands clasped like the hairy claws of his favourite seafood around its sweaty black circumference.

He walked up and down, up and down the harsh wooden deck of the trawler, itself a floating lie, for deep within its barnacled hull revved a tremendously strong engine and locked away down there also, were enough armaments to sink a small navy.

Ho Fat could only see scrublands with an occasional spartan tree imploringly pawing toward the sky. Over on the furthest hill he could make out some unswept graves, marooned like sperm whales on a dry beach, but there was no sign of life anywhere. Rather an anomaly, given that Lamma Island was so close to the massively meandering metropolis that was Hong Kong.

If Ho Fat knew any English at all he would have been familiar with the cliché 'like looking for a needle in a haystack'. But since he was resolute in both cigarette smoking and Cantonese, he was mouthing grotesque obscenities, spitting into the spray and sucking deep on his El Cheapo bootleg cigars, smuggled in via Lau Fau Shan during the last few weeks.

They were getting very sick of and increasingly bad-tempered with this continual search for that cocksucker, Godfrey Woo. The bastard seemed to have developed invisibility, along with his other traits of overripe gambling and never paying back his exponentially increasing debts to the Wo Sha Ni triad. Ho Fat Kit – as chief enforcer – certainly had a vested interest in locating Woo once and for all and dealing to him big time, for it had been he who had O.Ked the plethora of loans to Woo.

If only they could find him.

Rumours had been threading in that Woo had somehow managed to elude them in Kowloon and – again, somehow – had inveigled himself onto and into Lamma's broad back-blocks, surviving on cut-price instant noodles and rainwater, sleeping rough, bathing in the secluded coves when night fell.

Yet no one could pinpoint him for sure and Ho Fat's big brothers were getting increasingly irate. He spat again into the lurking swill and paced once more up and down, up and down, using his binoculars as an extension of his own macroscopic need to spot and then swat Woo, once and for all.

Woo could see just about everything from his hideout high on Lamma's barren peak. No one could really nab him, just as long as he was vigilant and shifted his location reasonably frequently. Lately also he had been filching food from both restaurant garbage bins and from open windows – reaching in and snaffling as easily purloined, whatever some errant homeowner or shopkeeper had left. His long bare arms grabbed what was available and his long brazen gut just swamped down whatever didn't smell too bad, taste too sinister. He had ceased shaving some time ago and didn't want to look at his reflected image.

Not just because he knew he would look bad, but because he was bad and he knew any self-reflection might seriously disturb his sleep. More and more of late he had slunk into violent dreamology and the demons from his guilt-ridden past were haunting him, beckoning to him through a miasma of children's wails, wives' pleas, mistresses' screams. Woo had long since crossed the magic line between moral and amoral. Between fair and feral.

That late afternoon though, Woo was becoming just a little puzzled by that fishing trawler just off to his right horizon. It seemed to have been there for some considerable amount of time and – what is more – it seemed to be making zany zig-zags along the same sections of sea. Instinctively, Woo stooped his bony thin frame even more and swept his thinning wisps of no-longer-dyed hair away from his greasy broad forehead. He swept his puffy tongue once or twice over his filthy broken front teeth and snorted as he segued into the taut scrublands and hoped that the vessel just vanished.

Ho Fat was by now certain that he had seen something – or was it someone – high up there in the distance. Sure, because Ho Fat detected movement, sudden movement. He signaled to the bored skipper to slow the boat right down and to sweep one more time along the same channeled rut.

The sun was still high enough, still had not broken out into rashes of shadows, still could illuminate sufficiently anything weirdly untoward in a scene that rarely altered.

There. There it was. Something gray. Something protruding from the scrublands. Ho Fat tightened his focus another notch. He was by now reasonably certain he could discern spasmodic movement all right.

The trawler stopped functioning altogether.

Woo knew they knew. Something slunk into his mind to inform him that he had indeed been sprung. He also knew that if he got up suddenly and ran, he would be waving a red rag to a bull. What to do? He tried one last time to merge into earth, hoping that this might disempower his chasers. But deep down he also sensed they would not give up: the momentum in this cat and mouse race had built into its own freefall – the chase now ran itself free from human input.

He sighed and wondered what he could do. The boat seemed to have stolen into a Van Gogh seascape – it was that motionless - and he guessed that whoever was on board lusting after him, would be on their mobile phone to the land-based team, offering a vivid description as to his exact whereabouts. Not that Woo had ever heard of Van Gogh.

He sweated a bit more, until he once more ran out of it. His short pants were fighting his groin and his torn singlet was abusing him grotesquely. Only his twisted sandals offered him any support, as crouching as low as he could sustain, he manoeuvred his way off the summit and down, down, down to the rocky cove.

His thoughts were to throw off the inevitable dogs from his strong scent, by diving into the water and swimming over to the next bay, around the sharp promontory over there. Woo knew he had once been a good swimmer, good enough to represent his secondary school team in the across the anchorage event, years before it was shut down due to the lurking murk of Victoria Harbour. But, he never had been a victor.

Woo waited, breathing deeply into his skinny frame after slithering his slink down the hillside. Where he waited for the other team to make the next play.

Ho Fat was now yelling something in his Fukien dialect at some poor underling on the land side of Lamma; yelling so loudly as to be heard by diners at the nearest outdoor by-the-shore restaurant, specializing in whelps and cockerels served in a stew of turnips. If they listened closely and if they had any credentials in that Mainland tongue, they could hear something about, "dogs, now, dogs, now."

Wo Sha Ni wasted no time. Even on Lamma – some way away from the urban thrum – there were steady connections among the merchants, the restauranters, the cleaners, the fishermen, the ferry crews. Wo Sha Ni wanted Woo's head – and a few other bodily parts here and there too - and would never back down or away until they recouped all of their large amount of gambled-away money. Including the huge swathes of interest owing. Failing that, there would only be severe torture of the offending party, causing unmitigated and prolonged pain, preceding his or her demise.

The dogs were already coming to the lonely beach, like toy statues cast on the small and fast skiffs run by zippy little outboards, usually used to flee the Coastguard, on their frequent nightly smuggling flits to the Mainland. The canine tribe were sniffing and pawing and yelping, wanting so much to bark, but under threat of savage beatings if they so much as opened their jaws.

Ho Fat waited further offshore, until the job was done. The minions would grab and nab Woo and throw him at Ho Fat like a sick flea, ready to be expunged after his last ooze of dollars had dried up. He motioned the captain to smooth the craft over the waves until they were anchored just offshore, slowly transmogrifying into the dropping dusk descending everywhere into the permanent hazy carapace lambasted over Hong Kong.

As he paddled deeper into the sea, ducking every so often when he believed he saw a light off-shore, Woo smelt fear: his own, dripping duly down his whippet-like torso and co-mingling with the wave scum.

It was quickly getting much darker and Ho Fat was cursing even more than his own steady norm, for no dogs had yet been seen anywhere near a climax.

Woo was keeping close to the rocky side of the beach, amongst the sharp pinnacles and trickling streams of skanky seaweed, hoping that nothing could track him down in this dark area.

Just as he rose a little higher than normal, he saw just over there, a small boat with flickering spotlights playing havoc with the waves. Uncomfortably near. He soon also heard indistinct voices, becoming blurrier every time he dunked himself further and more frequently into the tepid rinse. He was well aware that he would soon be out over his depth and was preparing to swim and swim and swim.

One or two of the dogs were in full whimpering mode, for they sensed something just beyond their range, could smell something and could not contain themselves in their lusting excitement.

Woo was stroking steadily further out to sea, hoping to circle well beyond any craft and to land back on the other broken cove further along the shore.

He seemed to have succeeded in avoiding the dog ships, for when he quite literally stole a glance adrift, he noted that he was beyond them, their attention riveted much closer to the shoreline now.

He was just beginning to think that he had been undetected, was alive to face another 24 hours, when the anchor chain hit him hard on the crest of his skull, just as Ho Fat was yelling at his small crew to tarry there and see what was going to happen.

Woo could have sworn that, just before he passed out completely and floated comatose toward the reef way out at sea and beyond anyone's immediate cognizance, the name of the vessel loomed fleetingly into his flickering consciousness.

He was almost certain it read, as scrawled lazily across the bow –
優勝.
Victorious.

27/4.

Norton felt physically ill. Nothing to do with the striations of the waves or the noxiousness of the diesel engines' vomit of bilious smoke deep into his lungs. More to do with a reaction to the vibrating synapses in his forebrain, stating that perhaps these recent deaths of close family members were indeed linked, were pre-planned; were part of something wider. He couldn't quite grasp the weft of the pattern, despite all of the phenomenological effort his brain was putting in to do so, but it was all making him feel decidedly unwell. He lay on his bunk attempting to subdue his ruminations via slumber: all to no avail. His brain just dashed on and on.

He still had rapid rivulets of guilt about Makere compounding the flow, as he began to admit to his essential inner soul that he was missing her. A lot.

He would liked to have run everything past Monaghan – as he usually always used to – but, of course, his now unavailable lawyer was even more inaccessible as a crony, as a sounding board. The trouble also was, Norton hadn't exactly kept in close contact with Monaghan these past few years.

Norton had not – as yet – linked Monaghan into anything to do with the slaughter of Trevor King and Makere. Why should he, despite Hemi Hemara's inebriate misgivings? However, he was puzzled as to why the lawyer-friend had seemingly vanished at this crucial stage of proceedings.

It was later – in the so-called wee small hours of the morning when only the dum-dum-dum of the ship engines made any spike into quiet – that Norton nearly sat bolt upright, as his mental nebulae slashed into his cognizance the fact he had earlier forgotten. Monaghan's office was in Auckland, while he was rumoured also to have been seen in Gisborne recently – possibly present, then, during the times of both slayings.

In fact, Henare Kupu - a distant cousin whom Norton had encountered at the RSA a few nights after his own ex-wife's *tangi* - had muttered words to that effect, after a drinking session there.

Something like, "Saw that Pākehā mate of yours' down in Gisborne last week…what the fuck's he doing in these parts, man? He was all dressed up like he was goin' to go hunting or something…"

But Norton – or rather his then addled-with-alcohol-mind – had soon forgotten that tidbit from someone he wasn't so sure about, as to regarding reliability at the best of times. Norton still believed Kupu had stolen from him some years before, namely the diary Norton had once maintained pretty regularly before he became a meatworker. Besides which, Norton had never trusted Kupu ever since he had served in Vietnam with him years before.

As had Monaghan, of course. Monaghan had been Kupu's platoon leader and had had Kupu do all sorts of undercover behind-the-lines type stuff – at least that was the rumour. Norton had himself never been too closely involved with all that sort of shit – while he never really got too close to Henare either. "Just in case, eh," as he had once put it to Hemi.

So it goes.

Or so Kurt Vonnegut reckoned anyway.

Norton had long since stopped reading Vonnegut. Or anything much else for that matter.

His whole life – particularly right now – seemed more of a fiction than any novel: yet more of a novel than any documentary. Words could not seem to describe it. Here he was on the very far outskirts of Puerto Princessa, as an illegal immigrant, about to jump overboard and land up the coast a bit, on the ship's motorized and leaky launch. Along with a cargo of armaments for the MILF rebels, who were stashed steadily among the backwaters of Palawan, Philippines. He didn't expect to see any rebels however, because Eric Canlas had told him that Norton would be soon escorted to some of Eric's friends, "for a while" – before they would get him across to Manila – and then, "*kaibigan* – it's all going to be up to you."

It wasn't the first time Norton had been to the Philippines, but the one and only other time had been around forty years previously, on leave from the skirmishes in South East Asia that he had been involved in. He had gotten drunk and frequented the innumerable girlie bars in downtown Manila and out in Makarti. He also had the requisite fight or two with some foolish Americanos, who seemed to think that they owned the place. Other than that, he remembered SFA about the jaunt – except that Monaghan had been there too. And that, on reflection, Monaghan had seemed to get along very well with these selfsame Americanos, the same ones whom Norton had tried to bludgeon into stasis on more than one occasion.

While he was waiting for the launch to be launched, he reflected on Monaghan again. Yeah – it dawned like a cliché on his brain – Monaghan had also taken a long leave in Manila for some family business back around then. It had always seemed bloody odd to Norton that his mate had no family in the Philippines, let alone only a few in Aotearoa New Zealand – and even in that country, only in some small back-alley township that the census often forgot, because it was so nondescript. Monaghan's American mother had passed away two years previously, or at least that is what he had told all his military mates - and some of his clients later on.

Come to think of it, as Norton now was again doing much more of, what was an Irish-Armenian ever doing in Aotearoa New Zealand anyway? Monaghan had said his father was some sort of diplomat and that he had changed his name from Mondaugen or something similar.

Norton was then told to get into the lurching launch, so his brain shut up shop for a while. Like it had done for too many years already.

28/3.

Back down in Pampanga. Ruby, her mother Acquilina and her sister Ivy went to
Euris' wake and then the burial – leaving Cross to look after himself in Manila. He
had the money, he could buy his way around for a few days or much longer, if
need be.

All the cousins and aunts and uncles were at the burial – except the many
Overseas Foreign Worker ones, who couldn't afford to come back home and
indeed hadn't been able to come back home for years since. There were also a lot
of Euris' classmates, all in full grievance mode. The priest said the right homilies,
they sang the correct hymns, they then went down to the overflowing cemetery and
watched as Euris was lowered slightly into a far too thin piece of remaining terrain,
that would only flood when the rains came.

Later, Grace put on food for the closest relatives, and the few hungry hangers-on.
They sat quite silently chatting small talk to each other and occasionally casting
swift looks up at Euris' old, faded full-face photograph resting on the mantelpiece in
the living room.

"Have the police made any arrests yet?" enquired Ruby to no one in particular, only
to receive shrugs all around.

Silence pretty much ruled the remainder of that afternoon.

Grace later shared with Ruby and Ivy and their mother – her aunt – that the police
had disclosed that it was 'no sex crime, this one,' but that maybe the offender(s)
had wanted people to believe that it had been.

"So who do they think killed the poor girl?" nagged Ruby, herself one who could
never bear procrastination and things left undone.

"They say they are not too sure at this stage," replied Euris' mother – herself
remarkably sanguine about the loss of her oldest daughter, "but they also said that
Euris was in some sort of socialist youth group and that they had CCTV footage of

her trying to break into the American Embassy a couple of months ago…at night."

"What – all by herself? That place would be heavily guarded."

"No – apparently there were a few of them who tried to create a disturbance and one or two tried to get in through the gate. It didn't work, of course – but they reckon Euris was one of them."

"That doesn't sound like the Euris that I know - I mean knew," stated Ivy, matter-of-factly.

Grace paused to clear away a few dishes and to tidy up the scraps of this and that, that and this as left by the by now departed guests. Then she murmured something to the point that, "Well, Euris changed a lot recently. Had some funny ideas. Went on a lot about José Rizal and freeing the Filipinos from *putih* imperialism…I just thought it was all youth stuff – yunno – just growing up."

"And what about Rustico, her boyfriend?" nagged Ruby again, "How come he wasn't at the wake? We saw him today only at the cemetery? How much does he know about all this? Was he at the embassy too?"

Grace merely shrugged in response. For her, Rustico Tuazon had been a prime factor causing Euris to recently go off tangent; had radically influenced her daughter. Yet, she wasn't going to share her feelings about him just yet. Grace wanted to learn just a bit more about the boyfriend's motives.

"It was a pity that we could not see her in the coffin," mused Ivy some time later, to no one in particular.

Grace picked up on the comment. "They said that, her body was not suitable for viewing." And left it there as she farewelled her grieving relatives and turned tiredly to clean up her home.

Before Ivy was driven back to her Manila condominium, her mother, Ruby and she were taken by Ivy's driver to the large church at the end of J.Pintella. The sisters had always called it a cathedral, because to them when growing up, its height and the huge tower in the centre, seemed far too massive to be those of a mere church.

Inside, the atmosphere was like stepping into a kaleidoscope, for the sun's still rampant rays were filtered through the giant panes of multi-coloured glass. Inside, the ceiling seemed distant, stretching upward toward where heaven thrived. Inside also – immediately – all three feel into peace, for all was silent. Clear. Vastly deferential.

No one else was there. Just hymn books piled obediently on a pew or two and sets of dried flowers and their colourful living cousins spread here and there around the wooden walls, as garlands.

Ruby glanced up to sight the pained expression on the uplifted face of a Christ carved in wood, lashed to a cross that stretched for metres upwards and sideways. She knew that she was not as devout a Catholic as her mother and sister, but right then and there, she knew she craved the respite, the sanctuary, the tranquility the church offered. She prayed in her own erratic fashion, for her family, her cousin Grace, her own children. She asked for resilience. She requested repose.

Ruby sat back and waited for her mother Acquilina and her younger sister Ivy, to finish their own reflections and ruminations. Both had their eyes closed tightly, while Ivy clenched her rosary like there was no tomorrow or, indeed, the day after.

As they slowly left, all three turned and genuflected toward the altar and the wooden lectern stooping as a sentinel directly behind it.

Ruby suddenly felt emptied of worry, of doubt, of dependence. As if her entire unsettled inner being had somehow been sucked out of her mouth and discarded in some waste place well outside of this place.

 Outside, the din, speed and sheer weight of people and vehicles hithering and thithering everywhere in the evening almost overwhelmed them, as Mother and daughter slowly walked back down their street, after saying their goodbyes to Ivy.

Hand-in-hand back to mother's home, just around a few bends in Pampanga. There they soon after went to bed, although Ruby couldn't settle. She toyed with ringing Cross, back up in Manila, but put that idea aside quite quickly. What could he possibly say or do to help her?

She probably wouldn't have been able to get through anyway, because he was already on the telephone, ringing a number internationally, which he had been given by his American mentors quite some time ago.

Monaghan however, missed that call, as he was now finally in transit to somewhere in Asia.

29/2.

Woo, for reasons he could not fathom, had been incredibly lucky. It seemed he was fated to survive – still free at this stage – and remain alive, given that he had huge bruises all over his high-domed and balding forehead and that he had almost drowned.

Somehow, he had struggled back to the surface, to find himself many metres away from any launch lights and well out of earshot from any receptive, probing strobes. His head throbbed all over and his lungs were rebelling big time.

But Woo could float – something his mother had instilled in him as a young boy, when they all went fishing together off Sai Kung – so as to be able to survive until someone could save him completely.

So, here he was floating way out at sea in the dark, yet towards another small island to the west of Lamma. Actually, it was more of a rock outcrop and it bore only a couple of decrepit stone cottages, home to the sometime fishermen who rested there during storms.

Luck swam deep that night. For as Woo floated on his back, half-kicking in unison with the tide, he arrived on the scrambling shingle and sand shoreline, just under the one cottage, which had an inhabitant, a man named Ah So. Who was right then filleting some of the many snapper and cod that he had netted earlier that afternoon from the decks of his one-man launch. Which was now ferreted around the hidden side of the islet, away from the potentially prying eyes of the maritime police and the Hong Kong Fisheries Inspection teams. For Ah So was no ordinary fisherman. Rather, he was a smuggler for hire, who went out to fish because he was not only good at this trade and actually made money from his plentiful catches, but also because by going out on his launch at fairly frequent intervals he could give himself cover for his more illicit activities.

As the sun struggled to saunter early the next morning and as Ah So was wandering down to the sea to chuck away all the unusable slivers of his catch from the previous day, he noticed what looked like a man laying right next to the water's edge. So close in fact that it looked as though he was breathing in the wavelets.

Ah So ran down to the figure and – quickly kneeling – pulled him over onto his back – for it was indeed a man – and away from the water. The man was still breathing shallowly and Ah So soon had him gulping more deeply, as he pounded his back, after dragging him away from the shallows.

He helped Godfrey Woo back to the hut and made him a cup of heavy *cha* over the portable gas stove, muttering, "Man, you gave me one hell of a turn just now. I thought you were dead" – in his native Cantonese.

Woo didn't register for quite some time that he was still extant. In fact it took him a couple of days to even remember more fully what had happened to him that night before. But it slowly crept into the crevices of his brain that he was indeed alive and – even more amazingly – that he wasn't going to be shopped to or chopped up by, the triad – or the *jing cha* for that matter – just yet.

Ah So followed the code of all criminals – never backstab one of your own. He wasn't going to dob in this fellow, nor was he going to ask him too many questions about how he got there as a form of seawrack. For his part, Woo was in no hurry to go anywhere either, mainly because he had nowhere to go.

So the two stayed on the rocks for two days. It suited Ah So to do so because the seas were running rough and he still had to keep filleting and deep-icing his catch. He strayed around to his boat most of both afternoons to work on some dicey throttle problems, too. Woo was content to dry out and sleep and de-bruise and lay low. The weather was pretty shitty, so he kept indoors in the one room shack and wrapped himself in a blanket and made noodle stew from the copious provisions Ah So had stored there. There was no fresh water source, so all water came in bottled form – from a crate, which the fisherman-smuggler had lugged around himself a few days previously.

The two didn't say much to each other either, so it came as a bit of a surprise to Woo when Ah So looked him in the eyes and stated matter-of-factly, "I reckon you will want a ride with me on my boat soon. I'm leaving tomorrow."

It wasn't so much a remark as a command.

It wasn't until they were out at sea a bit the next day that Ah So looked across at Woo sitting right up against the bulwark in his scrawny clothes and his days-old beard and added, "I'm going across to Shenzhen tonight, so I will drop you off just outside of Lau Fau Shan."

Woo was heading back to where he had used to live all those years ago.

And he had no real choice in this matter either. It was hardly as if he could ask to be taken somewhere else. And he didn't much care to jump overboard and taste the swill all over again.

The only real thought of substance he had just at that moment was that he hoped none of his family, who were still living in the area, recognized him. Or that Ho Fat Kit was not back in these, his first haunts. Or any of those other swarthy guys with swarthy crew cuts, all dressed up in black and smoking their brains out like fumaroles.

30/3.

Eric Canlas and Norton stayed at one of his cousins' shacks, way out the back of the capital of Palawan – out of the way of tourists and cops and politicians. The others in the launch had set off further down the coastline with some of the big stash of firearms and God-only knew what else. Seems Canlas was going to go back to Pampanga sometime soon for, "a break from all this sailing, man." He wanted to go and see his grandmother while he could - and she wasn't getting any younger.

They stayed there for three days, eating rice and fried chicken and bugger-all else, which was tolerable for Norton, because there was also a fair supply of Red Horse beer with which to guzzle everything down. Besides which, he had paid good money back on the East Coast of Aotearoa to be ferried all this way, with the promise that he would be accompanied for a bit, "once we reach Philippines – our guarantee," as Canlas had stressed. Norton even went swimming a couple of times in the warm and blue-as-Paul-Newman's-eyes seawater cruising and lapping languidly onto the white sand beach they stayed nearby.

It all would have been heaven – whatever that might be – if it hadn't been for the torrential downpour on the third night, which made arrant mockery of the thatched roofing and which had more chance of drowning them than the sea outside their huts. It was then that Canlas said that – tomorrow - they would jump on another yacht, which would take them to Subic.

"Then," he repeated, "you are on your own *kaibigan*."

Which was a mantra Norton was beginning to get sick of hearing. He had no idea what he was going to do over there, but figured that he would be able to meld in for a bit, with his brown skin and low profile.

He had forgotten that he was pretty profusely tattooed with multifarious *moko* and that he didn't actually speak Tagalog – let alone understand it.

Then again, he had forgotten rather a lot these last few years. He seemed, in fact, to have slopped down a rather steep character slope; had misplaced emotions such as love, fear, remorse, with a more general spew of vapidity and torpidity. Makere's mantra of, "You're not the man you used to be," was on endless replay inside his skull and the only way to switch it off was to dive deep into the sweet blue sea.

31/3.

After the latest developments in their lives, Ruby by now knew for sure that she had indeed had enough of the Doctor's procrastinations and prevarications.

He hadn't wanted to come back down to Pampanga for the wake, which had lasted in essence several days, and he hadn't bothered to call her more than two cursory times. It seemed he was dealing with what he called, "urgent matters to do with his own national security issues," which was a complete surprise to her, for he had never previously even touched on said issues.

More, he had spent most of the last five or so months laying around her mother's home, eating the readily-cooked food, crapping and copulating at whim and sleeping at will. Yes - he did pay his fair share and more of their accumulated bills and yes - he had never physically lashed out at her like that bastard Godfrey Woo had more than once. Such as when she had disturbed Woo wanking over computer porn or fornicating with the latest betting pages of the local Hong Kong newspaper. But, all this recent aloof treatment from this *putih* Doctor was stuff she could do without.

Ruby wanted proximity and loyalty in her men - she provided it for them and couldn't comprehend why it could not work both ways. She had decided to get rid of Doctor Cross when the time was opportune. She wasn't exactly going to double-cross him - and she smiled at her own wordplay there - but she wasn't going to cross his path for much longer if she could help it either.

She had gone back to her mother's home after the sad and wailing wake at her cousin's place and only muttered, *"hindi ko alam,"* when her mother finally enquired as to where the *putih* was.

She did telephone back to Hong Kong too — for the first time in quite a while - to check up on her kids. Not that they were kids anymore of course, but she liked to hear their voices now and again, given that they both had their own lives these days and were pretty busy.

She was amazed to hear from her son that he thought he had seen his rapscallion father last week, skulking around Tin Shui Wai. Or at least, "it looked a lot like him. *Ho nan*, Mummy."

Ruby told her son that he was probably mistaken - Woo had been gone for so long now that they had all assumed that he was dead. "Probably just someone that looks like him," was all she could stutter back.

Ruby went out back and chatted with her mother, who was once more doing the washing by hand - eschewing any washing machine. Ruby had once offered to buy her one – with the Doctor's money, but her mother didn't want to know. She liked to wash clothes by hand. Gave her time, "to relax and to think," as she once confided to her daughter.

Later that afternoon they strolled together down to the small local market and bought some chilies and dried fish.

No need to worry about what the doctor might want to eat now.

And they would eat it with their hands too.

<table><tr><td>

My sister – as recounted by Ivy (magna cum laude, Asuncion College, Manila)

Ruby was a fulcrum.

Everything seemed to revolve around her. Whether it was because she was dynamic, ever active, positive, or whether it was due to some flicker of fate, Ruby was most often at the centre of the storms and their later lulls in our family.

Her luck with men had always run out at some time and after she had cast her mind back during her few periods of inactivity, she told me that she realized that she should have seen their inadequacies coming, especially as she grew older and supposedly wiser. Maybe all men were as ultimately useless, undependable, inadequate, as all of the men she had had encounters with. She told me, more than once, that she thought briefly about Godfrey Woo and then shuddered at this very thought. What had possessed her to have ever gotten involved with that 'ugly bastard' in the first place? She knew her own answer – her own naivety, youth, loneliness – and the very fact of being a Filipina in a discriminatory World.

</td></tr></table>

She knew she also needed and wanted men. Not merely for sex, although that was always on her wish list, but for their companionship and quite honestly also, for the money they brought into any relationship. Money, however, never translated into security, as the relationships eventually wilted, failed, wound down to entropy.

Ruby often sighed. She said that she couldn't talk to her mother much about men as, quite frankly, our mother didn't really want to talk about her long deceased husband, our father, because of the mean man ways he had treated her. Our mother was happier now than she had ever been with him, even during their early honeymoon days.

I am also completely frustrated with my own chain-smoking husband, but rather resigned to keeping the bond going, so as to ensure a future for our son. I too, just do not want to parlay about men. For good reason. Thinking about them always gives me a headache.

So Ruby tended to keep such conversations to herself and to determine that in any future relationship from now on, she would always straight away, make sure she would not be hurt, by making certain also that she would not get too close to the potential partner. Have some fun, yes, but no more long-term commitments to anything much else.

She would be the fulcrum for only her own self and her own family from now on. Ruby told me that she became consciously deliberately selfish.

She had to in order to survive. And survive she would.

And, as she confided to me, she also pledged herself to out the killers of Euris and to do justice to the bastards, even if it took the rest of her life. That pledge would never be far from her mind from now on, even as she smiled her beautiful smile and considered her next moves. Blood was blood, after all and Euris was her close blood.

And mine.

32/2.

Godfrey Woo lay among the cardboard cartons he had scored from out back of Wellcome and Park 'n' Shop stores in Chung Fu Plaza, in the North West New Territories of Hong Kong.

He was sleeping and living rougher in the nullah out back of Lau Fau Shan and scoring a few dollars by loading and unloading various swags of counterfeit bootlegs, on a semi-regular basis. Labouring for the Mainland sharks who paid him irregularly in lank wads of notes, sometimes dripping with the salt spill from their launch decks, and as always carefully checked by Woo, to ensure they too weren't counterfeit bills.

He had grown a spindly beard, freckled and flecked with grey badinages and he hoped that no one would recognize him anymore from around these parts, where he had indeed lived and brought up his family quite some time ago now. Before he had deserted them for that Shenzhen honeypot, who soon lost her flavour.

Woo kept well to himself and avoided eye contact. He wasn't the sole nullah-liver by any means. Times were always tough out in this City of Sorrow, as Hong Kong's portly politicians liked to paint it – and yet none of them had ever been sighted this far out from the dense throb of the central city, where they spent all day and half of each night playing plutocrats..

33/2.

Monaghan and Dr. Cross had never actually met, yet both had irregularly worked –
if that is the correct term – for the same company for most of their adult lives.

They were both rather oddball, who because of their respective eccentricities, had
fallen into the company despite some actual distaste for much of what they were
now supporting. Cross disliked most Americans, yet was a dark-skinned one
himself, at least via the African heritage on his father's side. While Monaghan was
a Pākehā New Zealander via upbringing, who fought alongside Americans and
continued to stand staunch for what he identified as a top cause. He was even
more staunch, in fact, than most American citizens.

Both then were highly dangerous, because their company had the best weaponry
in the world, combined with a trove of seemingly unlimited funding and a tendency
to be able to obfuscate their employees' identities so successfully that not even
their mothers would have known what they were doing.

And what were they doing?

Basically anything to ensure the American regime remained transcendent and
regnant and impervious to anything that supposedly threatened its worldwide
valence. And anything meant anything. More, their regime hated being
embarrassed by this truth being made common knowledge. So it would not pause
to eliminate any outspoken whistleblowers. Or writers.

These two conquistadors, then, were lethal in that they were chameleon-skinned. It
was as if they could be remodeled in plasticine anytime their company needed
them – sometimes a lot all at once, sometimes not for months, years. Even
decades.

Here they both were in The Fort, Manila, drinking coffee at the diner that
specialized in supposedly Americano treats. They weren't actually sitting together
either, because they had never seen each other before. They had spoken only
briefly on a supposedly secure telephone, just once a few days previously

They were just awaiting instructions on what to do next – or rather whom to do next - because they specialized in eliminating what the company nominated as threats to the flag.

Dr. Cross, for all his apparently amiable ambience, and Monaghan, for all his legal training and stature, were assassins.

They killed to order and then just went about their normal routines.

And they just loved the money they were earning.

Monaghan looked around him, over his oversize mug of café latte.

There was only one other guy in the room, masquerading as a customer. He was a rather darkish-hued man, who was scanning the newspaper, whilst still wearing shades. When he looked up he caught Monaghan's less-than-glance and beckoned for the latter to come and join him.

Which Monaghan did – shaking hands when he neared the American. No names were exchanged. It was rather like a Hollywood movie, or how a Hollywood movie would unveil itself. In other words, as scarcely credible, as hugely coincidental, yet still massively present. Inerasable absurdity.

They both knew that it had all been arranged for them to – finally – meet up here. They had separately received their oral orders only a few hours previously.

Small talk wasn't on their agenda either. Instead, Monaghan listened for a bit as Cross – for of course it was he – outlined this agenda. They were to take out another young student who had been generating too high a profile of late and whose continual and popular blogging was causing too many questions to be raised in the Philippine Senate. All of which was hugely embarrassing for their off-shore paymasters, who counted on their ex-colony to remain pretty much that way, despite its nominal naming as a Republic.

The problem was though, that this student was IT savvy, a bit wily and was traipsing around a fair bit – even jetting as afar as Hong Kong, which would be no real matter, because it was yet another ex-colony of the American's first cousin – England. They all spoke the same language after all.

And the Anglo-American complex was also damned determined to keep their lingua franca foisted onto paying customers, in not only their ex-colonies, but also well beyond.

Cross told Monaghan that he – the paler skinned killer – was to do the job as soon as possible, while he — the far swarthier of the two men and the more senior - would have to now travel to Hong Kong to tie up a few loose ends, as recently unraveled by this 'punk kid'. As he put it - just before sipping on his own cappuccino with a pink marshmallow poised somewhat obscenely on its froth.

"And that's all I have been given," averred Dr. Cross, who really didn't want to know anymore anyway.

Secretly, not so deep down, he had enough of this place also. He would telephone Ruby to tell her some believable bullshit and that he would be back soon enough and would let her know when he was about to land at Clark. Little did he know about her recent decision. He had never deigned to really get to know her.

He wasn't too sure anymore if in fact he would come back and work for the company for a while. He had more than enough funds to semi-retire – or at least until the next wave of redactions and renditions. After all, he had amassed quite a tally of them in the Philippines and other parts of South East Asia already.

Monaghan, on the other hand, was musing that there had to be some serious shit going on in the free world when he had to depart another English-speaking colony – his New Zealand – and then to fly half way around the world and actually meet another killer in the flesh. Especially his being directed to go to a country he had only ever been to previously for short spells and where he knew almost zero of the local lingo. "Who makes up these schemes?" he had queried to himself, on his business-class flight over here. "It's like something from a cheap novel bought at an airport."

The other side, the communists or radicals or insurgents or activists – or whatever their new categorization was these days – must have been powering up some steady steam for such a turn of events. In his own compartmentalisable mind, he felt he had a duty to protect the free world from such riff-raff, even if a small part of this selfsame mind, trained as a legal expert, was rebelling with rumblings of assassination not equating to justice. He – Monaghan – spoke into his coffee though when he mumbled, "Fuck this shit", so the American beside him didn't hear anything, except what he took to be a burp from the Kiwi.

Mind you, Monaghan liked money too. Which was probably also the main push towards gaining that law degree, after he had been demobbed all those years prior. His mother would have been extremely proud of him too.

After Dr. Cross – if that was ever his real name departed – Monaghan for some reason couldn't help but begin to wonder what was happening to his distant and consistent client, Norton, whom he presumed was still back on the East Coast of Aotearoa New Zealand, somewhat scared shitless and witless about what was happening in the big picture. He shrugged inside his own mind, "That's just the way it is. That's just the way it is."

And he looked more closely at what the documentation actually stated about his next victim, and where he had now to travel.

One thing is for sure – he had never before heard of San Fernando – except in a pop song from eons ago – and that one sure as hell wasn't the place he would be traveling to tomorrow.

To kill. And maybe to take some photos of interesting things too.

It didn't ever enter his mind that his masters were either increasingly desperate or inordinately incompetent – or both – to have ordered his inclusion in this, their latest special project. As good as he was as a killer, maybe one of their best, this jaunt smacked deeply of being an uneasy amateurish gambit. Then again, Monaghan had never read about their invasion of Granada back in 1983. Or had forgotten all about it and other such fiasco.

Mind you, recent American politics increasingly trumped rational explanation.

JC Monaghan got up to return to his semi-luxury hotel and passed by the newspaper segment lambasting the coffee bar counter. *The Philippine Star* headline of its thin international section, read, 'Snowden leaks more.'

Monaghan merely sniffed and scowled to himself. "That's another bastard we will get."

34/3.

Norton was struggling here. It was was hot, very hot - and there seemed all too few places to find some shade, inside the shack he was staying in temporarily, well outside Subic. There sure as hell was no air conditioner in sight in this two-room abode built out of scrap timber and old unpainted roofing iron.

Canlas had brought him here after their latest small boat had departed Palawan, and had introduced him to the old woman, Belinda, who was to cook and wash his clothes for him. Canlas then vanished for days at a time, only to pop up again like a beaming energizer bunny to announce that was into some new scheme to make money, and to check on Norton.

The food was minimal and the drink filtered down to Norton as bottled water and local beers. He was beyond bored and was wondering why he had let Canlas lead him over here. No one particularly bothered him and he occasionally went out to check at a local Internet café to see if there was anyone looking for him either in Aotearoa or even internationally. But other than this, there was SFA to do with his time, except to brood and to self-drive himself nuts. The newspapers were flimsy and not hot on world news and anyone he encountered wasn't so interested in speaking English. None spoke *te reo* Māori either, eh. They all sort of looked at him oddly when he couldn't fathom their Tagalog or – in some cases – Kapampangan, although there were, in fact, several words all these lingos had in common.

The only good thing about his misadventure was that he was a brown as most of those he encountered and – externally, at least – may as well been one of them.

Except for the tattoos cavorting his body.

35/2.

He had been back 'home' now for nearly two weeks, when he heard the sirens coming too close-by – somewhere just behind him in Tin Yan. Maybe it was yet another jumper from way up high in one of the many anonymous housing blocks.

Even Woo could not resist a stroll over to the increasing commotion from the solid swell of folk scuttling to have a look at just what was going on.

The police had already formed a yellow-band cordon around the body and were also keeping all and sundry well away in their relatively quiet noseyness; because most had seen all this before. There was a fair bit of gossip though and Woo stretched his big ears to pick up on what the buzz about this body was.

"He wasn't from 'round here," he heard one old man stutter - and that guy would have known, for Woo recognized him as an ex-neighbour from many years before. Which is possibly why the old guy scanned and stared Godfrey for longer than any norm.

"Yes," muttered an equally aged and weathered old woman hunched across her walking frame, "no one lives in that apartment anyway."

Woo followed her bent neck upwards to the designated jumping site, where a flimsy plastic curtain was fluttering triumphantly from the open window. Already some of the uniformed tribe was up there, measuring and notetaking.

Back at ground level, the police were endeavouring to flush away the burgeoning crowd, most of whom were unemployed or gerontion, or unemployed gerontion. The schools were still in operation nearby, but the teachers had kept their students well away from their windows. Someone, a couple of metres closer to the yellow tape, was confidently stating for a fact that the jumper was, "quite a young guy – well-dressed too – he wasn't anybody we know."

By then the ambulance had wielded its way into the gathered throng and its minions were already packing up the limp carcass. Death was always quick and just as quickly over in Tin Shui Wai – no one could afford to linger too much ruminating about it, as everyone was just too busy trying to prevent their own early demise anyway.

Later – two or three nights later in fact, after Woo had a caller come to tell him more moving was on that midnight – he casually asked one of the illegal immigrants, as they shifted giant cardboard boxes of abalone for some fat punk cadre up the line somewhere,

"Have you had heard anything about the young guy's cascade down from about the 30th floor of Tin Yan Estate?"

The Illegal just smirked and said something rough in Mandarin, to the effect that the kid had been biffed out the window as an example to others not to challenge the status quo.

When Woo looked completely bewildered by this, the other lifter just winked and spluttered further words to the effect that, "the Party doesn't like stirrers."

And that fellow wasn't going to say more that night, as he casually lumbered away from Woo and towards the launch, hefting a sizeable carton like it was a wet towel.

36/3.

Monaghan hired a private car up to San Fernando. He could afford it and money went a hell of a lot further there than in New Zealand – and in many other places, actually. It was easy to see why many *putih* stayed in San Fernando too, because of all the beautiful young women everywhere. That was about the first thing the sex-starved Kiwi noticed when they arrived at the bustling hotel where he was going to stay, while he checked out his next to-be-killed.

The receptionists there were unilaterally gorgeous – or was this vision of his purely and simply a lust-filled epistemological overflow? He couldn't care less, as he flirted ostentatiously with all of them. Monaghan did have some very rudimentary Tagalog from his brief vaco-leave days in Subic and Clark during his two crazy stints in and about Viet Nam, decades previously. As well as from his escapades once or twice in the seedy sex-spots of suburban Manila.

'Salamat po babae magandan maganda' was his stock answer to all the queries about how long he would stay and how he would pay and did he need breakfast and so on and so forth. He smiled what was his best come-on smile and went up to his mid-range room and squatted under the air-conditioner to read more about one Rustico Tuazon.

It seemed this Tuazon had to die because he was upsetting too many political allies within the country - due to his honesty and inability to keep to himself the facts that he had investigatively unearthed. Facts about their connections – the fiscal and hegemonic links to Los Americanos in Washington and, indeed, anywhere else where Halliburton-clones made their mints from the vagaries and vestiges of war and potential war. Tuazon, quite simply, had to be shut up once and for all. Being a journalist or reporter of facts in or near – or even far away from – Manila was not a safe haven, and now that the Kiwi gun for hire was nearby, even less so.

Monaghan had learned through the grapevine – which was basically Dr. Cross – that Tuazon's girlfriend had been put away some week or two previously. "Pity," was all Cross had leaked out of the side of his mouth, "she was a cute kid – but she blabbed too much, if you know what I mean." Cross, of course, had never confessed that he had been heavily involved in the disposal of his own girlfriend's niece. Never would either, as he had conveniently shelved that fact in an airtight compartment in his brain.

Cross however, had droned on a bit about, "They needed to call you in up here because there's just so much going on – these people are all interconnected on the Internet these days and their gossip just spreads too fast. Besides which I'm needed elsewhere." He had as a sort of afterthought, affixed just a bit more, "And they thought we could rely on you to do a good job at short notice..."

After switching on the television to find innumerable boring programmes about the NBA and several badly dubbed Korean movies, Monaghan decided that he really wanted – no, needed – to get laid. There were indeed plenty of less-than-cryptic yellow pages ads for massage. However, Monaghan had been around long enough to learn that most of what they said was a pile of crap and that the services that he did receive would cost the proverbial arm and a leg.

So he sauntered down the stairs to see what – rather who – he could find to help in this particular quest. He next strolled outside and soon began chatting in broken English to a security guard type who was wearing shades and abutting the front gate – sort of scanning cars as they lazily putted in from the roaring main highway outside.

Turned out that the guy's name was Romeo and through his somewhat broken front teeth, he soon sputtered out what Monaghan really wanted to hear more about.

"Hah. Girls. Yah – plenty o' girls. Over there near the casino," Romeo was waving his right arm vaguely over there, where the name *Casino* was fluttering in broken lights. Seemed – after a bit more 20 *peso* investigation by Monaghan - that there was basically a brothel between the diner and the actual casino – up on the first floor – which, inevitably, was run by the local cops anyway.

"Good luck," was all Romeo could get out as he shook his head at the receding back of the white man, who was cruising rather quickly in the direction he had roughly indicated. Romeo took another swig of his Fundador and waited for his mates to come and get him soon – the cockpit would now be in full bore and he was eager to win some more *peso*. Besides which, his new job was so boring.

Over there, Monaghan had already broached the stairs and was squinting through the tinted glass doors into the gloom of the dark air-conditioned room. His initial sighting that there were several scantily-dressed women inside, turned out to be true when he actually slid the doors apart – except that straight away he could tell that there were as many *bading* or lady boys, in there as true feminine genders. He would have to be bloody careful as to who he ended up with, because he prided himself on being a straight, macho type of man.

A multicoloured hair woman, with a big mole on her cheek, was semi-smiling at him from behind the old wooden desk and asking him how she could help, "Sir."

It must have been fairly obvious to everyone why the white man with a distinct tattoo or two was there, because soon he – and her name turned out to be Rosita – were fucking each others' brains out all over the fake fur eiderdown on the single bed in a back room. Monaghan had chosen her as she was petite and pretty and she had given him the eye straight away anyway.

After the usual cum-grunts and the spool of jism jerking deep into Rosita, Monaghan rolled over and shut his eyes for a while.

She was already in the tiny tinny shower, where the thin shards of lukewarm water exploded like hailstones on the thin metal walls. Monaghan – for some obtuse after-sex reason just then – was again wondering what had happened to his old war buddy and faraway client Norton. Whether he – Norton - had actually managed to find another legal mind to help him out of the deep quandary he would surely be in. With two dead close relatives – and you couldn't get much closer than an ex-wife.

Monaghan was another one who had the weird ability to strategically separate his mind into watertight sections and there was absolutely no overflow between the compartments labeled Norton as client; Norton as friend; Norton as stooge. He sighed and opened his eyes to see Rosita's perky tits flailing under the vigorous rubbing of her towel.

Rosita was smiling. Not at or for the tattooed man, whom she had just fucked silly. "Screw him," actually, was her thought at that moment. No, she was smiling because she now had reached her target sum and would be able to take her daughter out to the birthday dinner after all. No other way to get *pesos* that effortlessly and that quickly and – every once and a while – to get a bit of visceral pleasure at the same time. But now she would have to get rid of this guy as soon as possible, so that she could move on to whatever – or whoever – might be waiting downstairs.

Monaghan hadn't yet got any hint. He was guessing that if Norton wasn't at least locked up for good by now, that he soon would be. He also reached out to grab Rosita's tits, but she slipped away, grinning, "that's gonna cost you, sir."

He sighed again and sat up straight on the spindly mattress. He would have to go and kill this kid Tuazon – if he could find the kid – because that was his job right now. Soon, anyway.

Yet, while his newly-encountered killer-crony, Dr. Cross – or whatever he was named – was flying across the Philippine Sea, or South China Sea, as others named it, the irony was that Monaghan didn't know that his war buddy Norton was only a few kilometres away near Pampanga right then.

Mind you, Norton also had no glimmer at all that the man he once trusted and who had suddenly disappeared on him away from Aotearoa, was right at that moment plunking down a few hundred more *pesos* for a slim brown girl to give him another blow job and then to fuck his brains right out the door.

It would be a really great birthday for her five-year old, now.

37/3.

The few days had led into nearly a fortnight, when Canlas came back again and said to him – "I'll take you down to SM Mall today – you will like it there, man." Canlas was with his cousin Fred and the latter's jalopy was revving along outside the shack. Norton squashed into the back and settled for the drive into Pampanga, and more specifically the large mall.

And indeed Norton did quite like it there, given that it was air conditioned, bustling, and – more importantly – was full of food stores and restaurants. He wolfed down a variety of yummy chicken and beef varieties from a variety of chicken and beef serveries and sat back and enjoyed the manifold parades of passers-by, dressed for the occasion of malling. Today, at least, the recent *whānau* killings back in Aotearoa receded from the front avenues and slunk deeper into the far-flung back alleys of his mind.

He actually smiled for the first time in what seemed like months. Canlas was raving on about how he would have to go back to sea soon and that – yet again - he – Norton – "was his own man now."

For Norton it was indeed time that he did something authoritative about himself – especially since he had come into the Philippines with no visa, let alone a passport. By now, he and Canlas had left the streamlined mall and were wandering around the local fresh-food wet market, over the footbridge crossing the busy road outside.

It was just then that he heard Canlas cry out at someone, who must have been passing by their latest food stop.

Next minute he was shaking hands with a real Filipino beauty. That woke Norton up big time; for the first time in a long time.

"I'd like to introduce you to my cousin Ruby," was about all that Norton's ears could manage right then, because his eyes were on overload.

Wow!

She was a mature woman who had maintained her looks, her poise, that effervescent smile.

Norton zoned onto the here and now for the first time in a long while.

38/2.

Woo woke the next day of his algorithm of meaningless days, with a monster headache. His broken wisdom – or lack of wisdom – teeth were bothering him no end and he had no real funds to do anything about the situation. The best solution he could find was to scuttle to the nearest Watsons and buy the slimmest packet of Panadol-type medicine he could scrounge. There was some palliative pleasure for just a while, before the throb began once more.

What's worse it was raining – a thin typical-to-Tin-Yan rain that seemed only a caress, until you realized you were soaked through and had started to develop flu-like symptoms within the next 24 hours.

Woo had also seen a terrible apparition in the pharmacy mirror: a tall, stooping man with receding hairline; unshaven; bedraggled, wet; with bed-black eye bugs and a twitching pulse in his left temple. It could indeed have been a 3-D monster from any recent C-grade Hollywood movie – let's make that any Hollywood movie, as there's no real sub-division in that bland product range.

But, of course, it wasn't a 3-D monster: it was Woo himself, it was what he had become.

He crept back to his under-the-bridge cardboard mattress and attempted to steal some sleep from the day. The ache of his rotten/rotting teeth receded for a while, as he counted down the hours before he would have to struggle back to the boats, the cold slick sea and the cutting acerbic rocks under his aching feet, with the heavy contraband-filled boxes ramming his breaking back into total submission. And it may well still be raining.

When he awoke from his semi-snooze, the rain had lapsed into a form of intermittent trickle – still enough, unfortunately, to keep him wet. It was now allying itself with the haze creeping down from the Mainland of P.R. China. Where Woo was loathe to go for fear of running into further enemies – such as his Shenzhen mistress and her triad relatives, who were threatening to cut off all of his – Woo's - fingers and toes. And anything else that dangled in between.

He was – to hone a cliché – caught between the devil woman and the deep grey sea.

He stumbled to his feet and shook himself. It did seem hard to believe but it appeared the sun was trying to exert itself a bit more up there in the left hand corner of the sky. Was that some warmth Woo could feel hit his feverish temple?

Later that afternoon, as he sat smoking *El Cheapo* brand roll-your-own tobacco outside the local tea shop, above a lingering and lukewarm *lai cha*, he almost shat himself at the recognition of the face looming out from the front page of the free local newspaper. It was the kid who had jumped/been pushed out of the window in Tin Yan estate the day before – or was it now two days ago or more? Woo could not recall, as time for him these days seemed to ebb and flow like a worn-out rubber band. It may have been a week ago, for he had no watch, no calendar, no sense of what day it was.

Reading on further, as the newsprint dissolved into his own sweaty fingers, Woo learned the name and age of the victim. For victim he was. It seemed – from preliminary police investigations – that the young man named Lok Mai Chun had been pushed – no, thrown – out of the upstairs window by a tattooed man, or – maybe, men – whom police were now seeking to 'help them with their enquiries.' It also seemed that the dead young man – aged only 25 – was a promising graduate student from the local university in Tuen Mun and had been intending to go overseas soon to further his studies in Internet Technologies.

Finally, Woo read - as the new sun started to burn his balding patch – that Lok Mai Chun was known as a rather ardent student activist and had been at the forefront of recent massed student protests against the several American navy visits to Hong Kong. Against the resulting occasional violence, frequent hassles, overcrowding in bars and intimidations that inevitably occurred during such shore-leaves. Mind you, the rapidly disintegrating front page didn't actually state the last part at all, but it was fairly common belief out here in the New Territories that sailors from afar, always caused havoc and panic in Wan Chai and Lan Kwai Fong.

Whether it was a fair belief or not.

Woo sniffed as the cold trembles started to set into his depleted frame. He yawned. These reported tattooed men could only be triads. His shuddering deepened, as he thought about Ho Fat Kin and his men maybe still searching for him. Perhaps they had thought he drowned last month after all. He hoped so.

Woo looked up and around. Pretty much the same here day in, day out. He squelched the dismal dregs of his cold, lame tea around his teeth, as a form of tooth-brushing, and got up somewhat shakily.

It was only then that he noticed a short fat guy staring at him from behind heavy horn-rimmed spectacles. Unblinking. Steady. Unsmiling.

Woo smiled a thin half-smile at the squat guy and attempted to disappear. It didn't work, for as Woo scurried toward the dank harbour, he sensed the guy was following him under the lame afternoon sun. It was like one of those silly Jackie Chan movies Woo used to take his son to all those years ago. He would have smiled if it had been funny. But it wasn't.

He felt the chopper glance off his left shoulder and the cleaver pain jolt through him, knowing that he hurt bad. He slumped a little, but, conversely, also picked up his pace into a slow loping run – gaining distance from the shorter and much more corpulent assailant.

Up around the corner, under the nullah overpass and in the shadows, Woo was wiping away a thin trickle of flesh wound blood gingerly with his right palm.

He wasn't quite dead yet, but it seemed that he was being steadily dismantled – the complete opposite to a paint-by-numbers portrait build-up. This was character assassination in the flesh.

When Woo squinted back out into the now brazen sunshine, the short, fat chap seemed to have vanished.

Woo finally disheveled himself to the harbour front, just as the sun began again to falter, where he managed to swamp several small buckets of oily seawater over his thin torso and only stopped to see if the equally thin red trickle had also ceased to flow.

Later, when he thought all was staunch, he clambered back out of the brush where he had hidden himself to soothe his wounds, put back on his dusty top and went to report for work.

The new wound gave him little trouble, but his teeth were hammering away like hell on a rent day.

Woo tried his best to ignore the ache as he bent once more to unload the steady stream of handed-over-the-side cartons, all stamped 'Fragile' on one side.

So it went.

39/1.

It took some time for the New Zealand authorities to even notice Norton wasn't around. Then again, they had never been known for their percipience. No one had thought to send his passport down to Wellington H.Q. and he still hadn't yet been charged with any offence.

The news media had no whiff of his absconding until about a week after he had left, when their own inside sources picked up the scent from the local constabulary. That they had, "sought out Norton at his Matakaoa refuge, only to find no trace of him and nobody who could – or would – throw any semblance of light on his vanishing from their purview."

His cousin denied having any inkling where Norton had gone and sure as hell was never going to tell the 'pigs' anything anyway anytime. Hemara hated anything to do with the police, probably because he had spent far too long at both Waikeria borstal and then Paremoremo prison. Even if he had any idea where Norton had gone, and how, he sure wasn't going to tell these bastards. Especially Fatso. Fatso had trundled down to the Coast like some big-time city cop and had been seen zooming around asking all sorts of dumb crap.

In fact Aotearoa – as opposed to New Zealand – did have a reasonable idea that Norton had skipped out of the country somehow, but they just feigned being dumb Māori whenever anyone who looked like a detective asked them leading questions. "Fuckin' good job," was their main comment to one another over a few quiet beers in the RSA. Even from the mourning ones who believed that Norton had murdered his wife somehow and who still remembered that sad morning.

Eventually the New Zealand authorities relayed the wanted man information overseas – including to Interpol.

Trouble was, Philippines police were not so accommodating toward Interpol themselves. Their attitude roughly translated to something like, "shit New Zealand – we can't ever get there without sucking up for a visa, and even then, there's been no direct flights from there until last year anyway. Let them wait."

Besides, they had enough strife going down of their very own. Let alone worrying about tracking down some Māori guy covered in tattoos who might have killed his ex-wife and could be anywhere in the World. *Hindi ko na problema iyon.* Not our problem. Indeed.

So, Norton wasn't actually an internationally hunted man – yet.

Monaghan did hear later that his old wartime buddy was not locatable, but he sure didn't dream Norton was this close. Monaghan, after all, did not work for any New Zealand authorities, while his American masters did not have Norton on their radar – yet.

Besides, Monaghan wasn't attuned for any of this. His immediate focus, after fucking his brains out, was to find the boyfriend who knew too much. And spouted too much. He was reputedly in Pampanga, close by, and now Monaghan was to hunt him down and expunge him. Then to smash all the computers he may have trammelled. In his arrogance, Monaghan believed this job would be an easy one.

Back in Tikitiki RSA, Hemara was having a good long laugh. He was pretty stoned, after a mighty toke on a mighty smoke, but he was also pretty chuffed that his crazy cousin seemed to have eluded everyone in a uniform.

Mind you, Hemara didn't know just how close his cousin was to the guy that Hemi had never liked. Something about Monaghan had always rankled with Hemi: he had never seemed real somehow. Monaghan had always spouted on about how proud he was to be a Kiwi, because he was raised in that skinny country. For Hemara, that meant nothing at all. So were millions of other Pākehā.

Hemara chortled and turned to Julie Delamare. "Want a fuck?" he said, matter-of-factly.

He only kept on laughing when she spat back, "Go fuck yourself. Arsehole." He laughed even louder when Fatso and a couple of his cronies sort of sauntered into the bar, dressed as civilians, but with haircuts stolen from a GI Joe comic.

"Good on ya, cuz," was what he was muttering, beneath his shades, to no one in particular.

All the time in the background Billy TK's Powerhouse were varoooooming through the lounge from the jukebox someone had fuelled up large with $2 coins.

40/3.

Norton instantaneously found the woman attractive. She had long hair swept back and free-flowing, and what is more she has had it dyed to a lighter hue than the natural colour, so that she automatically stood out among her peers, for her hair contrasted more starkly against her tanned brown skin.

Mind you, he mused later on, she would have stood out anyway, because she was pretty. Her dark eyes had flashed full-on at him when her cousin called her over to meet them both, and her full-bodied figure also appealed to him – he could feel an automatic clench ripple down his groin when he saw her front on.

"Hey Ruby – come and meet my friend," Canlas had yelled amid the market roar, so loudly that more than her head had swished around to see who had made such a bigger din than the residual background humming of voices; the yelling; the generators fuelling some of the stalls.

Ruby smiled at them and walked over to see who the brown-skinned guy with all the tattoos was, standing somewhat shell-shocked-looking next to her cousin, whom she rarely ever saw and hadn't in fact seen for months – and months. The fact that both of them spoke in Kapampangan only served to make the stranger look even more bewildered, as he stood there squinting in the noonday sun and imbibing all the heat and smells.

The cousins spoke rapidly and caught up with their respective slivers of news, after exchanging the usual questions about how their mothers were and how their kids were and the usual suspect banter about how they were both looking, "O.K. but a bit older, eh."

Canlas seemed to have forgotten about the man he had brought along. So, it was Ruby who had had to use her eyes as a semaphore grid to get across to him that they had better do something about the increasingly fidgety friend whom he had recently incorporated into his life.

Canlas told her that this guy was, "a good man, who was having a bit of trouble

back home" and that, "I had brought him along in an effort to help him…" Canlas
thought about saying 'hide' but also thought somewhat better of it – "to have a
break. Do you know anybody who could house my friend for a bit, cousin?" he
enquired.

Ruby asked for how long and – of course – how would this be paid for? Canlas
said that he wasn't sure exactly and that he – Canlas – had to go back on a ship in
the next couple of days, but that he knew the guy – whom he now named as
Norton for the first time – did have funds.

"Let's go and find somewhere to sit down and think for a bit," she said, meaning
herself actually. She knew that opposite her mother's place there were several
apartments of various sizes and scales and that some of them were unrented and
that the landlord did accept short-term leases. She was also thinking that maybe
she could score some extra cash by providing meals for this guy. Perhaps doing
his washing, although she knew her Mother would be the one doing this. She
hadn't yet thought much about him, let alone whether he was cute or not, as she
was now seeking to get out of Pampanga and to go back to Hong Kong. As soon
as. She needed funds to do so.

They all went over to the tin-roofed cafeteria, with the low slung chairs and the
rickety tables and ordered some San Miguel with ice. All the while, the two cousins
were chatting quite animatedly and the other guy, the accused/accursed outsider
figure, was bringing up their rear like a stray dog.

Canlas asked Norton whether he wanted to eat anything else. When the Māori
said, "yes, I wouldn't mind something to eat" - when in fact he was still hungry -
"and to have a piss" Canlas directed him, "to go out the back to the toilet walling up
the creekside and take a *mimi* up against the old sheet of tin, while I will order us
all something to eat." (Norton later realised that *mimi* was not only his word, but
meant the same in their respective languages.)

Ruby seized the two or three minutes Norton took to ask, "does this guy have
money to pay for his lodging and food?" and when her cousin said, "I think so, yes,"

she stated right out that, "I will take him with me on a tricycle to show him the rooms across my street. After this meal."

And that's how Norton eventually moved into J. Pintella, met Ruby, and soon developed a wicked taste for Red Horse beer. He did have plenty of money from his freezing works pay and back pay and bonuses. While another of his cousins back in Matakaoa had also finally reimbursed him the five thousand New Zealand dollars that he had once borrowed, with a promise of, 'I'll pay you back, Cuz, honest', as financed from his cousin's dope-selling operation out back of the Horoera Valley.

But Norton wasn't going to let any of these Philippine people know any of this money stuff. He was just thinking that it would be good to sit in one place for a few weeks, to catch up on his sleep and to work out exactly what was going on and what he could do about it too. That was sufficient for him. 'Stay in the present,' was his mantra. To try and balance out all of the emotions shooting through him like fireworks at Chinese New Year, would be a bonus for him right then.

Besides – he had had another look at this lady's backside. And he liked what he saw, eh.

41/2.

Dr. Cross had landed at Hong Kong International airport early a couple of mornings ago. He spat onto the pavement in joy. He liked coming back to Hong Kong, where he had some great fun over the years. Indeed, he'd once even been married to a local lady, a real *leng loi*. She hadn't wanted more than one kid though and they had drifted well away one from another culturally. A pity, as for him, she was a beauty. He still fondly remembered Ki Ki. Yet he had kept in only sporadic touch with their daughter – such was his way.

Cross had come to make a quick killing. Not on the stock market either. Nor at Shatin racetrack either, actually. He literally had been enlisted by his somewhat shadowy masters back in continental USA, to eliminate yet another of these young revolutionaries who used too much Twitter and Facebook and aroused too many opponents to what these masters had vested interests in. Which, of course, were the usual matrixes of oil, armaments, power, money. The masters were, of course, all mongers with fingers also in politics and probably also up each others' bums. It went without saying that they had massive stashes of moolah in the Cayman Islands, all tidied away by swanky law firms created solely to operate that rort. As well as cavorting with tax returns that meant even more millions came their ways. Cross never cared about all this; only that some came his way.

He never carried weapons to countries – they were already planted somewhere for him to pick up, if need be - while millions of dollars also magically transcribed themselves as bitcom into his bank ledgers every time he made a hit. He, however, preferred to have his own, exponentially augmenting offshore funds stashed somewhere in Panama.

Cross caught the downtown hotel transit bus that was waiting there, throbbing, out in the bays behind Terminal Two. He was the only passenger, and he settled back to skim the paperwork that had been provided to him back in Manila. He was a veteran by now and an always-trusted agent who never seemed to stray into error.

The photo was recent and showed a young unlined man with a pleasant demeanour. Trouble was, he was an intelligent and radical young man – the type that was especially detrimental to these military/industrial Americans, in their united worldwide efforts to squash what they viewed as revolutionary. Left-wing idealists were anathema to Rule America. Meaning dangerous to their domineering economic and all too often, environmental, pillage.

This young man, Lok Mai Chun, had a degree from Harvard and he had returned to Hong Kong an articulate, pretty much on-to-it organizer and a stirring make-sense activist – more particularly to the quite alarmingly large and growing local student audiences. He was also like so many of his countrymen and women: a computer and Internet savant. His fame had begun to spread beyond the Special Administrative Region. The clichéd alarm bells were sounding in the dusty corridors of not only the New York stock exchange and the sweaty Washington DC senate locker rooms, but also more penetratingly in Langley, Virginia, where the CIA and innumerable as yet undiscovered secret clan-destinies met and fomented frequently in a sort of sibling rivalry.

The bottom line was that Lok had to die and die soon. 'He hanged himself', was a pretty good line and had worked quite frequently in the past – especially throughout Mainland China – and that was probably how Cross would stage-manage the next scenario.

But, first he had to locate the victim. And before that Cross wanted to eat. First things first.

Cross checked in and had a brusque shower before he went out in search of food. He knew exactly where he was off to too. A trim bar in Lan Kwai Fong, where they served up marinated steak to die for. His largish lips were already salivating somewhat at the thought of what would be coming up.

He had hardly even thought of Ruby, since he had scarpered down to Manila at the urgent summons of his division, and now was no time to begin doing so. He had left quite a large stack of *peso* for her anyway and he knew Ruby well enough – or at least he thought that he did – that she would be content for some time yet without him.

Anyway, they weren't married or anything. What did he really owe her after all? He shut away any further thoughts about her into a locked mental room without windows.

Dr. Cross was enjoying his coffee when he saw the photo of Lok Mai Chun lambasted all over the front page and identified as having died somewhere out in the New Territories under, 'suspicious circumstances', while police were 'still investigating.'

Cross by now was semi-choking on his shard of prime beef. "Shit," he thought rapidly to himself, "what was going on here?"

Who else had wanted this kid – for Dr. Cross anyone under the age of thirty was still a kid – so dead? And more to the considerable point for the good doctor (Ph. D from the University of Wisconsin, majoring in Nichomachean Ethics) was, what was he – Cross – going to do next? He hadn't come back to Hong Kong just to chew food. What about his precious bounty now?

Cross read on and then picked up his mobile phone with the security toolbar. He rang back to the USA H.Q. and asked exactly that question.

Trouble was, no one on the American bench had even gotten this latest news about Lok. For all intents and purposes, Lok was still in the land of the living and due for a quick departure from this land very soon. All the Stateside division manager could bluster to Cross was to, "stay on the ground for a bit and we'll get back to you soon."

Cross merely snorted once more and turned to watch the direct stream baseball game filtering through the giant screen barnacled to the bar. He kept on chewing, vaguely reflecting on how his recent acquaintance – the Kiwi guy, with American mannerisms – was getting along in Philippines. "What was his name again," Cross mumbled to no one in particular, "Monroe? Monaghan? Mondaugen? He never talked much, that was for sure."

He guzzled on his umpteenth beer and trusted that his masters would soon get back to him with some updates and more importantly, some new directions. Until then, he would ruminate further about writing another book about jurisprudence and espionage.

He would probably title it *When Three or More Wrongs Make a Right*.

42/3.
Monaghan woke up late the next day.

It was already noon.

He was hungry and he was pissed off that he had missed the breakfast-that-went
with the rent of the room.

He showered again, after another long night's fucking, and went downstairs –
having dressed as anonymously as possible – to search for food at the hotel's
diner.

He ordered up large – *bifsteak*, pork *adobo*, rice and ice lemon tea, and finally
fitfully unsheafed the bulky dossier that Dr. Cross had handed him, just before they
had parted in Manila a few days previously. 'That guy Cross never said much', was
his reflection as his fingers scrambled through the pages.

Seemed he had to expunge this Rustico Tuazon – yet another one of these smart
college kids, who blogged too much and bantered too much and broke open too
many embarrassing secrets to the slower moving and dilly-dallying local press.
Tuazon – it seemed – had already quite a sizeable slew of supporters and they
were shimmying solidly along like a Wikipedia trail.

Monaghan sipped his *minum* and read about how one Euris – [name deleted] had
been exposed and deposed about a fortnight earlier and that she had been this
Rustico Tuazon's girlfriend, as well as his leading confidante.

Since then Tuazon had vanished back into the provinces and was probably hiding
deep down there somewhere in Pampanga, where his family and closest cronies
lingered too.

Monaghan looked up just then, chewing his pork and rice and thinking that he had
heard a very familiar voice – of someone speaking in English. Sounded like Norton,
of all people.

"Shit, no way," he muttered, shaking his unshaven head a couple of times as he masticated a bit more and went back to peruse his papers. "Fucking Norton. Fuckin' waste of space now that one," he continued out loud to the near-empty diner.

Of course, it had in fact been Norton himself, strolling through the foyer of the hotel, because that's where he had been told to meet up with one of Ruby's young nephews, who lived in the same street as her. This was after his also being told earlier to stay a day or two in the nearest hotel, until his room was ready back in their *barangay,* on J. Pintella in particular.

Norton was on his way to this room, by *jeepney* with this nephew – for they were ready for him now.

43/3.

After he came to his new living quarters, from the enforced two-day lag at the local two and a half stars hotel, sent there while Ruby and her mother got things ready for him, Norton then slept for the best part of a day. For a couple of reasons. One, it was so fucking hot he didn't have much choice. His body couldn't repel the heatwaves smacking him about like a wet fish in the face, a bit like in a Monty Python's Circus skit.

But the main reason he dozed most of that day was because – for the first time in what seemed like years - Norton felt more relaxed, a little unburdened in his existential self. His subconscious had somehow given up its angst and had said to him, albeit unknown to his conscious self, 'Chill, man. No one is here to grab you, to isolate you and to hassle you. Here you can merge unasked.'

Yet, those lingering guilts still rippled to the surface on occasion; rather like another cunning fish just waiting for a bite of bait. Norton had by no means gotten over the sudden demise of his ex-wife; hadn't even really faced it full-on/frontally. He also knew he should have somehow resolved the friction with his own two daughters. He was only too aware he should have been a better man, but had let himself drift into the abyss. He remained the inauthentic individual that he had become too long ago; the *salaud* one he had read about so much in his younger years, when he still looked at books.

Mind you, Ruby's mother was anxious and asked her daughter more than once if the *putih* was O.K? Part and parcel of her overall nature and Filipino custom per se, was such concern for the wellbeing of any guest. It was just that deep in any *barangay*, there was a tendency not to be too manifest about displaying too many emotions.

"*Walang problema*," Ruby must have soothed her own Mother seven times that afternoon. "*Walang problema. Ma.*" 'He will be fine,' she mused to herself.

For, of course, Ruby was facing up to several large issues of her own.

44/3.

Norton spent much of his first few days in the thin rutted street, accommodating himself to the noises there – especially the call outs from the traveling salesmen, selling everything from ice to ice creams. The barrage also consisted of tricycle drivers honking and the big SUVs rummaging the raw surface in vibrating fury. The schoolkids, always immaculate in ironed white, gamboling in the early afternoon sun kill. The occasional long gray shark-like *jeepney* skewering the street in an elongated thrust.

Then there were the sudden tropical downpours, which came from absolutely nowhere and then went straight back there in a matter of minutes. At least these ensured cooler interludes, but then the sun hit again in full-on frenzy.

Norton ate at Ruby's house, cramming himself full with the *masarap* taste of her mother's cooking. He just couldn't get enough of the *adobo* and *menudo* and banana fritters, let alone the mango and onion salad.

And it didn't take very long to not get enough of Ruby herself. He was naturally attracted to her and he soon began to think dirty old man thoughts about her. He found himself scampering more and more over the thin lane to her mother's house, rather than ruminating in the rental.

One afternoon, after maybe five days - for time always seemed to lose itself in the heat - of just lying around and sleeping after eating and watching the few free TV channels, Norton started to chat her up big time.

They sat outside on her verandah at dusk, when it was far cooler, and bonded over even more Red Horse, which Ruby's Mother had sourced from a near by *sari-sari* store. They learned a little about each other, although he never mentioned to her that he was a hunted man for murders he would always claim he didn't commit. He did mention Makere though and was a bit silent when he told her that Makere was dead now. Norton didn't mention their kids at all.

She told him about her Chinese ex-husband and how he had deserted her and their two kids back in Hong Kong and how she had had to survive in that 'racist place' all by herself for quite a long time, while she struggled economically to bring her kids up. She told him about Dr. Cross, but not by name. She also omitted to tell him about bulk other things. But then again in an incipient romance, who does latch onto the exact truth anyway?

Just when Norton – who by now had had way too much to drink – thought he might push his luck and get a bit more cuddly with the very delectable Filipina, someone started to bang on the closed front gate, under the now dusky streetlight patrolling down on them from just outside.

Ruby didn't bother to say 'excuse me'; just got slowly up and went over to the half gate and swung it wide open.

She kissed on the cheek the guy who was waiting outside, clutching a small bag for all it was worth. They spoke in rapid-fire Kapampangan for a good five or ten minutes, just inside the gate, while Norton sat there, rather ignored.

Then Ruby brought her nephew over to met the Māori guy who was sitting outside her mother's cottage in the middle of Pampanga on a thin Tuesday - or was it Wednesday - evening, sculling Red Horse like it was going out of fashion in the next day or two.

"This is my brother's oldest son, Rustico Tuazon," she introduced. As Norton shook the thin young man's hand, he noticed he was also shaking somewhat – Rustico, that is. There was something wrong with his entire bearing: the kid was frightened about something.

Seems Rustico Tuazon had a pretty heavy tale to tell. But he only began it once his aunt had assured him that Norton, "was O.K." Once he had a meal ever-ready inside.

It seemed that he was another of Ruby's relatives, this time a nephew. He indeed had seemed a little perturbed – just a bit edgy – but remarkably self-composed and confident for a young man who had recently lost his girlfriend. And more.

Rustico sat and – after supping on a Red Horse and after having a good munch on the usual delicacies Ruby's mother routinely seemed to have in the fridge in the tiny kitchen, out back of her house - he was ready to talk. He started to regale the now sobered Norton and his aunt with a tale that could well have been sourced from the pages of a bad novel. That is how incredible it came across.

Rustico had been a politics major at Atenao University in Manila, drafting his Ph. D thesis on the American presence in Luzon. He had necessarily been in touch with a wide raft of contacts, both in and out of academic research circles – including fellow Filipinos studying stateside and also the several Filipino servicemen and women within the American armed services. Subsequently, he had been uncovering piles of straight-out evidence that showed the Americans not only wanted to grab back their earlier presence at Subic and Clark air-sea bases, but to further expand their hold over the Philippine nation. As well as to capture large swathes of the Pacific and the Philippine aka South China Sea, by first building big bases in Palawan also.

More than this, Rustico had learned via his multifarious and varied channels of information – which nexused in his tiny apartment in Pasay City – that the Americans envisaged a vast territorial toehold right across all of the Indian Ocean as well, itself centred on Diego Garcia, where, ironically, several Filipinos were working. The Middle East and Africa were to be the next targets – all of this smoothed over with a spin-doctored patina of these sites being mere informational facilities. But in all truth, they were sheer imperialistic steps to build up, spread out and solidify and maintain a mighty Yankee empire. A base nation indeed, in every sense of the term.

None of this was ever meant to be common knowledge, given that much had been leaked out anyway. But it was the rigorous detailing that set Rustico's trove well aside from any previous glimpses into the American lebensraum. Some of the material Rustico had stumbled across via his own resolute and relentless research;

more of it came to him via secretive information drops into his home computers or in couriered parcels from outside of his homeland. He now had amassed a poisonous mountain of enough material to sink a million American battleships and aircraft carriers.

This is why his girlfriend Euris had been despatched and why Monaghan had been sent to convey Rustico Tuazon to an early grave – not that the latter had any idea of the former's name, or when his demise would eventuate. Although, of course, Rustico knew he was well and truly high on the Hit List pioneered and patrolled by Washington D.C and Langley, Virginia.

Which is why he did not go to Euris's wake, much as he desperately wanted to and – concomitantly – why he was right then at his grandmother's abode. For Rustico required some practical help from Ruby. Today.

She had asked him almost straight away, "Where were you when Euris was murdered?" and to which he pleaded, "Wait, *Ate*, wait – and I will tell you."

It seemed that by now there was quite a sizeable network of Rustico clones around the ever shrinking globe, some of whom had been garnered by him, some of whom had actually engendered him through their own initially separate missions to seek out and publicize more widely what the American empire had in store for their own respective climes. Thus, Rustico had contacts elsewhere in Asia, in Central Africa, in the 'Stans of Central Asia, in Micronesia: all areas where the expansionist regime was firmly aiming to entrench itself. And, of course, in Diego Garcia, which was by now the throbbing heart of the beast.

Rustico Tuazon wanted out of the Philippines as soon as possible and he knew all about Eric Canlas' ability to smuggle people. He also knew all about Ruby's public housing estate apartment back in Hong Kong, where he – Rustico – had particularly close anti-American comrades in the struggle in what they liked to nominate as the Anglo-American plot to domineer the World.

More than this however, his Hong Kong allies also hated the machinations of their own Motherland – P.R. China – to do exactly the same thing.

Now Norton had listened to all of this and had started to put 2 + 2 together, qualifying his equations with a further thought that what Rustico was spouting was very probably true, but surely dashed with youthful naivety as well as helpings of oversimplification.

Still, Norton, quietly reflected, what the kid was delineating somehow made sense when he thought about the recent stabbing deaths of Trevor King and Makere. He reflected then and there what his own cousin Hemi had told him about their being members of an Indigenous 'rebel' group back in Aotearoa. Whose manifest bonding was to explicate and extirpate the very imperialistic conniving that Rustico was steadily rattling off, and which was similarly crawling like a cockroach through his native land of Aotearoa.

Tuazon made a lot of sense to Norton, who himself had fought in an American-fired war in Vietnam and its immediate environs many years prior and who had had crazy R 'n' R stays at Subic with quite nutty American officers. Who genuinely seemed to believe that the world was theirs' and who had in fact shown a universal ignorance as to where New Zealand even was, let alone to be able to comprehend the word Aotearoa.

When Norton had jokingly responded to their bluff ignorance by asking these selfsame officers if they had ever studied geography at school, they had looked straight back at him with somewhat dumb stares and said that, "We don't do geography in our schools."

Norton thought he would do what he could to help this kid flee: after all they would both be renegade refugees then, if they were not already. They were also sharing the sudden recent loss of women oh so close to them, given that Norton had fallen out of love with his ex quite some time before.

Or had he?

He dug into his wad of *peso* and handed Rustico several thousand, while Ruby
wrote down the address where her own son lived in Tin Shui Wai, way out in the
New Territories of Hong Kong. Where, incidentally, Cross, her ex-boyfriend, was
aiming to cruise to on his own murderous mission and where, purely coincidentally,
her ex-husband Godfrey Woo, was reconnoitering just about every corner 24/7 to
obviate any potential threats to his own seedy existence.

Ruby also promised to try and find Eric Canlas' contact number – which she didn't
have with her right then.

They ate some more and drank well into the night – but lightly, for Rustico's serious
spiel and his obvious grief for Euris – shown by the tears he sprayed around at one
stage of his rant - was seriously restricting anyone's desire to gulp down too much
alcohol on that particular evening. Everyone was also all too often sinking deep
into their own reflections about Americans and their self-centred and quite
iniquitous meddling into the affairs of communities that didn't want them around at
all. Or – worse – who didn't even glean that they had been meddling, day in, day
out, for years and years and years in countries they had absolutely no business in.

Some time, about midnight, they all went to bed, just as Norton was about to say
that he had some idea who possibly could be after Rustico right now. However, he
bit his own tongue on the name of Monaghan. The notion that his erstwhile friend
could be involved in a loose string of international murders just seemed way too
strange on a late night in a *barangay* thousands of kilometers way beyond his own
tūrangawaewae. Besides, he had no evidence whatsoever that his former buddy
was in the Philippines at all.

So, he kept that possibility to himself for a bit longer. It may have been only an
alcohol-fuelled idea, after all. Norton's new paranoia now bit quite deeply.

Euris and me – a confession by Rustico Tuazon

Ate – I loved Euris beyond anything else. I still do, of course. I cry every night when I am by myself, wherever I can find sleep.

I could not come to the wake at Grace's place, because I knew that they were after me: it was far too dangerous. It was only because I had to say goodbye, when I crept in to her burial ceremony for a while. *Ate*, Aunty – please believe me. I swear on the Bible.

I was not with her the night she disappeared, *Ate*. Euris was her own person – you know that. She had her own ideas and opinions and she was very determined to protest at the Embassy. I warned her about this several times, you know, but…

Euris was so strong-willed. Much more than me. She kept telling me that Filipinos had shot José Rizal, but only because they were forced to by the Spanish, who had their own troops there as back-up anyway. She kept on reminding me about how Rizal turned to face these executioners, just as they fired on him. How he also refused any blindfold. She too was that brave. That committed to the truth and to freedom for our country.

As soon as I saw her name lambasted all over the press, I knew who had killed her, or at least the organization behind her disappearance. It had to be someone who was paid by our government, but who was in league with the Americanos, standing directly behind them. Because of what I had been working on, I knew all right.

And I would be high up on their hit list. I had to keep hiding. And running. I have to keep doing so.

Help me *Ate*. *Tulungun mo ako.*

Natatakot ako. I am afraid.

45/3.

Monaghan got the word early the next morning, not long after he had been woken up in his hotel room, due to the steady drip drip drip of the air-conditioning system plunking onto the tin roof of the half-house next door, directly below his second-floor room windows.

The phone rung soon after, as he screwed up his eyes and rubbed all traces of sleep from their squinty corners, wondering where the hell he was and why it was so bloody hot there.

Then he recalled that he was in Pampanga, Philippines – alone – in a small bed in a small room, out back of the MacArthur highway in a nondescript mid-range hotel.

He picked up the plastic landline handset and said, "Hello."

The contact spoke mannered English, rather like they were feigning an American accent, when in fact they were a real American by the name of Walter Wyshnowski, calling from a command H.Q. somewhere out back of Pasig, Manila. From inside a neutered cinder block assemblage that was actually the CIA nexus for the entire Republic and which was sanctioned by the Philippine government, in return for several million dollars paid annually as part of an aid package.

Wyshnowski, who of course gave no details about himself, including his name, merely said, "Target is in J. Pintella, Santo Tomas," and who then hung up the phone at his end.

Monaghan had long since ceased to think about how come the Americanos knew so much detail about everyone's movements, yet had missed out on eliminating their target earlier. Something to do with satellites and proxy killers, maybe. Responsibility and no responsibility. The USA could kill anyone anywhere anytime, but not be seen to be so doing. Just as long as they located the target first.

It also never seemed to cross his mind that he himself was a mere stooge: the very role he had accorded Norton. That he was in Philippines, in fact, as someone his mothers' country could completely disown if necessary, never entered any of the several sealed chambers of his partitioned brain.

Up until right then, of course, Monaghan wasn't to know that in fact two of his recent projects were in J. Pintella – the one he had been sent to eliminate/exterminate/eradicate – and his own war buddy/crony and client from Aotearoa New Zealand. The former, the Americanos, for all their perceived wisdom and strategic finagling, had not known was that close by until some snitch had informed them about Tuazon's immediate presence. Until then he had eluded their elaborate grid-like radar schemes, while Norton was still not on that radar.

Monaghan shrugged. "Screw them," he thought, "I'm going to eat."

So he did – breakfast was all-inclusive. He strode to the restaurant within the hotel compound and ate the scrambled eggs, white toast and spindly solitary *longanisa,* in a few mighty gulps.

"Shit," he continued to muse, "that's not enough to feed a sparrow." So he ordered more and put it all on the bill – the CIA or whoever were his employers could pay for everything. And were anyway. Par for the course as far as he was concerned.

Later, Monaghan went to the front desk and enquired where J. Pintella in Santo Tomas actually was. They had absolutely no idea and had to consult their own street directory and maps.

According to one of the petite receptionists, it seemed it was, "just a few kilometres across town, sir."

He went outside to find a taxi driver skulking on a lounge chair, which needed hip replacement surgery pretty badly. Probably because this particular driver was rather corpulent.

After negotiating a price, Monaghan was now on his way to scout out the surrounding territory and – maybe, if he was carefully lucky enough – to actually sight Rustico Tuazon.

But even if he did, he wasn't going to kill the kid just yet. It would be too obvious, too much in the clichéd broad daylight, given that *barangay* lore was always the same regardless. Namely, that guys were bashed and shot and knifed every day somewhere in San Fernando, in Pampanga, in Manila, anywhere at all in the Philippines. Often by their own first cousin or their local police chief. Or by their own first cousin who was the police chief.

"No," Monaghan continued to ponder - on his way through the steady snarl of the *jeepneys*, tricycles and scooters - the actual elimination would be quick, as untraceable as possible, and only when he was ready to then slip away to Clark Airport straight afterwards.

That time wasn't quite with him. Thus, while he checked out the skinny back street, he merely filed away that information for the proverbial rainy day.

He looked quite closely at the rumoured potential abodes where this young snitch might be and marked down instinctively the entries and potential exits, the possible entrapments and endangerments, the passers-by and the lingerers-around.

He didn't note any look-alikes to Rustico Tuazon and - even if he had any idea that he was there - he sure as hell did not sight his ex-comrade-in-arms Norton. He did note however – with his usual robust roving eyes – some beautiful Filipina womanhood strutting along the lane and with that randy material more in his mind, he called out for a nearby tricycle driver. Who was Romeo's cousin Soto, who just happened to be one of those passers-by – and went back to his hotel to resume what he did rather well – at least in his own opinion. Which was to fornicate with local prostitutes.

He would give himself a couple of days before his big move to murder.

And bugger any legal consequences, he thought – and he chuckled within earshot of a somewhat bemused Soto - as he ruminated that, here he was a lawyer who filled in his ample spare time and made even more money from the death habit, than he ever did from his circling-shark antics within the courtroom.

All Soto had thought when the *putih* had descended from the tricycle cab and had thrust a wad of faded *peso* in his somewhat sweaty hand was, "Fuckin' *putih* always on the move, always with the money, always think they own this world."

Then Soto Quesadilla spat into the dry dust outside in the carpark and drove himself off to the Burger Machine to squat and talk shit for the rest of the afternoon with his cousin, over cheeseburgers and copious lashings of Fundador brandy.

Inside the hotel walls, Monaghan was checking his yellowing yellow pages of the local telephone book under, *'Massage Parlours and Escorts.'*

He was ready to kill in another more extravagant sense altogether right now. Murder could wait a bit longer.

46/2.

It was, of course, inevitable that Ho Fat Kit and Dr Cross would meet up, primarily because they both had the same paymaster.

They were directed to convene in Tsim Sha Tsui to streamline operations, according to the Director's directive, fresh from Virginia, Stateside.

For it had been the minions of Ho Fat who had been out in Tin Yan recently and who had pushed the Lok Mai Chan kid out of the window onto the hard concrete creases so many floors below. Ho Fat had told them straight out to, "Kill the kid – no questions asked."

The Wo Sha Ni triad needed funds fast and would take on anything anywhere anytime to get them: thus this murder. They didn't give two figs about any American rationalizations – because they were also hired guns for Yankee dollars, especially at a time when the ICAC or Independent Commission Against Corruption was hot on them and their drug-running scams and when their prostitution rings of floozies from the Mainland weren't prospering.

The Americans on the other hand were also entirely pragmatic. They had needed this particular student rebel out of the picture and didn't really care how, just as long as they weren't seen to be directly hands-on. Cross they could always disavow as one of their own, as he had been out country for so long now and his profile could easily be muddied into disbelief. But, as permanent pragmatists, they also saw fit to contact their shady Chinese gang affiliates for this job, just in case Cross did not accomplish this task quickly. And it didn't matter to them if these guys were really nasty characters who pushed hard drugs and cut off fingers and killed people with choppers.

Just as long as there were no smart arse voices letting on how Americans ruled the waves and as long as there was no illumination given out as to how they were sealing and stealing all the access to their perennial lodestone – oil and gas and now rare metals – they couldn't really care less how such outspoken folk were de-tongued. Just as long as they were.

So Ho Fat and Dr Cross – their supposed Asian expert - had been guided to discuss business, to ensure everything was covered up and so as no loose ends unraveled. The fact that Ho Fat couldn't speak a word of English and that Dr. Cross was skint with Mandarin – and all this in a Cantonese speaking city – didn't ever occur to the Director and his gang of razorback haircut players back on their own Yankee version of the Mainland. Arrogance does that to a foreign policy.

One thing for sure, though – Lok Mai Chun had not been an idiot. He had kept records. Not as many as these Americans – that was impossible, for there's was an inexhaustible tranche. But sufficient, nevertheless.

47/2.

Godfrey Woo slunk around corners these last few days, with his head somewhat similar to a turtle rammed into his spiny shoulders.

He didn't want to go out any further than his cardboard box space under the bridge beside the nullah, but he had to go and shift the bootleg and the contraband goods from and into Lau Fau Shan as much as possible, so as to be able to even eat.

So, when he had to travel – albeit as late in the evening as possible – he tried to avoid being seen as anything resembling a human being. He now knew for sure the triad knew he was very close by and he now also knew for sure that he was probably working for the very band, which wanted to see him expunged. If Woo had any notion of irony, he would have been laughing, even if only for a couple of seconds.

But his life was by now so severely fucked up that laughter – let alone smiling – was a luxury for free, rich bastards.

He sniffed in the cooling evening air and shook in his ripped singlet and slunk – head down – to the beachfront, where his boss was giving out directions about what to lift up and what to pile down.

It hadn't always been this way, he now daydreamed. He had once been reasonably successful as a businessman, running his own garage and bringing in thousands every week. He had a lovely wife and two well-behaved children and always enough money to go out to eat in fairly expensive restaurants scattered around the territory. He could always afford good presents for his kids – the latest toys, for example – and they'd even gone to the Philippines on a few occasions. He wouldn't have minded seeing his kids at least one time – and he suddenly wondered where they were now and what they were doing? Woo drifted back into dream-space.

But Woo was a fatally divided sort of character. He loved to smoke and he loved to gamble on the horses. And then – after being introduced to Macau by one of his so-called pals - he loved to bet even bigger on the tables there. Where there were also lovely young ladies from the Mainland, working at the same time the selfsame tables and the gamblers who liked to think they could buy their way around. Like silly Woo, who began to spend nights away from his home and his kids and to neglect his business and his family and his wife, Ruby – who soon began to wonder just what was going on with him.

His marriage fell apart, he borrowed money from his own mother and sisters and even his brother, who once worked for him. He developed a further penchant for sidling over the border to Shenzhen, where he made his first mistress very happy. The devil named cash did that – while it lasted. His daydream soon became nightmare.

Woo had had to vanish from sight, as he had become a pariah even for his own flesh and blood and he by now owed so much money that no one would have believed him even if he had had the stomach to tell them. He lost his family as quickly as his own hair fell out and – soon – his teeth had begun to default too. He managed to hide in his used car scrap shop for a while – but that didn't last either.

Now he was a bit of a social disease who really had run out of places to flee and who had – of all places – scarpered back to where he had run from, like he had been sketching some gigantic warped-out-of-shape circle for the last dozen years or so and the lines had finally knitted back together.

From nightmare to incubus.

He bent down and picked up some boxes, aware that no one was taking much interest in him here at least.

But, deep down, Woo knew it was all just a matter of time.

He noticed the chopper blade lying quietly minding its own business, where one of the fishermen had forgotten it – maybe because it was so rusty.

Woo bent down quickly – or as quickly as was possible for a man with a ricked back – and flicked the blade into his trouser pocket, making sure it was turned outwards, so as not to cut his balls off.

If he was going to be dealt to soon, Woo mused, he had to put up some sort of fight. Another blade could only help.

Ho Tai Chung yelled at him at that moment to get on with it – for Woo was once more standing there dopily, lost in his own distracting thoughts. A state which had become more frequent of late, as Woo began to search inside himself for solutions and to rattle of the many 'if onlys' that now came to his mind as a result.

Ho Tai Chung was the foreman for the illegal shipment of the wide raft of goods at this little port across the Bay of Shenzhen, as well as being Ho Fat Kin's second cousin. He never actually knew Woo's history and wouldn't have cared even if he did know. He only cared about his own cut from the traffic he could steer back and forth to the Mainland across the bay.

Woo hated what he was doing. He hated it with a vengeance. He shuddered as he thought about returning to cocksucking. Besides, where could he continue that craft?

Sure as hell not out here in Yuen Long territory. No one had any money and no toilets were accommodating enough for his service there either. Anyway, he detested that service even more. "No way,' immediately lit up like a cheap neon strobe in his mind.

He sighed when he saw Ho Tai Chung glaring at him, so he bent down and – grunting – lumbered up another massive carton of abalone, destined for the same rich suckers who had had their cocks blown by him in downtown Central and throughout Tsim Sha Tsui.

Part Five: Mainland PR China

48/5.

Several supposedly undercover, but so ostentatiously obvious, Chinese agents
actually helped dispose of Dr. Cross soon after. Disposed him to a safe house
back in the back of Xi'an actually. He is in a black jail right as you read these
words, located in a disused factory premises in Fung Cheung #2 Lu. He never
really knew what hit him a day or two after his, what he presumed to be cordial,
liaison with Ho Fat and some of his subordinates.

Cross had been last sighted eating some high-density carbohydrate meal in
Delaney's Bar & Grill in lower Tsim Sha Tsui, flushed down with a couple of
draught beers from Denmark.

One minute he had been a USA point man in Hong Kong, the next second he had
vanished completely, and it took quite some time for the American Legion aka CIA
office over in Central to even learn of his total disappearance. After all, he had
never been obliged in his role of Eliminator, to report regularly to anyone in
particular. Assassins had a fairly free range with the Virginia lads, primarily
because the latter never wanted to be seen as in collusion with their killers'
completely illicit goings-on.

Speaking of collusion, the Chinese had never wanted any American suchlike in
their own master plan. They hated Americans. Always had, always would – these
were like two dinosaurs from different eras, with different genetic make-ups. They
used Dr. Cross and his information and then knocked him out, bundled him up and
swept him via Shenzhen up to their original capital. That quickly and that invisibly.
They knew that the Americans could not kick up too much of a storm, if at all, as
everything about Dr. Cross was *très non de rigueur.*

Until the Americans negotiated some sort of trade-off, Cross was stuck in the cold
North West of P.R. China quaffing stinking black coffee and chewing on stale mung
beans, *pak choi* and rice. With a continual headache, wondering when the SEALS
would charge through the roof on a rescue mission that was never to be.

What the Chinese wanted was no American involvement beyond what was only vitally necessary: ultimately no American anything at all in fact. They had wanted to exterminate Lok Mai Chun themselves under their own terms – for their very own reasons, which had absolutely nothing to do with his divulging secrets about America, although they did have some interest in this.

They wanted to eliminate the promising young man because he had deigned to operate as an anti-American agency, without any PR China governmental qua communist cadre sanction. Independence of mind was not at all high on their radar, especially if it incorporated Internet communication, therefore freedom of speech. And even more especially if he also had divulged rather too much about his own administration's connivance with the American machinations. Indeed, independence of any sort wasn't on their screens at all. Ho Fat had been assigned to literally chop him down to size.

Ho Fat, then, served many munificent masters. *China is Kafka*, after all – just like the poem says. (That book of poems, ironically, was published in New Zealand*.)

So the three really crewcut hairstyle, black-suited-two-sizes-too-big for them chain-smoking Mainland Chinese agents just swooped in to Tsim Sha Tsui on Ho Fat's information. They could have been any Mainland Chinese tourists, after all. They swept out again with a comatose Dr. Cross, under a thick blanket, posed as a drunk *peng-you,* into the back seat of a waiting taxi. Which drove them all pell-mell up to Lo Wu where everybody quite successfully crossed the border. For by this time, Cross was stuffed inside a suitcase the three had trundled on its trailer past the check-in counters and into Shenzhen, before his quick flight up to far away Xi'an.

And, of course, while Wa Sha Ni triad and Ho Fat the boss man had had some inkling all this might have been going on, they were never privy to official P.R. China manouevres. The triad was - sometimes, just sometimes – a handy mechanism to be employed on just such occasions as this, and no more. By whoever could pay them the most.**

Meaning Ho Fat Kit, along with his fellow triad kin, was a free agent – within limits – to source and silence – for his usual fat fee – the next young man with any key information about just how nefarious both the Americans and the Chinese government were in their delusions of collusions. Of course Ho Fat never mentioned to his Chinese bosses, anything about also being paid by the American regime to eliminate whomever they saw fit to redact and rescind.

Meanwhile, Dr. Cross was wondering when he might be allowed to shave his several days' stubble. He was also thinking – far, far too late by now – how he should have remained in Pampanga, eating Ruby's mother's excellent home cooking. He had indeed been completely double-crossed.

Meanwhile also, Lok Mai Chun had – before his sudden death syndrome - been in touch with Julian Assange and already delivered a zipped parcel of quite tasty morsels about the cross-scheming machinations going on in Hong Kong. Information as all whipped up by a *pot pourri* of people who no one would have ever dreamed of being so involved. Trouble was, of course, Assange had his own hands somewhat tied together, having spent years in the Ecuadorian embassy in London, with no sight or sign of any end-of-tunnel light and with only a cat to play with.

One had to give some credit to the Americans however. If someone was perceived by them to tread on their splayfooted toes, they trod back twice as hard, so as to make the alleged perpetrators lame. Ask Kim Dotcom, another ex-Hong Kong boy. Still marooned in New Zealand, but for how long, after the local police had burst in American gangster movie-style to his overfed home, pried open the doors and left his pregnant wife barefoot and shivering in the cold, as they continued their over-the-top raid and ransacked their mansion?***

And they were still trying to nab Edward Snowden, who – very interestingly – had also first touched down at Chek Lap Kok airport in Hong Kong - en route to Russia.

If Norton had known any of this, his mind may well have dredged up the idea of a *karass*: Vonnegut's notion that there are many odd connections between cliques comprised of seemingly unrelated components. However, Norton was nowhere nearby and nor was his memory right then either.

So it goes.

[*Rapatahana, Vaughan - *China as Kafka.* Kilmog Press, Dunedin, Aotearoa New Zealand. 2012.]

[**The Mainland used any available means they could, so as to maintain their fairly cynical control of Hong Kong S.A.R: while they pretended that it was one country but two separate jurisdictions, the reality was – and almost always had been - one country and one system. Increasingly so nowadays and most certainly totally, in the immediate future - from **Radical Wikipedia.com** 2018.]

[***She is a Filipina. **Radical Wikipedia.com** 2018.]

49/3.

Their lovemaking when it exploded, came as a surprise to Norton, as he had basically given up on Ruby ever coming to the party, especially while her younger relation Rustico was still around.

But the next day Rustico went what he termed as deep undercover somewhere. And Ruby herself had what she later confided to her new, Māori lover, 'woman's needs'. She'd had them for quite some time actually. She still wanted a confidante as well; maybe for a little while yet.

Perhaps it had been further fuelled by that evening beforehand, when they all had bonded somewhat more familiarly and she had seen Norton's genuine interest in what her young nephew was extrapolating. And his obvious concern for Rustico too.

Their fervent sex came when they were making a bed in the middle room together and she had brushed up against him, when bending over to fold in a sheet on top of the thin mattress. Earlier, Ruby's mother had strolled off to the local market, where she would take a couple of hours haggling for fruit and vegetables, but more likely gossiping – *chika chika* – with her own elderly relatives and friends in the immediate neighbourhood.

Norton had always been one to seize any half-chance, let alone a quarter chance, and on this occasion he was certainly no different. They fucked in frenzy, yet there was also a measure of tenderness in their rapid-fire thrusting and mutual ejaculations. If anything, the act served to slam them even closer – they were now co-conspirators in the secrets of Rustico Tuazon, as well as the co-minglers of their own most recondite body fluids. It would seem now that they had a sort of pact to protect their newfound knowledge of Los Americanos - and to cover each other's backs too. As well of course now – to uncover their fronts, whenever the opportunity would arise.

And afterwards, as they lay quietly on the thin mattress reflecting slightly and cliché-like gathering their thoughts, Ruby could not help but muse about an

American of her very recent acquaintance and where he might be right then. As the geckos flicked around the slow-churning overhead fan, she could only reflect that seemed a long time ago now and that yes – her nephew, Rustico Tuazon, was right about that particular culture. They were definitely not to be trusted, they with their closet agenda.

Little did she know that Dr. Cross right then was spitting out a horrid-tasting fish congee in the depths of an industrial zone in Xi'an, Peoples' Republic of China. She would have laughed out loud if she had known.

Similarly, as he lay staring at the selfsame busy lizards rummaging to and fro above him on the faded in-need-of-a-paint ceiling, a warm thrumming/humming zinging throughout his formerly rather jaded being, Norton flicked onto a thought he had retrenched the earlier evening. Where was his old war buddy Monaghan right now? What was he doing? Was he – now at least – potentially a dangerous ex-crony? Who killed Makere and how did they get away with it? His thoughts returned to their well-worn rut. It could only have been someone very skilled and surreptitious. And damnably good with a knife.

They said very little to one another and anyway, Norton had been a man of few words for a very long time now. They spent their conversation smiling at each other.

Little did Norton know – as he clambered upwards and out towards the only-cold-water available shower in the narrow back bathroom – that his erstwhile army mate was not very far away at all and was just then preparing his own minor small-arms cache, in readiness for his next major, hopefully undetected, kill.

For James Monaghan had recently received the word that his prime connection in these parts, Dr. Jehovah Cross, had somehow gone missing in action and that he – Monaghan – was – for a while at least – just a little bit alone on the frontline that was illicit North American rendition activity within the wider parameters of Asia. The word that had filtered through from the connection deep down in Pasig, Manila was that he – Monaghan – "had better move onto his hit pronto and then getta the hell outta there – because we won't acknowledge you son, if you are snapped." He never once pondered as to where all their other undercover enforcers were or why he had been selected from among what he presumed were several others.

Any cogent reader would have thought that American espionage would be far better organized, of course. Truth be told, however, they weren't and never had been - and indeed their entire so-called subversive history was a litter of error and oversight. From Baghdad to Benghazi and well beyond, their missions were all travesties of arrogance and oversized male egos. Testosterone territoriality.

It looked like tomorrow might be a big day for all, because Ruby hadn't yet told the Māori that she wanted to get out of the Philippines for a while and that she wanted to reconnect to herself back in Hong Kong. As for Norton, he hadn't any concrete plans whatsoever – fairly typical of him. He was still a curious admixture of grieving ex-husband, lost potential villain, lonely and still disorientated illegal immigrant, and vindictive and well-trained killer. "Just keep livin'" was always his steadfast riposte, if anyone ever asked what his best advice was. Jus keep livin' was about all he was doing right then.

Historical note:

Norton once also had a somewhat more visionary aspect to his multiple personalities. For example, he used to have been able to have visions of the future - and to talk to the dead. He was *he matakite*. But this especial ability seemed to have divorced itself from him quite some time ago – the more he mingled away from his family roots and the more he slept and the more he slowly loitered away from his true indigenous self. Norton also seemed to have completely forgotten all about what he had read as a much younger man about J.W. Dunne's theories of serial time; about the latter's notion that past, present and future were all continuous. And contiguous. They exist in a meaningful interconnected continuum. (Which he should have intrinsically remembered, as this is a key aspect of being Māori.)

That linear time sequences were bogus. Were historically assumptions rather than an absolute truth.

Any distinctions between self and environment, mind and matter is a further assumption, as is causality. As such synchronicity is the norm, not the deviant.

So anything might happen next.

Anytime and anywhere.

As it tends to do.
Anon

50/1.

Ngā Wahine Toa were practising again. Taking their guns apart, cleaning them, re-assembling and then firing them at the targets down the far end of the paddock. Practice was somewhat restricted by the fact that they had a limited amount of ammunition.

But the women were keen, whether they had sufficient equipment or not. They had been congregating for a couple of years here, high above Ruatahuna, ever since one of their leaders, Te Matekairoa Cairns had made that fiery speech on Waitangi Day.

The women had flocked to her straight afterwards, resolved to fight back an administration that continued to ignore them, vacillated about all the proposals *Ngā Wahine Toa* made, ostracised their platforms and petitions. It had now come down to arms training, because it seemed to Te Matekairoa and her lieutenants in what they termed *Te Nonoke*, or The Struggle, this was going to be their only direct way to achieve some of their aims. Aims via arms.

Because, Māori were still at the bottom of the socio-economic pile in Aotearoa; still formed a majority in the nation's burgeoning prisons, still had among the most drastic youth suicide rates globally. And Māori women were still being bludgeoned – often to death – by their partners. Men who required training of a different type.

"Time to finish up? "was the suggestion from Sheila Raumoko, as she looked across to Te Matekairoa. The latter nodded, "*Āe, tika*. We'll meet up again next weekend, eh."

The sun had married the moon by this time and darkness was among them. Just before they climbed into their cars and trucks, Sheila counted. 55 women and young women. Not too bad, considering that initially there were over 100. Many had found the rhetoric too powerful and the subsequent physicality of their training too arduous. Anyway, mused Sheila, as she shifted the gears of the utility into reverse, there were always new recruits coming in, especially since the latest news about the government abolishing separate Māori representation in parliament. She had noticed, for example, those two teenagers who had come to check things out today.

"They are Makere's daughters," was how Te Matekairoa had introduced them to Sheila.

"Have they found their bloody father yet?" replied Sheila.

"No. Make sure you get hold of some more ammo," directed Te Matekairoa, through the open back seat window of the old Ford, being driven by one of her own *whanaunga.*

Will do, "replied Sheila Raumoko, thinking that she would have to go once again to the gangs to secure whatever she could in the way of firearms from them. She would make sure she stirred them up a bit more too – too many lazy bastards there and the time for retaliation was heating up real quick.

And then the moon won out completely and the hills merged into the sky. All she could see was a few speckles of vehicle lights, bumping down to the sparse township glow.

51/2.

The late Lok Mai Chun's twin brother, Lok Yi Yi, went swimming, believe it or not.

He found that the best way to relieve the incredible amount of pressure that he had put himself under, was to swim under the water for as long as he could hold his breath, deep down from the surface, for as far as he could possibly travel. The serenity and still far exceeded anything in the rampant noise machine that was anywhere in Hong Kong. Because, even the so-called country parks there were mobbed by screaming Mainland visitors who seemed to believe that their raucousness was how you were meant to communicate. They were inevitably on full throttle endlessly - with a measure of spitting erratically anywhere thrown in.

He sighed as he crested the surface of the town pool, where he had illegally jumped over the fence much earlier that morning, so as to be free of any spies and – worse still – any enforcers from anywhere. He was not quite sure who exactly would be after him, but knew indeed that they would be Mainland agents of some description. Whilst his exponentially augmenting paranoia – as fuelled by all the hacked state secrets he had either been entrusted with by his brother, had garnered himself, or had been sent by his own anonymous international network – only served to keep his entire body on permanent edge.

Then there was the terrible reality of his brother's recent death and just how his brother expired. He was too unsafe to even think about going to his brother's funeral.

Lok Yi Yi had secreted his rather voluminous files onto a series of encrypted flash drives, duplicated them on equally clandestine discs and had also managed to send some of the most serious stuff overseas. To contacts whom he had never met, but who seemed to share exactly the same dawning awareness that he and his twin had engendered for themselves in the last two years. The information – if ever revealed in any extensive manner to the majority of the citizens of the several most incriminated countries – would blow a massive hole in any of the joint Mainland blandishments as to world peace, stability and social justice.

The facts were themselves rampageous. The United Nations was actually a major front for continent-wide money laundering. Halliburton was in league with the Chinese communist cadres to manufacture and sell even more armaments to North Korea. The USA was hell-bent on expanding Diego Garcia with Philippine labourers - with of course more Halliburton influence - and to hell with any Chagossian input. England had a closet deal with the Scottish Nationalists to remain with a balance of oil power - just as long as these Nationalists received a fair share of the mineral and petroleum booty the English mine-owners and bankers would unravel in league with Chinese monetary input. Meanwhile Russia was not sitting on any sidelines, as it shared its space technology with American drone-dom, and reached concord whereby any new petroleum zones were to be split 50/50, incorporating Thailand, which had been specifically mandated for them to plunder.

Meanwhile, Robert Mugabe was holidaying just down the road in the Peninsula hotel; as his daughter had taken over their mansion on The Peak: and he was probably laughing his head off too, as he luxuriated in his satin sheets and his gaudy silk pyjamas in his lascivious retirement. As for those buggers The Illuminati – the Vatican was actually a not-so-hidden front for people trafficking of all ilk, sizes, genders and faiths. The recent spiel in TIME magazine, Asia edition, about the potential first Chinese American President, was way closer than most would imagine. His name would not be trumpeted about until it happened overnight, unlike one of his eponymous predecessors, who remained locked away in some tower in New York somewhere.

There was just so much a person could take. Indeed, Lok Yi Yi did not have any head space left to consider the recent rush of rumour concerning Israel and Syria somehow joining forces to fight Turkey.

Lok sighed yet again and began to feel his brain melt into a gooey mass; there was just too much information. Anything once identified as truth had long ago disintegrated and merged with its newfound cousins nominated as bullshit, crap, double-speak and gallimaufry. Fake News. Politicians were chronic split personalities and if they were not, soon succumbed schizophrenic under the thumbs of money. Or else they were either expunged, emasculated or imprisoned. Just like the journalists who ventured to publicize anything approaching reality.

Lok dived down again, deeper this time, and when he came back to what even he didn't consider as a dangerous surface, he was startled beyond fear by the sight of shadows playing over there by the other side - luckily-for-him - of the large poolside area. Two black-suited, chain-smoking men with minimal haircuts, were plying their torches along that side of the pool and talking in an undertow of rapid undertones. One of them seemed also to have what looked like a long black banana in his grainy fist, clenching it rather as a baboon does. But, when the bullet spat out across the surface of the water, sending off little errant sprays of malice all-too-close to him, Lok panicked even more.

He was already at the supposed deep-end of the pool, but so lusty was his fright that he was almost under the concrete underlay of the bottom. The next solitary bullet he saw swim like a dopey shark, about a metre above him and then with a *blub blub blub* of ignorant silence, it slunk to the selfsame bottom, where it lay like a dead man.

He held his breath for what seemed like two hours, but of course it was more like two minutes. He was fair pissing himself through the droplets of fear forming on his skin, water and all.

From his depth-charge position, as he squinted slightly upwards and as the sun thankfully began to do its business at long last, he could not sight any shadows, so – primarily because he had no choice except to drown himself – he slopped to the surface and took a breath beyond measure.

The two men had merged further into the far distant backdrop that was the usual Hong Kong pall. Lok Yi Yi surmised that at least until they turned and/or returned, he was free to gasp a bit more air, before what may be his next submarine mission. One thing was for sure though, these two guys weren't there to sunbathe.

When he thought he may be reprieved and that the agents from the cadre clique –

for it was so glaringly obvious what they were – may be on the way out, one of
them suddenly turned around for a further reconnoiter.

Did he see Lok Yi Yi?

Lok didn't know, as he had dived down deep again, but this time more cunningly,
for he had now swapped pools and lay not only under the water, but also under the
blue plastic covers that still hid this smaller lagoon, before the pool staff arrived in a
few hours to cleanse it again.

All he knew right then that there were no more silencer-sent bullets floozing around
him and he wondered if the earlier fusillades were merely the aimless actions of
two very annoyed men.

He became increasingly water-riven as the sun scrawled on the sky – 'Hey I'm
here, please let me be seen.'

But like oh so much in this Sino republic, no one was listening and both Lok and
the sun would have to hang around in their respective plights for just a little longer.

52/3.

When Rustico Tuazon resurfaced a few mornings later, he immediately realized something had changed in his aunt. She seemed fresher, happier, prettier somehow – while the other guy he had been introduced to earlier, seemed more deferential, more smiley, more relaxed even.

However, Rustico didn't have too much time to ponder such, as he knew also that he would very soon have to escape Pampanga, indeed flee the Philippine nation completely. After a few more frantic text/SMS messages and after a frenetic phone call or two from his student cohorts and cronies back in Manila, he sensed his time there was basically up. He hoped his aunt could now help with those specific contact details.

He wanted to get to Hong Kong to try a find a bit more sanctuary, but more importantly to compare notes with another recent contact – a Chinese student whose name he could not quite remember, let alone pronounce – who had in fact sent him reams of quite revelatory, quite-shocking information about – not Americanos this time, but about PR China. Material concerning its equally nefarious influence in exactly the same places, with the Indigenous populations there not having the means to self-defend. And not having the wherewithal to thwart their all-too-often-own Cadre kin, who were also profiting from and profiteering away at the huge expense of the generally subdued and suppressed majorities in these zones – whether they be rural or the cities where all-too-many Chinese had to travel in an attempt to source income.

What made the Chinese guy's information more queasily worrying, was that on many occasions it actually seemed that the Americans and the Chinese were working together in some sort of tenuous unholy alliance.

Tuazon needed to go and he needed his aunt to finally give him the information about how best to find Eric Canlas and a boat out of there. He also wanted her to give him her Hong Kong address, so as to lay low there, yet to later also spy and set up a meeting with his newfound confidants in the Special Administrative Region.

Much more than this, he inevitably continued to suffer from his continual grief at the loss of Euris; something he had tried somewhat valiantly to suppress, but which kept coming back to bite him very hard. He had not yet shared with Ruby, the glimmers of information he had picked up from his own Pampanga relatives. Which was that they had themselves heard an Americano was purportedly the killer of Euris. In fact, yet another of his relatives, Joey Rodriguez, was convinced of this, because a Manila contact of Joey had described seeing a man fitting the description of Dr. Cross shadow Euris on more than one occasion over the last few months. Given that Joey had not always proven to be 100% accurate in the past, as he ensured he was not captured by the President's vigilante squads, by any means possible.

So, Rustico was rather twitchy right then. As opposed to the newfound serenity he espied in these two much older folk, who both were bearing wide smiles as he slunk in through the large iron gates he had noisily slammed on.

He would have to tell Ruby this latest snippet, today. No telling when he might see her again.

Rustico had at that moment no way of knowing, of course, that a tall, sun-glassed guy with quite a good physique and a shaft of silver grey hair, had him in his sights from just across the road. Indeed was sizing up exactly how best to send the young Filipino into quick, anonymous and undetected oblivion.

Monaghan, on the other hand, also did not know that behind these selfsame gates, his ex-colleague and client and onetime confidante – Norton – was sitting in the noonday sun, eating Ruby's own fine concoction of chicken *adobo* and rice and slurping on cold water reamed and rimmed with ice chunks almost as big as his own fists. Monaghan had only seen his prey slide through the gates and had no way – as yet – to see beyond.

So he waited. And waited.

It was toward late afternoon when he saw the gates open quite widely and he viewed not only Tuazon, who very closely resembled the photos the Pasay contacts had proffered, but he also sighted someone who could not possibly have been standing at the front with him – Norton. Who looked good and if anything – trouble-free.

"Well fuck me," was Monaghan's immediate expletive, as he stooped lower beneath the upstairs windowsills opposite. "This is fucking amazing." He didn't know either, of course, that he was right next door to Norton's erstwhile lodging, given that Norton rarely stayed there much anymore. He found himself rubbing his eyes for the truth: it could not possibly be him.

When next he stretched a bit higher to see what was going on and to reconfirm it was indeed Norton and not some doppelganger stunt double, both the figures he had just sighted had vanished from view, while the gates were again firmly clenched.

"Fuck," he swore louder this time and ran down the backstairs, out into a side alley to sneak a better glance as to where they had gone. He sighted Tuazon strolling carefully away down the lane, while of his buddy/client there was absolutely no sight whatsoever.

Monaghan grabbed his revolver from his small kit bag and sauntered – as inconspicuously as a non-Filipino male can way out in the provinces – after his soon-to-be-he-hoped his next victim.

Meanwhile, Norton had just finished giving Ruby a big kiss full flush on her lips and had turned around to re-open the large front gates, so as to call for a tricycle, so they could journey down to the local café for a while.

On his first step out into the street, he knew it was Monaghan as soon as he saw the steadily receding back view of the man.

It was almost as if he had been expecting it.

Norton turned and called to Ruby that he had to do something quickly and that he wouldn't be long – and he vanished himself. As the third component of this unlikely triumvirate under the late afternoon sun, still coruscating without slumber as it beamed down from asunder.

It was all more than a bit like another Hollywood movie - that stilted, staged and, if you ever thought about it too much - quite unbelievable. Pure fiction in essence.

For here – in a narrow, partly unpaved and rather dusty provincial Philippine back street, swerving to avoid swerving tricycles and the odd lost *jeepney,* were three men following each other, yet with the first two not knowing each was being tailed by another. And, yes indeed, one of the men had his primed pistol at the ready. He would use it too, for he was quite the accomplished assassin.

All the while the sun grinned down crazed, rather in jest at this odd harlequin parade so far below.

Tuazon was already hot and sweaty, as he was perennially worried about his own back these days, a condition that was all the more flustering because he was also really excited by soon meeting up with fellow whistle-blowers in Hong Kong. There – somehow – he would be sharing with them the atrocious news about high-level cabals of supposed enemies actually working together, despite all appearances and the manufactured news reports of their being the direst of opponents.

Tuazon also knew – because he had obtained direct proof – that P.R. China and the USA were actually in league to take over the Philippines, in a sort of squeeze-play. Whereby one would work on the Spratlys and the other would inveigle the local administration to therefore have to be re-invited to occupy Subic and Clark bases, in order to counter this perceived Sino threat. But – as Tuazon saw it – this would mean only one loser – his own sandwiched nation, colonized once again, yet again. He was really twitchy now.

He had no idea however that these two powers only connived when it suited them. He had never shared experiences with Dr. Cross, after all.

Monaghan also had hands that were leaking perspiration. Not merely because it was well over 30 degrees out there in the lane, but because he wanted to make his kill as fast and efficient and as undetectable as possible. So that he could get the damned hell out of there and back to Manila for a bit of R 'n' R, before sidling back to his law firm in Aotearoa New Zealand, pretending that he had been luxuriating on an extended Hawaiian vacation. The irony was, of course, that his emolument for this hit was going to get him to Hawaii for precisely that. For several months in the best hotels if he so wished.

He was gaining some ground on his prey, but also had to avoid being seen as too obviously chasing him down. He could almost see the end of the street up ahead, because there was more traffic on the prowl just a few more metres on.

All this time, Ruby felt more than a little miffed. Here was another lover as absconder, without any explanation. "What is their problem?" she asked the shabby dog sprawled out in the sun over by the gate.

"Are all men so crass?" she then asked herself, as she combed her freshly-washed hair under the jovial sun, out in the backyard where little lizards frolicked unperturbed. Ruby was beginning to believe so, even more than before.

53/2.

So, Godfrey Woo slunk and slunk and slunk lower every day, almost to the point where his feet were higher than his head. Not quite that drastic, but you can well imagine how he presented himself.

In his effort to be invisible, he thought himself into behaving like a worm, or more accurately a caterpillar, and attempted to creep low everywhere. He didn't want to be identified or discovered, because he knew Wo Sha Ni would be lethal. Wipe him out via evisceration or a quick couple of *slash, slash, slash*. They knew he knew they knew about him now being out here somewhere, slinking in or around Tin Shui Wai.

And Woo had to survive. Even a caterpillar has to eat and exercise to some degree.

Here he was creeping around every corner, sliding down the alleyways of Lau Fau Shan, to go and laboriously labour every day, or part of a day, loading and unloading illegal counterfeit and expired cargo. Cargo going either to the Chinese mainland to be sold at foolish profits, or being stocked away there in Hong Kong SAR for just as foolish profits. Chinese robbing fellow Chinese without any thought of cadre comradeship and only motivated by one gross factor: sheer and rampant greed.

This day was no different. He was up off his pile of rotting cardboard cartons early, before the sun had started to even think about kissing the sky, and was well on his way to the seashore. Passing just a couple of other unshaven men en route, who looked almost as worse for wear as him. No eye contact. No greetings. Nothing.

It was as he got close to the seafood restaurants and diners, of course all rampantly closed at that hour of the day, when he saw someone cycling his way. In other words, back towards the very cartons he had departed about 30 minutes earlier.

As the young man cycled by, Woo had a distinct impression that he knew him from somewhere: he looked that familiar to him. But Woo couldn't quite put his finger on it, to utilize an awful cliché right then. He even scurried a back flick of a look at the departing cyclist, but that merely led to further puzzlement. The young man looked like he was delivering something.

Soon, however, Woo was bending down and hurting his spine even further, as he gruntingly lifted and shoved further cardboard cartons - but not of the flattened kind – onto the narrow deck of the small craft, bouncing by the rocky shore. The sun still hadn't even raised its hand to recognize the day. And he had already forgotten about the rider of the rickety black bicycle with the far-too-big handlebars.

At snack time, Woo had been handed the usual silver dish of hot steaming white rice – *pak fan* – with a sprinkling of *pak choi* and this time – dried fish – which he literally wolfed down like – well – a voracious wolverine. He was at least fed by his boss, who – fortunately for Woo – was a bitter rival to his own relative, Ho Fat Kin and who would never have shopped him in at any time, such was his own competitive hatred of the stronger triad headman. Mind you, Woo's boss was hardly ever sighted out there and it was his couple of factotums who organized the trade and the contact with men like Woo, who had no real choice in the matter. They paid him too, when it suited, and sometimes it didn't suit. They yelled at him infrequently too.

Still it was – marginally - better than sucking cocks. Today at least, when fish were served up.

Godfrey sucked instead on the dregs of a butt of someone's used cigarette, which he had filched from the open-topped ashtray outside one of the restaurants: he was in no fiscal position to replenish any holistic supply. He had of late returned to the fold of smoking as much as he could and his few remaining stalwart teeth were quite hideously stained a yellow varnish, of a hue that no self-respecting paint store would ever want to sell.

Then it was back to the backbreaking dross of making money for someone who wasn't even around.

It was only later, during another quick snatch of puffing away on a used butt, that it flashed into his terribly faded mind, that the man on the bike, the youth in fact, was probably his own son. Whom he hadn't seen now for about 6 years – ever since Woo had first run away to Shenzhen and left Ruby there in Tin Shui Wai to bring up their two kids all alone.

It was the way in which that teenager – or young man, by now, he mused – moved – all awkward and jaunty and uncoordinated - that made Woo think of himself as a young man. They had to have been related.

54/3.

Norton, however, was not as hot and bothered as his new prey. If anything he was cold in his choler, for he had figured what Monaghan – his former buddy – was going to do to the relation of the woman he now thought he already loved rather deeply. That, combined with his own rage at what Monaghan had perhaps done to his own ex-wife – and possibly also to Trevor King, the least of his worries, and would likely try now on Tuazon – meant Norton was fulminating for a fight, for a showdown with his now nemesis.

Norton had the advantage of being somewhat of a guerilla fighter, something he had honed in that earlier Asian pseudo-war and in the meat works, where there was always some sort of putsch being pursued. If he didn't have the ability to hit and hide, slink and slide, he would have been expunged from there years ago. As it was, he was a master in staying away from the full-on frontal clique battles and never sided with any faction as regards bosses and workers. He had managed to survive at the Works fairly untroubled for nearly twenty years.

The only problem was, there he had felt his inner being slowly turning into something as drab as a chilled side of beef. He had lost whatever it was he had had as a much younger man – some elan, some *joie de vivre*, not to mention his former abilities to see well ahead and beyond. He had distilled his *matakite* or seer faculties into a mismatch of too much beer, too much sleeping, bipolar marital relationships and the sheer drudgery of trying to make a living. He had also become a man of fewer and fewer things to say, as his vocabulary desiccated over time.

Now, for the first time in what seemed like decades, Norton could actually feel some sort of chill thrill vibrating through himself: the dopamine was firing into small crevasses that hadn't been nourished since he had fallen in love with Makere, all those many years ago.

He strode quite elusively through the increasing traffic, oblivious to the few questioning stares from the locals who could even be bothered to even look at him in his passing. Just up ahead he glimpsed Monaghan's own back pushing its way through the throng of pedestrians, who were there at the junction outside the hoary church. Of Rustico Tuazon he sighted nothing.

Norton twisted the hasp of the sharp pig-carving blade he had borrowed from Ruby's mother's kitchen, a knife that he kept well-hidden under his shirt, a shirt he was now carrying, to pretend that it was all too hot to wear on such a stultifying day.

Norton ignored the newly erected traffic signals, just as Monaghan so obviously had done, and strode across the crossroads towards the market over on the near horizon and the tall church steeple looming saintly above it.

The showdown – if there was to be one – was going to take place there it would seem. Quite appropriate when Norton thought about it – near the local butchery, by the squealing pigs.

Rustico Tuazon was already deep in the market, camouflaging himself among the sellers of grain and fresh fruit and plastic chairs and straw brooms. He wanted a refuge for a couple of hours, somewhere to gather his thoughts for a while, before he slunk off to a mate's place to sleep. And then to hopefully escape Luzon completely, armed with the new information his Aunt Ruby had provided.

He hadn't seen that the tall white man, wearing shades and bearing arms, was almost directly behind him and that he was raising quite high in the air what must have been a slim pistol.

And he most certainly would have had no idea that there was yet another guy in this concatenation, who was not so far away from the middle component and that he had a long silver blade in his hand, just lusting for a stab or two. Here where the sunlight was neutered somewhat and all the smells and scents ran into one pungent whiff.

The first bullet – subdued in sound by the lengthy shiny aberration on the end of the pistol barrel, a clever silencer – hit Rustico fair in his upper arm. He recoiled upward, before crashing down onto cartons of Coca Cola stacked way too high. If anything, it was this first shot that saved him, for in its ferocity, he was involuntarily impelled away from the follow-up, which glanced on by innocuously.

There was no third bullet because James Clement Monaghan couldn't shoot any more. He was already dead, a bloody red mess sprinting away from his twisted corpse, mid riff, where the knife had discovered his life and taken it from him real fast.

And Norton, adroit as he was, thought he had managed to vanish back into the now screaming throng and the furnace air outside the cathedral, untroubled, unmolested, unnoticed by anyone at all.

Or so he thought.

55/2.

Lok Yi Yi had a damnably sore back right now, after stooping almost motionless under that damned canopy in the broiling sun for so long. It was deep evening and no one had come in to clean the pool or even to check it. He couldn't figure why until much later, when he realized the pool was not yet open for business and that he had pre-empted the summer season by about a week.

He squatted down and tried to encourage his back to relate to him better. But it still wasn't quite on talking terms with him, so he had to scuttle over to the entrance way and skulk around there for a while, as much to give his spine a chance to rehabilitate, as to spy the terrain.

When he was pretty certain that there was no gunman or hatchet man awaiting for him close by, he creakily walked out of the pool environs, hailed a taxi and went deep into Kwun Tong, to crash at the apartment of one of his many hacker cronies. Just one of a skilled network of stealth merchants sprinkled far more frequently than would be expected throughout the Special Administrative Region.

For Lok – rather like Rustico Tuazon – a fellow recent online acquaintance, now incidentally recuperating in the home of one of his own brethren in Puerto Galera, where he had fled to, wounds bandaged and all – had copious allies, all of whom had plenty of insight into just how things were in the World and how things ought to be. Who all pored and pawed over their computer screens day in, day out, assembling more information, more incriminatory material, to one day reveal all to everyone else who would listen. Their time wasn't just yet, and they didn't have the guns or the requisite funds; but the information dump momentum was going their way and their numbers were increasing steadily. Lok Yi Yi and his late twin brother had, after all spent a giant part of their youth in front of computer, mobile phone and I-pad screens. It was almost as if they were extensions of their technology, components in fact. This is the Hong Kong way.

As for the goons, the ill-fitting suited picaroons, who worked and sometimes shirked for Ho Fat and thus de facto for the P.R. China cadre elites, they mostly couldn't even operate a computer and relied on brawn and being yelled at, to ever accomplish much anyway. Their yellers, however, were a far different kettle of fish and they were adept electronically, so were fairly *au fait* with these young anti-regime corps. They were fellow savants never that far behind and all too often beside the Loks and Tuazons who opposed them.

And when The Americans shared their satellite imagery and their reconstructed scenarios – spasmodically and erratically – with their supposed political foes, well then all hell was likely to break loose. The trouble was, Dr. Cross was in lock-up. And no satellite knew that as yet. So nor did Wayne Wyshnowski, his ostensible boss in Asia.

Lok Yi Yi slept well that next evening; aching back and all. His crony had welcomed him, without any signs of fear.

Mind you, at first, Lok himself had no real idea of the extent of support that he had in Hong Kong. He knew one or two close buddies and realized only later that there was some swell of empathizers, from the support that he had received to his initial blogs and to his later exchanges of tight information with others of his ilk. Albeit such exchanges were encrypted, given the nefarious network of Mainland hackers and subterranean Internet ghouls, who were largely sponsored by a freedom-denying Chinese administration as they continued to cement into place their Great Firewall of censorship.

In other words, there was a definite international market for the information he had helped rake in: it was just that he had no idea of the scope of such a market.

He did know one thing however; that several other earnest governments, who sometimes worked in tandem, but more often arbitrarily and quasi-independently, had also marked him down as a rogue element, which had to be eliminated. He also understood exactly why they wanted his elimination: precisely because what he had garnered and shared piecemeal here and there with cronies, was ultra-explosive. If anyone with any modicum of nous had picked up on it, who wasn't part of the mighty exploitative chain, which stated and maintained the cabal lies, there would have been one huge spontaneous rebellion and the so-called modern world, as it was known, would be seismographically upturned.

Lok would have smiled at that thought, but he was far too tired after hiding at suburban swimming pools and evading bullets earmarked solely for him.

Thus he had indeed slept quite soundly that night, deep in a Kwun Tong tenement; knowing that one day would be enough there, but that two would be setting himself up for a certain death.

The next morning, he entrusted a couple of flashdrives loaded with sheer shock, to his cousin Ah Lee Hok, who was a bus driver back up to Shenzhen and who therefore sometimes had interesting connections and insights. Ah Lee, in other words, had far more than an inkling of what P.R. China was really like, how manifestly corrupt it still was and had always been and indeed, just how Kafkaesque it was. Namely, eerie beyond words in any language or in any of its remaining dialects, which had not already been smashed by the enforced use of the Mandarin Chinese tongue, a veritable elephantine *lingua franca*.

He nodded at the much younger Lok Yi Yi.

Ah Lee offered his cousin some congee, which he noticed disappeared with quite some relish – he then asked him, "What will you do today?"

Lok didn't really mutter anything intelligible, but later Ah Lee thought he had said something about, "I'm going out to Tin Shui Wai."

"Don't you think that is dangerous? After all, what happened to your brother out there? I do not recommend going there..."

Lok Yi Yi merely frowned and didn't utter any response.

Ah Lee shook his head and muttered, "Silly boy."

And went off to drive buses.

56/1.

Meanwhile, back in Aotearoa New Zealand, the skinny country as one of its leading novelists had once designated it, Hemi Hemara had finally been cajoled and had cajoled himself into joining up with the guerillas. Who were locked into an ultimate showdown with the countries' puppet administration: mere marionettes, they believed, of Anglo-American master puppeteers; copycat minions who merely mocked the Māori, despite their equivocations otherwise.

Basically, Hemara had had enough of being poor, having no prospects, having to wander down to the local welfare office, when his marginalized farm ran dry and his stock had begun to die. There had to be a better way of life than having to scratch around to find some dollars to buy food and the occasional ale or two. Too many others had a sweaty hand on the marijuana market and Hemara had already been busted for growing it on his own property, so jail time wasn't an option as far as he was concerned. Been there, done that and he was too old for more.

Besides, he had pretty good firearm aptitude – his cousin Norton had taught him all he knew, which was a considerable amount.

So Hemara ran around the back blocks with like-minded men and women and honed his survival skills and his combat readiness. And they all bided their time. Mind you, they all also comprehended that any one of them could be murdered at any time – just as Trevor King and his sister had not so long before, ostensibly because they were rebel sympathizers and prime stirrers. For by now, Hemara had pretty much placed his mate Norton's lawyer nearby the scene of both killings and had not been backward about regaling his allies with this observation.

And he kept well away from the likes of Fatso, who had been asking far too many smart-arse questions of late, especially since he wasn't even based on the Coast. It was like the cops, the D's, as they were called there, were sniffing around big time, now they knew Norton had scarpered off – somewhere.

57/3.

Norton, actually, was in rather an invidious position.

He had just killed another man for another time on foreign soil and in pretty much the same fashion – quickly, noiselessly, reasonably stealthy. But not – this time – without being seen by others.

Whereas Monaghan's victim, Tuazon, had been patched up pretty swiftly and sent to Dr. Munoz's nearby clinic to have his glancing bullet wound stitched up and was now all bandaged and en route south beyond Manila to stay at another one of his auntie's, Norton wasn't so fortunate.

He wasn't injured and he still hadn't managed to be rid of the bleeding blade. Several market vendors and their wanna-be customers had followed, were staring at and pointing at him. No police were there – yet – and the couple of security guards were still twitchy about what exactly had gone down, let alone about what to do next.

Ruby had also since arrived – impelled by the sight of the three men following one another snake-like down her street, as much by any concerns for her loved ones' safety. She had no knowledge that Monaghan knew of Rustico and that her new beau, Norton, knew of Monaghan – who now lay sprawled bloodily on a swathe of broken concrete, half under a fresh mango drink stall.

So she grabbed Norton – who had sort of sidled away outside from the immediate scene of the crime – and pushed him away even further, back toward her mother's own home, but via another interconnecting lane, that offered some obscurity.

As soon as Norton comprehended what she was doing for and to him, he responded and they started to merge away from the still chaotic site, to emerge about twenty metres from her mother's small abode.

He wouldn't be able to hide there too long, they both assumed, without as much as a word between them – time for discussions later, much later – because it was sure as hell certain Norton would be found very quickly. A killing was a killing, even if it was ostensibly to prevent another killing. So, Ruby needed some time to think – and to think real fast.

58/2.

Walter Wyshnowski had now been dispatched – pronto! – to Hong Kong, after his recent jaunt to Palau to oversee the building of the massive new U.S. consular cathedral hidden away in the countryside there, openly concealed in fact from the majority of Palauans, who rarely visited the Big Island. He was to make enquiries as regards a 'missing American citizen', whom had recently been in Manila and who then travelled as a tourist to Hong Kong and consequently had seemed to disappear.

Enquiries in Hong Kong revealed that the missing American had not left the Special Administrative Region and therefore he must still be there somewhere. No immigration control records revealed his exiting Hong Kong, so it was of some concern that the man had vanished, without apparent trace or rationale or record.

Wyshnowski knew how to play the game, because it was by no means the first time that one of his own men had been taken out of the gigantic board contest the sometime contestants were usually quite adept at playing. He knew that Dr. Cross – the name that was being used here – was no fool, had always been very professional and cool under duress, so this sudden vanishing and lack of any communication whatsoever was extremely worrying – especially at such a stage when so much was at stake. He also knew about the tryst between Cross and Ho Fat Kit – because he had organized it.

Wyshnowski had to undertake negotiations with the Chinese rather delicately, for both parties were making use of each other in their endeavours to eliminate these recent burgeoning and annoying intrusions into their respective netherworlds of corruption, malfeasance, double-dealing and hypocrisy. He couldn't out-and-out accuse the Chinese of snatching Dr. Cross, but all pointers were stretching in that direction: especially as there was absolutely no trace of Cross in Hong Kong whatsoever. After all, the Mainland special forces were adept at exacting Hong Kong residents more easily than any wisdom tooth; most especially if they were journalists who may turn up several months later, if they turned up at all.

In other words, Wyshnowski wouldn't have been sent back to Hong Kong unless the stakes were huge and unless more routine surveillance had failed – as it had here. The USA seemed to have misplaced one of its very own – and they certainly hated that. Someone or something would have to pay. Sooner or later.

Of course almost all of the administrators in Hong Kong had no clue as regards the sheer deviousness of their Mainland overlords, had no idea what actually was going down with any potential kidnapping of Cross - and so were quite honest when they stated that they had no idea what may have happened to him. In every office he knocked on the door and politely enquired of the bevy of faces inside, all Wyshnowski received was a mass of shaking heads, shrugged shoulders and "*Ngo ng zi.*"

All of which, quite naturally, made Wyshnowski even more worried. It was fairly apparent to him, early on, that the people behind the vanishing of Dr. Cross were not stationed in Hong Kong and sure as eggs were not anyone regular – if, indeed, anything was regular anywhere in China.

He soon retreated, back to an alternative H.Q. in Beijing, to attempt to unravel all of the skeins of this intrigue.

59/3.

Eric Canlas was minding his own business, loafing around downtown Puerto Princessa and waiting for the new trawler to trawl back off out into deep water. He had already been several days on leave and it had long since started to become boring. When he answered his mobile phone and listened to his cousin, Ruby, he was instantly eager to assist, as much through having something stimulating to do as to help her and her immediate family out again. He had to suppress a laugh when he heard that that Māori guy needed to be moved away from where he had initially escorted him – and as soon as too.

"Sure, cousin, sure. *Walang problema*," Canlas drolled into the phone, as he toyed with the near-empty Red Horse beer bottle he was guzzling down one-by-one in the afternoon scorch. "But how will you two get over here – my boat isn't headed to Manila this time around – we are going to Taiwan…?"

Ruby must have muttered something incomprehensible, for Canlas was screwing up his eyes in confusion; not so much at what she was saying, but more because he couldn't actually hear what she was saying. It sounded like her and Norton would be travelling to Puerto Princessa tomorrow – somehow or other. Eric just shrugged his shoulders and hugged the now empty bottle closer to his side. He sighed, "O.K. then – see you tomorrow. I am staying at the Kings Royal Hotel downtown. We sail Friday."

Time to get another cold beer. Canlas was not the sort to worry too much anyway. Whatever was going to happen would happen, regardless of anything he could do. Anyway, there was a prime live band on tonight at the bar and sure to be some talent for him to gawk at, chat to and chat up and, who knows…? Palawan was a lot like him, actually – laid back, warm-blooded and ready to party at any time.

He didn't notice the guy over there on the other side of the main intersection, getting out of a black SUV and glancing around everywhere, sort of nervously as he held his left shoulder in an arm brace. And he wouldn't have even known it was one of his own relatives-in-law anyway – after all, it had been years since he had seen Rustico Tuazon.

Canlas walked back towards to the bar, humming something by Freddie Aguillera. Probably *Anak,* as that was the only song Eric remembered all the words to.

60/2.
Lok Yi Yi quite literally didn't know what had hit him.

Because, he died instantaneously from the first chop to the back of his neck. His spine had been severed, such was the severity of the blow and the force emanating from the wrist of one of – perhaps - Ho Fat Kit's strong men. A killer, who had fled the scene in a back street of Yuen Long, by merely merging into the late night crowds permanently engulfing the overcrowded streets of this North Western New Territories cosmopolitan zone.

Lok's quickly lifeless body plunged onto the footpath after first ricocheting off several rather alarmed bystanders who – also quite literally – didn't know what had hit them and who hadn't even noticed the blow, such was its swiftness and almost invisible dexterity.

The blood wasn't even spurting, primarily because there wasn't any to spurt – Lok was basically decapitated by bone, not flesh, weird as it seemed. The killer was obviously well versed in his lethal skill.

If Lok had had any luck, it would have been in the fact that the day before he had come on out this way to surreptitiously greet and to grieve with his family, he had deposited all of his manifold files with colleagues in Kowloon, for them to hide a bit more clearly. The only thing he had on his nearly headless torso was his Hong Kong I.D. card, a few hundred Hong Kong dollars and a couple of business cards with what seemed like hieroglyphics scrawled all over them – it certainly wasn't in Chinese script at all. Seemingly, the secrets of his particular anti-cabal cabal were safe for now. Ho Fat and his minions – if indeed it were they – would have to source these files somehow else, so as to sell locally or to give them to their Beijing masters at the highest possible price. If not these alternatives, the market stretched well beyond Asia.

If the assassin was not one of the triad's members, who else did the deed? If anyone had paid any attention to the man dressed in black from head to toe and wearing a collar-less dark jersey and nicotine-stained fingers like gloves, who just elided into the mass, they would have correctly surmised that this was no Hong Kong killer, but a very sure thing, a Mainland man. Down south on P.R. business. Maybe the truth would be revealed on one of Lok's usb drives somewhere – for he had indeed compiled lengthy lists of the establishment's prime movers and shapers, as well as their messengers of mayhem.

If Lok Yi Yi had ever heard of Thomas Pynchon or Jorge Luis Borges – or even Dan Brown – he would have thought he was himself all caught up in one of their ultra-complicated hermaphroditic sub-plots. But, of course, now he was very dead. It was now far too late to read anything and certainly not in English, a language that had been forced on him and all of his school peers by the previous Anglo administration and ever since maintained by an elitist bunch of English school-educated local politicians.

The brothers Lok Yi Yi and Lok Mai Chan grew up in their tiny New Territories apartment reading Cantonese-language comics, if they read anything at all beyond their networked computer games with their constant mayhem and accompanying sounds – sometimes depicting people being decapitated, as just one gory example, actually.

Certainly not books replete with deliberately created intricate plots and sub plots either; with a myriad of obscure characters at every turn. Who had the time to even write such labyrinthine stuff, let alone read it? Certainly not Hong Kong twins screen-gazing in high-rise apartment blocks. They had long since thrown away their Hong Kong Advanced Level Education study guide to the English novel in one of the large rubbish skips lurking at the rear of their complex.*

No one there would ever be bothered to retrieve it, let alone the aged and wrinkled pensioners trying to find something to sell, to supplement their pathetic fruit money entitlement. One look at such an alien script would have seen them bury the study guide deeper into the morass of trash.

[*see Addendum].

Meanwhile, back up in Beijing, Walter Wyshnowski was swearing under his breath at these deliberately evasive Chinese politicians, who kept shaking his hand and offering him copious cups of tea, but who never revealed anything. Unctuous wasn't quite the word for their behaviour, but it certainly came close. All he received was an ubiquitous "*Wo bu zhidao.*"

Wyshnowski scratched the scurf from his balding pate and watched as it floated down to settle inside the semi-drained teacup. It seemed to reflect his very own freefall from Manila to here – quite powerless and at the whims of others. He had kept on trying to impress the serious desires and wishes of his American government on these guys, but all he could get in response were slight bows and smiles and gushing gusts of total ignorance as to where this Mr. Cross might be. These guys were so good that they actually seemed totally puzzled as to who Mr. Cross might even be, let alone where he might be. They weren't even inscrutable in their denials.

It was only later, when Wyshnowski was getting a blowjob from a male prostitute he had hired by the hour, that he clicked onto the fact that these guys also probably had no idea what he was talking about, precisely because they had no idea at all.

After he ejaculated fulsomely all over the young skinny kid and bade him farewell with a slight *yuan* tip, Wyshnowski began to ruminate a little more and scratch his head with more force than before. He remembered a clichéd saying from his upbringing back in Chicago, about the right hand doesn't even know what the left hand is doing, and considered that maybe – just maybe – that's what the state of play was here.

He had been seeing the wrong guys completely.

 It wasn't government functionaries and factotums, or even triad foremen whom he needed to question, but the far more clandestine cadre who lurked around every corner, shadowing, firewalling, hacking and bashing into submission, anyone who they determined was not in the Sino states' best interests.

Trouble was Wyshnowski had no real idea how to even go about finding these agents. Even although he was a career diplomat, he was nonplussed in Beijing.

And no one was going to tell him anything there either.

62/3.

Norton had not killed anyone for a number of years now. His swift – what he saw as retributory - swiping of Monaghan with a sharp blade, until today had been the first such considered hit for him for quite some time.

Retributory not so much because he felt any great need to support Tuazon, whom he scarcely knew, other than through Norton's lifelong sense of 'fair play'. Retributory more because of what Tuazon had sent more swiftly to the forefront of his – Norton's own brain – all about the deliberate Anglo-American mega manipulation of Indigenous and indigenous populations, for what seemed like centuries. More fully retributory because of what Monaghan and he had been through during and since the crazy Asian war of nearly half a century previously; the deviousness and deceit of which had been a hallmark of what Rustico was trying to implant into citizens' consciousness more widely across the globe. Norton had to accept that he had been – back then at least – an unwitting agent of the Anglo-American compote. Complicit. Doubly complicit, as he had betrayed Māori. He had traduced himself.

But even more fully retaliatory, how Monaghan had completely, pitilessly and deliberately betrayed Norton, his wife, his *iwi*, his people and therefore himself. Mongahan had, after all, married one of Norton's own cousins, several decades previously. In his own odd way, Monaghan was a relative of his killer and at the same time possibly a killer of his killer's own relatives. The latter point was something Hemi Hemara had initially intimated to Norton and which had grown as more and more likely the further Norton pondered it. Had grown even more concrete by Monaghan's surprising presence in Pampanga.

For the first time in what seemed an age also, Norton felt better. His brain was now operating at something like two-thirds' capacity, as opposed to its usual sluggish plod. His eyes scanned everywhere all at once and his sexual appetite was overwhelming. Something about killing Monaghan in broad daylight had also unleashed something else primeval and instinctive within him: something he had not tasted for many years. All his recent half-doubts and semi-thoughts about potential conspiracies and cabals and sub-plots, where everybody was all mixed up with everything in some hieroglyphic sigil tune, had now coalesced into a clear burning paramount vision. Namely, that everything was holistically interconnected and that some clichéd clique of prime movers were consciously puppeteering the massive mass of others, all as part of their portentously greedy patch; as well as an unrelenting passion to retain their power, whatever the means.

The rune strumming through Norton's brain right now, as he followed Ruby to her sister's driver's suddenly-organized car, was that he would have to do a lot more about opening up the eyes and ears of all the other poor bastards who were being screwed by an imperium cluster made up of a select coterie of their fellow humans.

But right then there was certainly no place for fucking, even given the rampant libido drumming through him in the back seat of the SUV, as it sped off towards Manila to Ivy's condominium apartment. There was certainly no place either for delivering any sermon on how these bastards had to be even more fully exposed and thwarted. Especially to the rather wild-eyed Ruby who was sitting beside him, her own body tenor taut and tight, after having to say a quick goodbye to her very own mother and to try and knit a quick escape blanket that would cover both of them completely. Indeed, they had continued their non-conversation and only their eyes and body language corresponded.

And Norton didn't quite know it yet, but – finally - just about everyone was looking for him right now. Not only the Philippines police force to ask him about the bloodied body still sprawled in the Pampanga town market, beneath the durians and mangoes. Not only the police force from Aotearoa New Zealand, who after losing him in the first place quite some time ago, had failed to track him and who had recently also been intercepted by Interpol, the very agency they had contacted in their frenzy to start with.

But also – soon, of course – Los Americanos, who had initially sent Monaghan to the Philippine Islands to quell Rustico Tuazon and who surely would quickly put two and two together to place Norton as their own prime suspect in the quelling of his ex-war buddy and legal consort. Interpol were thus being impelled further by the CIA and the multifold other clandestine agencies, demanding to know his whereabouts.

Norton was too adrenaline and dopamine fuelled right then to be thinking in any Cool Hand Luke manner; was too busy formulating how to get back in touch with his own whānau to join the revolution in his homeland. An uprising, which had already begun without him long since anyway, as a form of Antipodean echo of the rebellions now taking place rather regularly in other, northern climes.

His tongue, however, had freed up more and he was getting ready to babble. Just not yet.

So – again - it was all left to Ruby to be practical. To escape from her homeland again; for different reasons than the socio-economic miasma she had departed from during her young days years beforehand. She thought that she might be in love with her new man, but still was not quite certain, because time had been too brief an acquaintance for them both. But she definitely knew that she had to protect her nephew Rustico and more significantly her own mother. By leaving the killing zone, this would be more than adequately achieved. Besides, she certainly had had her own doubts about Dr. Cross and his ilk, generally, and after listening to Rustico, she was pondering even more grievously his possible involvement in the sudden disappearance and purported death of her niece, Euris. In the very city where they were going to just then, albeit – she hoped – only briefly.

The money Cross had left her and subsequently dispatched to her from Hong Kong, plus Norton's sizeable wad of notes, as revealed when he had sailed in from Pampanga with Eric Canlas (namely his mighty abattoir pay-off) was more than sufficient to fly them to Hong Kong and beyond, if need be. While she had already – of course – left a fair sum with her mother for the not so proverbial rainy days. For soon it would be flood time in Pampanga all over again and J. Pintella could well be under water once more. Her mother Acquilina would be left to deal with its swampy aftermath of ring marks around the inside walls of her home all over again.

Nonetheless, money was no panacea, especially now Ruby knew that, as soon as she had the chance, she would go to church and pray. Pray for her kids. Her mother. For her family, from Rustico Tuazon to Euris to Grace, Ivy and each and everyone of her blood. Right then and there, she was clasping the rosary drawn quite tightly around her throat, in a sort of silent yet passionate benediction. To a God she had been raised to pray to – at home, at school, throughout her Philippine upbringing. A deity she had somehow sublimated until now.

They sped on down the highway toward metro Manila, her sister's apartment and the flight out the next day, at dawn.

Meanwhile Police Captain Ernest de Leon was scratching his head as to why this *putih* had been stabbed to death at 1.00 pm on a very hot San Fernando day.

Why, in fact the *putih* was even in the provinces, so far from any tourist spot whatsoever.

"I don't need this crap," he muttered over the telephone to one of his superiors in Manila, at the same time squinting through the filmy venetian blinds in his office, hoping to see something that would lighten his dull mood.

63/5.

So now – yet again – Chinese were infighting and competing one against another*
in an effort to obtain the golden fleece of whatever the brothers Lok had
discovered, and somehow hidden well away from their glares.

The infighters worked for different striates of Chinese society, which were
themselves in continual competition, rather like geographic shifting strata that were
in a permanent state of movement and could abrade one another and rupture this
entire society at any time. It wasn't clan based or tribally based, rather it was all too
do with power and money, with a large helping of male ego thrown in. And buckets
full of rice wine, accompanied by oodles of cheap and nasty smelling cigarettes.

Ho Fat Kit ordered his triad troops, based on orders rumbling through Hong Kong
from his own Big Brother based somewhere in downtown Kowloon. Quite where
this Big Brother obtained his information, Ho Fat never queried, but he was fairly
certain that Big Brother was well into local politics, ICAC and all. All Ho Fat now
knew was that this kid Lok Yi Yi also had to be removed and that any information
the kid had about his person had to be returned. Money was the main motivation
for this echelon of pursuit. Which is why Ho Fat Kin and his merry men were
always open to offer from anyone at all.

The Mainland vassals strode to a different drummer, based back in Beijing, who
essentially wielded far more potency than Big Brother, but who did not have the
advantage of knowing the home territory as well. Which is why their minions, black-
suited and collarless, had missed Lok Yi Yi on more than one occasion; that is,
except this last one This corpulent cadre insisted on having what was deemed
essential and secret information back in his own hands, for it really blew open just
how pervasively corrupt and intrusive was central China's own command system.
National honour was promulgated as the raison d'etre for retrieval here, but
quintessentially it was all about male ego, control, and power all over again.

[*China vs Hong Kong. Cadres vs crypto-politicians. It was all convoluted, bifurcated, complicated
and hermaphroditic: half the time the factions worked together, some of the time – as of now – they
worked apart. Much of the time they had absolutely no idea of what was going on, either each of the

All Walter Wyshnowski, the white man, surmised was that some Chinamen had Dr. Cross somewhere and it wasn't likely to be anywhere near Hong Kong.

And yet, he had been led to believe that for once he and NSA and all the other myriad Americano grab bag of miscellaneous secret security clubs, were co-operating with Chinese authorities. He had taken for granted the fact that both sets were akin to the cheapest of cheap desperate prostitutes of any gender. They would get into bed with anyone. Indeed, there were rumours of their patronizing nefarious Mexican drug-runners if need be…while they had absolutely no scruples sharing dirty sheets with a certain Mr. Putin either. Nor he with them, for that matter.

He was, of course, right off course. That while Chinese authorities were far more likely to be battling their own schisms, let alone their own public; one thing was as sure as Sam's Apple Pie: all of them hated Americans anyway.

More, they also wanted what the brothers Lok may have pillaged, as it also potentially showed deep American spyware penetration into their own secret espionage caverns.

It was just that Wyshnowski and his ilk had not as yet sorted this quite simple notion out. They remained defiantly obtuse, even with polite MI5 advice, which they chose to ignore, rather like benighted deep sea creatures. After all MI5 still retained and maintained their own not so secret espionage centre in their ex-colony of Hong Kong. Slap in the middle of Central and next to Marks & Spencers, appropriately enough.

The tectonic plates were always shifting and colliding and ultimately quite oblivious each of the other.

64/3.

In Pasay City, Ruby's sister Ivy wasn't home, because she was out working at her Korean bosses' travel agency. Trying to organize packages of wealthy Koreans to come over to the Philippines, to lie around in Boracay and Bohol, and spend their money on things Filipino.

And it worked, for Ivy had made it her business to get along well with her employer and his own immediate family, and so to become invaluable to them.

But she wouldn't be home for hours yet, because she did have to put in the hard yards, so to speak: to work six days a week, every week. To not only continue her invaluable role, but also to continue earning sufficient funds so as to maintain the hefty mortgage on her trendy and quite new apartment on the twenty-third floor. Overlooking the spanking new pool that glistened in the never-ending sun, so far above. Her own husband lived a somewhat separate life traveling between Korea, Bohol and Manila, performing as a tourist provider, although Ivy never really knew exactly what he did. He and she were somewhat estranged and had been so for a long time. Ivy liked it like that too. She – rather like her elder sister, Ruby – had had enough of men. At least for a while. The fact that she could never count on them to contribute to family finances made her work ever more.

So Norton and Ruby relaxed and drank some cold San Miguel, so thoughtfully left in the refrigerator, although Ruby sensed that it hadn't been left especially for them, because Ivy sure as hell didn't drink alcohol much, if at all. It had probably been left there by her sister's infrequently present husband, some time ago. But Ivy had provided the SUV to *zap* them to Manila, if zap was the correct term to describe the inevitable snail crawl inside the entrails of that vast, untidy city.

They made love quite soon after their arrival also – cooled by the cooling beer and by the incessant chatter of the air conditioning units throughout the apartment – and wanting to somehow cool down also their fevered emotions after the previous few day's events and the day's murder in the market. Sex seemed to be the thin dividing marker between going completely nuts because of these events, or staying somewhat sane and absorbing these latest developments. For neither of them had

– as yet – even mentioned what had happened or why it had. They had merely responded to events and then ran on from them.

Only now did Norton turn deep to Ruby and say that, "I had to do it, eh."

"What do you mean?" she replied. Ruby thought he had meant that it was because of her nephew being threatened with instant death that her new beau had acted as he had and she was rather alarmed when Norton then went on about an entire other rationale for the killing. She knew nothing about this *putih* Monaghan, whom she had never heard about ever and whose name Norton was almost chanting in the way he continued to say, "Monaghan did this, Monaghan did that," and thus, "he had to die, the bastard."

It now seemed, to Ruby, that Norton and this Monaghan man had been long-term acquaintances.

All this was of no immediate import for her however, for she had now concretized everything in her mind. She definitely had to get back out of her home country and return to her place of permanent residency: Hong Kong, where her now adult children were anyway and where she believed this craziness didn't seem to be so common. It couldn't be, surely?

That's why she had asked Eric Canlas for assistance to get her as close to Hong Kong as possible, and also as far away from mainstream airport terminals as possible. Her beau would be a marked man in such spots.

That's why they were going to fly on an old seaplane tomorrow morning to Puerto Princessa in Palawan. The old seaplane belonged to Ivy's Korean boss, who would never know that his Filipino pilot was not going to Boracay that morning to deliver supplies and pick up the month's takings, but flying somewhere else to deliver a fugitive and his new lover. Fortunately for all concerned, this plane took off and landed down beside Manila Bay, at a private airfield.

They didn't see Ivy that evening – she was kept at work until 10.00 pm – as a usual practice – especially during this busy season. And they were so tired with recent events and the strenuous lovemaking session they had both just put their all into, that they were both soon fast asleep and totally oblivious as to her late return to the apartment she owned. Sort of – if you took away the monthly mortgage repayments she somehow creatively accounted for - and which her semi-detached spouse sometimes erratically contributed to.

Meanwhile, back in Pampanga, Ernest de Leon still had no clues whatsoever as to why this murder had occurred or who was actually responsible for it. Different bystanders gave different versions of what they said they saw, while the Filipino victim – a young male with gunshot wounds – had vanished completely. It seemed that he had booked tickets on the Batangas bus, but when de Leon's men had stopped the bus and spoken to the driver, late that afternoon, his story seemed to show that no such man had in fact ever boarded his bus.

De Leon spat into the roadside dust and lit another cigarillo. Hell, he didn't even have a good description of the reputed killer, only that, 'he wasn't from around here' and that 'he might have been a *mestizo*.' That meant he could have been one of millions in Pampanga alone.

De Leon spat again into the tired dust. More fully this time, just missing a gaggle of girls out of school, but in uniform. They had slipped across the road in front of the new 7/11, where they had spent much of the day drinking Coke, for all the world to see.

65/2.

During all the action elsewhere, Godfrey Woo had – finally – struck a bit of luck. He had been given some responsibility in his cash only, always under-the-table job and now did not have to crawl to and from Lau Fau Shan like a neutered centipede. He had been promoted – that is what he had been led to believe anyway – and now was driving a light van, full of counterfeit goods, to and from the Lo Wu border crossing between Hong Kong and Shenzhen. He was busier than he had ever been and was quite happy in that he was merely a driver and did not have to do too much loading and unloading and certainly no actual smuggling of the goods – that was all handled by a crew of mirthless Mainland slaves.

Woo now could stand almost upright again and smoke new cigarettes and afford to have a haircut. His teeth were still broken and yellowing and he still needed a month of showers, but at least things had turned slightly towards him of late.

What made it all so much better was that he could now sleep in the back of the van.

It was such a change, that sometimes he almost forgot that Ho Fat and the Wo Sha Ni triad were still determined to get him. It was well that he heard via the local rapid-fire gossip, about the near decapitation of some young student radical guy nearby, rumoured to have been carried out by this selfsame gang, for it snapped him back into some sense of surveillance.

So, although Woo drove pretty much the same routes nearly every day in a van provided and topped up with petrol by his boss, he knew enough to be real careful. He drove slowly and always smiled politely at the motorcycle policemen. He locked himself in the van when he slept or dozed during the infrequent slack periods. When he ate he chose more out-of-the-way canteens, where no one would know him, let alone recognize him.

And always, every day without fail, he listened to the latest gossip on the street and feigned total ignorance of anything at all.

Woo was – almost – reveling in his new-found mobility and – to him anyway – near luxury of being able to hide and sleep far better than he had for a considerably long time. Meanwhile, the two-dead Lok brothers' cohorts in both the Mainland - and some would say its mega-slave, Hong Kong - were going overboard and spreading more and more of their information about just how cynically corrupt were so many cadre and civic officials in all echelons of their administration.

Heads were therefore literally beginning to roll, after this concerted upsurge in the dissemination of deleterious information about these officials – who were nearly all middle-aged men with their fingers in every possible pie imaginable. From pre-pubescent girls – and boys too, for that matter – through to the manipulation of accounts. The ripping-off of profits. The nepotistic awarding of work projects. The ingestion of massive bribes. The intimidation of poor people and the screwing them of adequate recompense for the land they had lost to rampant shoddy construction. Their having innumerable mistresses, as well as these sex-starved officials spread-eagling themselves in video shots with lush prostitutes – the list went on and on and on and on and on. The Loks' itemized audits of such behaviour, was – to utilize yet another abundant cliché – merely scratching the surface. But definitely right then a mighty irritant for those with too much to lose.

66/3.

After landing some distance from Puerto Princessa on a fairly secluded beachfront, Ruby and the still somewhat surprised Norton found themselves saying goodbye to the pilot, who was happy with the American dollars they had stuffed into his palm as an extra tip for this unauthorized flight. Everybody was happy with Americano dollars after all, even Norton with his increasingly anti-American feelings.

They trod their ways over the rampantly hot sand towards some manner of green vegetation and the concomitant shade it had to offer, where Ruby unleashed the bottles of water that she had had the foresight to bring. Norton guzzled noisily on one, while she sank the other far more decorously. Then they trudged a few hundred metres on towards the road that was somewhere close by, judging by the intermittent traffic noise they could hear.

Neither had had any real time to reflect on the events of the last few days or even to talk more than very fleetingly about their immediate futures, but now there was some sort of space, as they moved towards the road and therefore towards the township itself. For they could soon grab a tricycle to go into Puerto Princessa and meet up with Canlas in his designated hotel.

Ruby had had time to share with her new beau where they were going, but she had yet to ask him why exactly he had killed the man?

So she turned to look at him, full-on and said, "Why did you really kill that *putih*? Who was he to you, really?" His earlier rant had left her bemused and somewhat confused.

Norton stared her back and said something to the effect that he and the murdered man had, "a long history – way back, in fact," and that, "if he hadn't killed him" (Norton never mentioned the dead man by name this time, for it didn't matter) "the guy would have killed me first."

Ruby had long since surmised that was the reason, for she could not see why the dead man was even in Pampanga otherwise. He must have been looking for someone.

Yet, none of their conversation even touched on the fact that Tuazon must have been the prime target – from the bullets fired – not Norton. Ruby had always taken it for granted that Norton had been protecting her nephew, not himself, despite Norton's recent ranting about Laos and Luang Prabang. But she said no more at that stage, as a tricycle had done a complete u turn on the country way and – after their clambering in far too tightly into the back - was spluttering its steady way towards town and Canlas.

And Tuazon, who had done his own u turn days before and had flown straight there, bandaged shoulder and all.

The ever jovial Canlas was still smiling when he met them, for he thought it was funny that he would have to escape this foreigner all over again – this time out of the Philippines, and not in. He couldn't help himself from commenting on the fact that, "you are always in Palawan and you are always escaping," to Norton, who didn't appreciate the joke and merely scowled in silence. Anyway, Norton was tired right then. Tired of running and hiding and taking all sorts of shit for things he had no real memory of ever having done or had in fact done for reasons that made coherent sense to him, at least. He was hoping that all this effluent could just be flushed away and that he could live some sort of measured life for once.

But Norton also knew that now he knew far too much and that he couldn't just ignore it and pretend he hadn't listened to Tuazon. Or that he hadn't mused on his own missions from the past and the not so distant immediate present.

Which is why he and Ruby got roaring drunk on a mixture of Red Horse, San Miguel and vodka coolers at Canlas's hotel bar – nestled in a hot yard outside, with just a rudiment of shelter from the wayward afternoon sun – and eating the delicious *menudo* and *sinigang* the kitchen staff served up. Canlas, meanwhile, made do on a smidgen of Tanduay – he had to actually work on the boat tomorrow because two days later – ostensibly – they were set to sail to Taiwan.

When Norton had reached the percipient stage of his drunk he realized just how absurd the situation was – not merely his own – but everyone's on this planet they called Earth. All quite ludicrous actually - and what a waste a time it was for some asinine politicians and secret agents and cohorts and cliques to be so overwrought about their nefarious games and ploys. They were all going to die anyway.

Norton spat deep into the dust of the bar courtyard, narrowly missing the jandalled feet of some young stranger. He sculled another Red Horse and silently belched.

But at the same time the alcohol hit home with him that, given that everything appeared pointless and insane and just not worth getting so worked up about, he was in love with this now rather florid Filipina who was nestling quite close to him on her bar stool, laying into the *sinigang* and San Miguel with equal abandon. And for the life of him, Norton couldn't equate love with absurdity and meaninglessness and he remembered that he had always been useless in algebra and had been relegated to the bottom mathematics class in his dingy South Auckland school oh so many, many years before. And caned umpteen times for refusing to sing the British national anthem every morning assembly. 'God save the Queen' indeed. "Fuck that", he reflected. And then said out loud, too which Ruby smiled even more widely.

Monaghan, of course, had been in the top class. Except that he was well gone by now - as Norton spat again into the dust and Ruby had started dancing by herself to the band, which had recently started to play for the increasing number of tourists, now milling about and filling the yard.

Just as she came over to grab his hand and pull him onto the dance yard, Norton saw and heard a distinctive figure with a distinctive voice: Rustico Tuazon was shaking his relative's hand vigorously and the cousin, this time Canlas, was reciprocating as stalwartly.

Ruby waved at them both, seemingly unsurprised at seeing Tuazon, for she now had led her man into the centre of the yard and was dancing happily for all the world to see.

Norton just shrugged inwardly and gave up trying to put two and two together, as he shambled along to the beat. Mind you, he had never been particularly proficient at addition either.

And so the night segued forward into the misty recollections of the next morning.

67/1.

Hemi Hemara had sort of changed tack quite considerably these last few weeks –
ever since his close *whanaunga* Makere had died – seemingly murdered nearby an
urupā of all places, while she was herself attending the *tangi* of her own brother,
Trevor King. Who had also seemingly been slashed to death at his workplace in
Auckland. Heavy *tapu*.

Hemara had known that his relatives were considered Māori activists by even their
own peers and within their own *whānau* or family, but he certainly had not felt any
antipathy toward his own blood because of their fairly heavy political stances. They
had wanted total independence for New Zealands' *tangata whenua*, the Māori, and
were ready to turn to guns and violence to achieve it.

He – Hemara – had been swayed more than anything though, by another of his
passive cousins – Norton. Precisely because Norton seemed to have no radical
anti-establishment views whatsoever. Indeed, it was precisely because Norton was
being set up by the cops, that Hemara decided that it was time to stand up to those
clowns and to fight back. Hemara also could not see Norton killing his own former
wife at such a sacred place; he couldn't see Norton killing Makere ever.

And what really settled Hemara's stand was the fact that he was sure he had
sighted that prick James Monaghan down in Ruatoria during the *tangi* period.
Monaghan had quickly looked away when he realized that Hemara was staring at
him, but Hemara had thought at the time, "What the bloody hell is that guy doing
down here?"

He had never liked Monaghan ever since he had learned that the latter had served
time in the States in some sort of undercover capacity after the Vietnam war –
whatever that may have meant. Hemara had seriously doubted Monaghan ever
since and Norton's indifference to this fact only made Hemara more sure that
Monaghan was a spy or a double agent or something similar. Hemara had long
since learned that Norton tended to ignore what was right in front of his eyes, even
if he was told about Hemara's doubts. Why? Because he – Norton – was at heart a
romantic, who wanted to believe everyone else was basically good at heart.

Hemara knew better from bitter experience and he too had a very long memory of being forced to learn and then sing *God Save the Queen,* when he went to secondary school over forty years earlier. He never forgot his sheer displeasure when he looked around and saw that at least 80% of his schoolmates were as brown as him.

In short Hemara despised white men much of the time and Monaghan only made things worse. After Norton had vanished – taking Hemara's suggestion to, "bugger off overseas, who needs a passport?" to heart also – Hemara went west to the remote Urewera country and started to train big time with the many militia, and their armaments already there.

It had helped of course, that his immediate family had included Makere and Trevor King, lieutenants both in the burgeoning *Tino Rangatiratanga* movement sweeping Aotearoa New Zealand like a brume fire. They had been his easy entrée to the flames and had endlessly quoted at him the excerpts from the great Māori prophet, Mahon, a key harbinger to today's rebellion in the skinny country of New Zealand. It seemed this guy Mahon had long ago insisted on an uprising in Aotearoa, to overturn the entrenched white oligarchy there.

Hemi Hemara also knew that Norton had taught Monaghan everything he knew about knife play.

68/5.

The brother Lok's files – shared and up and downloaded everywhere in, about and around China and beyond – were now starting to have a massive cumulative effect and Ho Hamsap – the window-pusher killer of brother Lok number one - and his henchmen were way beyond angry.

Comrade Da Zei was the chief executive of P.R. China's rather sinister Central Investigative Corps, responsible for everything from the legions of supposedly undercover agents – who all dressed the same anyway and who were all so blatantly obvious what they were – through to the mighty Golden Shield project incorporating the Great Firewalls of China, of which there were many. He was also in charge of the burgeoning invidious and euphemistically named Time Out Camps for political re-education and psychological re-assignation. In one of which, in fact, Cross was still sitting and doing very little, except to think about how it was that he had ended up in this somewhat notorious Black Jail miles from anything like the American heartland he had grown up in; over sixty years previously.

Mind you, Cross was soon to be quite lucky. He was grabbed by his skinny shoulders - for he had lost a lot of weight existing on a diet of rice and *pak choi,* with meat he refused to eat as it was – to him, anyway – unknown as to its genesis, let alone gestation - and he was shoved without any sufficient explanation, into a black van. He was then driven quite manically to Beijing, loaded onto a plane and flown quite quickly back home, which wasn't quite Milwaukee, but Washington D.C, where he would have to undergo several days of debriefing from federal agents and the NSA and whoever else lurked under the bedsheets of American surveillance services, encryption and un-encryption. Still, Cross mused, as he gorged himself on a king-size beef burger from Max's Burger Chow House, this was a lot better than squatting and shitting away his life in P.R. China.

Sadly, Ruby had escaped his preoccupations almost completely. It was as if he had forgotten about her. Unless she was shut away behind one of his airtight mental compartments.

He later learned that he had been exchanged for two severely-wanted Chinese ex-officials, who had stolen billions of *yuan* and run off to the States several years before and who had to be brought back home to the Mainland. All of this in an effort by the authorities to deflect attention away from this latest scandalous information about current officials, being leaked and now indeed lambasted everywhere. Chinese politicians – like their erstwhile American ones right then – were eternally pragmatic and also right then, a little bit in league for their own not so ulterior motives. For them, Dr. Cross now also needed to be interrogated by his own kind, so as to find out how further to stem all these leaks and to – maybe – jointly help track down more of the Loks and Rustico Tuazons of the world.

Meanwhile, Comrade Da Zei was fuming impotently about just about everything. He wasn't making much progress on any front and the unwanted information deluge was exponentially increasing – even after he had enlisted triad assistance in both the homeland and in that troubling territory further south, with its dangerous ideas about freedom of the press and universal suffrage. He spat copiously in disgust, onto the pavement several stories below his offices, missing passersby by millimeters. Expectoration seems to rule Asia.

Short of killing a hell of a lot of people – and the thought had certainly passed across the forefront of his mind on a few occasions of late – he was running out of options.

He had even had to talk to that American fool Wyshnowski about their shared international concerns – but that had also led nowhere, as the American idiot was really living up to that appellation. Indeed, all Wyshnowski could do was scratch his rapidly balding pate and overextended paunch and claim that his, "best men were onto it."

Which was rubbish and he knew it. One was dead and the other only just released from a Chinese jail. Two sizeable snippets of information that he, Da Zei had only recently received.

Who knew if, in fact, there were any others to replace them?

69/3

By now, back in Manila, Captain de Leon had basically given up solving why the half-caste had stabbed the *putih* in Pampanga. He had filed the case in Unsolved – Pending, and retired to Bill's Bar for a sequence of Red Horse drinking games. With a few members of the detective corps – some of whom also doubled as night watchmen - security guards and gang hitmen in their moonlighting roles after dark. Most of them did as they had to, given their paltry *peso* pay; but some also rather liked the power rush such nefarious tasks after work hours gave them, as well as the stroking of their thin male egos it induced.

He sat firmly on one of the bar stools and chatted about one of the really important things in life – basketball. The PBA, indeed.

70/3.

Tuazon wasn't saying too much about how and why he had managed to get across to Palawan so speedily and about why he seemed relatively unconcerned about being sighted there. He seemed quite cheerful, in fact – other than his bandaged shoulder appearing rather grotesquely enlarged under his t-shirt – and smiled deeply when he saw his Aunt Ruby – and her bronze-coloured companion.

He merely muttered something along the lines of, "I have many, many contacts," and, "that in the Philippines, you can get a lot of things done that you couldn't in other places." While Eric Canlas laughed and Norton appeared puzzled, Ruby just turned to her new man and joked, "Only in the Philippines".

So they all continued to drink Red Horse and Tanduay mixes, until well after midnight and well after the band had packed up and gone home. Not a lot was said at all as to Tuazon's mission these days, about Americanos, about anything too serious.

It was still sultry, it was still festive, it just wasn't the time to talk about such weighty issues. As Canlas said more than once, and despite his own inner qualms as to what exactly was going on and what he was expected to do, "Life's too short *kaibigan*. Have another drink." Earlier he had also just shrugged when he and Tuazon had walked into the bar and seen Ruby and Norton there, dancing and carousing. Didn't seem much point in getting worried right then anyway. Or ever, come to think of it.

For Norton, it all was just too hard to get his head right around, that evening at least. Gave him a headache even beginning to think about it actually. He couldn't for the life of him fathom how Tuazon was there ahead of them, why he was there, and why – more significantly – no one was too upset by Tuazon's earlier revelations about conspiracies and Americanos and corruption and electronic eavesdropping and Subic and *blah blah blah*. Indeed, as the night wandered on, increasingly zany, Norton just drank, sat back and sang with the rest of them.

And the last thing on Ruby's mind was to reflect on anything other than having a good time. She felt she deserved a break from always having to be the organizer, the settler, the accommodator, the restorer, the empathizer, the key protagonist. No way, not tonight, no way. She slugged back on her Red Horse and munched on the *menudo* and rice.

With *halo halo* to follow. Of course.

Tuazon just smiled in his quiet way. He wasn't going to say anything about the fact that it had been an American who had financed his flight straight from a Batangas airfield to Palawan's Puerto Princessa. This was the same American, who was deep in with Tuazon and their internationally spread-eagled computer geek fraternity. Which had the keys to the kingdom of just how massive was the Americano spy network – almost as massive as the Americano bullshit machine that covered up for it, with its network of liars, spin doctors, fooled politicians, stooges and mercenary say-anything-to-anyone guys.

Because Tuazon knew if he said anything, if he implied that some Americans were actually fighting against their own countrymen, his whole sequence of efforts to expose that continent wouldn't have as much credibility. Yet some Americans were acutely aware of just how imperialistic, arrogant and belligerent their own American corporate mentality could be, and acutely concerned about where all the mass surveillance and manipulation would end up. Were as equally determined to expose what was happening, as the fellow countrymen powermongers were to maintain their tight control of everything.

Accordingly, right then, Tuazon just continued smiling and even dancing with a sore semi-shattered shoulder, after he asked a pretty young Filipina sitting a few tables away with a remote look in her eyes for a dance. Or two.

And so that evening segued to night and to near morning.

There were by far better things to do than be concerned about arseholes who wanted to manipulate and spy and inveigle. And rule the world.

Life was too short, eh, *kaibigan*.

Walang problema. Palagi walang problema.

Yet, deep into the wee small hours of the next morning, Tuazon plied a quiet toast to his Euris. He too would never forget her. Could never.

He had not, as yet, heard the new rumours about her either.

71/2.

'Māori *attack police station – scores dead.*'

If Woo could read English, in fact, if Woo could read at all, he would have seen the headlines of page 12 of the international section of the *South China Morning Post,* which had disentangled itself from its master copy and was whirling around the nullah like a drunken dervish. Woo would have had no inkling as to what Māori were – like 95% of his fellow countrymen in Hong Kong - and even if he did, would not have been particularly interested anyway, for money was a prime obsession with them and him. But it did seem that the Indigenous of Aotearoa New Zealand had not only fomented and fermented more fully a rebellion against the central government there, but that they were also having some success with it.

Not too many in Hong Kong or its Big Brother, P.R. China, of course, would be very keen to see such news too widely dissipated, so it was rather fortuitous that Woo saw that headline and just about everyone else saw nothing. Later editions somehow forgot to print this information. Didn't want to give the locals any ideas, eh.

Woo crumpled up the newssheet and tossed it out of the window of the van.

72/1

Around this time, Hemara – while he was not quite gloating – was happy to hold up the head of the much despised Fatso Smith, which he had very cleanly cut off from his overweight frame just a few hours previously, with an especially sharp machete.

Which he would place next to the others on an equally sharp pole outside the quite impressive and hopefully impregnable stockade, the so-called rebels had built to a centuries' old model.

The fact that many of these Māori 'insurgents' – as so labeled by the political prats in the nation's capital city Wellington – were also Pan *Pai Mārire** adherents had unified them into a potent fighting force, with a firm religious zeal. As well as their long list of grievances religiously compiled for well over 150 years

Hemara said his *karakia* and went off to join his mates for a *kai*. Among these mates were several members of *Ngā Wahine Toa*, who were allied for just as long as it took to attain their prime objective. Once *tino ranagatira* was accomplished, well then, many men were next on the list, regardless of ethnicity.

[Pai Mārire – literally 'good and peaceful' – in nineteenth century New Zealand this movement incorporated both biblical and Māori elements and promised its followers total deliverance from Pākehā domination - from **Radical Wikipedia.com** 2016]

73/4.

The boat trip towards Taiwan was pretty rough and tough and Norton was soon
spewing his ring over the side, ashen-faced and unkempt. After they left Puerto
Princessa, the seas didn't seem to want to behave that day. Ruby also wasn't well,
and it wasn't just because the drink and dance from yesterday was still lingering all
through her system: she was tired and more than a little worried about what would
happen next. Especially since her nephew Rustico Tuazon had drawn close to her
late in the early morning to share his suspicions about her previous Americano
beau.

Eric Canlas, however, was his usual cheerful self and ordering his two man crew
around all over the place, as the boat chugged slowly, a couple of hundred
kilometres off Palawan. He hadn't yet told his cousin Ruby and her new man where
exactly they were going and that he had decided to completely avoid Taiwan
anyway – hell, he felt, that port could wait.

No, instead he was heading to the Spratlys to find some decent fish first. He knew
of a lagoon or two where they could feast on fish fortune – if the bloody Chinese
weren't there blockading a Filipino treasure trove. He smiled inwardly too, as he
thought about the big guns he had had built into the boat.

Canlas needed to make up some money fast and fulsome – too much mucking
around sailing short trips and sailing bloody refugees everywhere recently wasn't
earning him sufficient funds. He was going back where he was entitled to sail as a
Filipino fisherman too, as these shoals had always been a part of his native land
for as far back as he knew. Certainly his own father had always taken him there
over the years of his youth and he saw absolutely no reason to change - even if his
own collusional and sometimes delusional government couldn't – or was it wouldn't
– assist Filipino fishermen to make a decent living in their own territorial waters.

Meanwhile – in between barfs – Norton was a little consoled by the fact that
Tuazon had shaken his hand goodbye back in Puerto Princessa, even although he
hadn't actually said, *'selamat po kaibigan'* for Norton saving his young life. Norton
had absolutely no idea what Tuazon was going to do now or where he was going

to go – and Norton really didn't know himself what was going on in his own immediate life situation, to care too much either just then.

The boat caroused the waves ever further and the coastline had long since run away with itself somewhere. They were seemingly all alone out there in the western Pacific Ocean, the Philippine Sea, the South China Sea – or whatever else it was called these days.

Ruby was trying to sleep away the burning din of the engines, which seemed too close for her liking – pummeling away just behind the warped tin bulkheads.

Norton had just spewed out the last of yesterday's *menudo*, Red Horse and his entire life up until then.

At last he could sleep with some sense of satisfaction.

The small craft ploughed on.

74/2.

Woo sort of sensed that he was not now – at least – number one on the hit list of
Ho Fat Kit and his merry men. Recently, he hadn't felt that he was being tracked
down, let alone followed and ready to be chopped to death, somewhere out back of
Tin Shui Wai. For there was absolutely no sign of any of the usual suspects,
covered in crude tattoo parlour paintjobs and jabs, chain-smoking and looking like
ketamine addicts high on withdrawal – which, of course, several of them were.

But what Woo did notice as he scrambled – still sagely and carefully, so as not to
attract any unwarranted attention – was a marked increase in the number of plain
clothed black-suited Mainlanders, always with ridiculously short cropped hair and
also chain-smoking: all looking quite obvious in their attempts not to look obvious.

They and more troops of the Peoples' Liberation Army – in uniform and marching.
Which Woo did find rather odd – and also rather worrying. "What was going on in
Hong Kong now?" he sort of mused, as he bit his broken fingernails deeper to the
quick. "Must be something serious." There was no one in earshot, but Woo had
grown used to speaking to himself.

But that was just about all of his wider concern. He shrugged his brain back into
oblivion.

He remained more tunnel vision focused on surviving and eating and sleeping,
than to consider why there was this heightened presence of forces, searching for
something just about everywhere he ventured, or was sent to pick up and deliver.

It wasn't until a few days later, when he was scrunching on some lame tasteless
noodle soup mélange, that he overheard some other customers saying something
about 'security broken' and 'confidential information', in rapid fire Cantonese. Woo
just kept on trying to eat and pretended he hadn't heard a thing. But later on he
rewarded himself with a half smile, because it did indeed seem that Ho Fat and his
Wo Sha Ni gang of thugs, at least, had bigger fish to fry than Woo, a relatively
small fry guy.

He quit smiling rapid fire however, when he saw a troop of Mainland security goons grab some young acned kid out of a nearby 7/11 and cast him headfast into the back of the big black van they were now prone to patrol the streets in. These guys sure as hell were not joking about anything - and that kid was scared shitless.

Woo drove slowly away in the other direction completely and parked deep in the Lau Fau Shan nullah, turned off his engine, swept himself into the back and slept fitfully for a few more hours.

75/4.

The voyage secured sunny skies and settled seas after the first two days and both Ruby and Norton started to feel better.

Neither had any idea where exactly the small vessel was lumbering to right then – they had been told Taiwan, before any possibility of moving on to Hong Kong - but both were much happier that the conditions enabled them to sit on deck and laze around a bit, while the small crew did all the manouevering.

Norton spent much of his time trying to get his thoughts into some better array than they had ever since he had fled Aotearoa what seemed like years ago – when in fact it had only been a matter of weeks. He still didn't say much and Ruby was quite content to leave him be, as she was similarly pondering what her immediate future might bring. She had left a tidy sum of *peso* with her mother – thanks mainly to her new beau's munificence, but also thanks to her old beau's quick departure, whereby he had practically thrown a wad of bills in her direction the last time she had seen him. She wanted to check up on her two adult kids who had quiet lives of their own in the New Territories of Hong Kong, but the need wasn't pressing.

Ruby also knew that the authorities back in Pampanga would not just let things die. They still had to deal with the New Zealand government's questioning as to what had happened to one of their citizens in the market and what the Philippines jurisdiction was going to do about it all…so staying in Pampanga was not a sensible option for them at that stage.

And there was always what to do about avenging Euris in her mind. The way she felt, after listening to Tuazon, her old beau, Dr. Cross, was a marked man. Should she ever meet up again with him.

They were snapped out of their respective slumbers by Canlas, who rather nonchalantly informed them that they were headed to the shoals to do some fishing and that Norton was welcome to go diving once they got there – he, Canlas, had the equipment if so. Quite why Canlas thought Norton was even proficient to dive escaped Norton, who said nothing much at the offer. They didn't question this interruption to their supposed route, being happy enough to loll in the sunshine and get some measure of composure after the last few days.

Way up ahead they saw some semblance of land in the form of a very low-lying prominence and a couple of bent palm trees supplicating themselves to the seas and strolling all over the scattered sand and shingle shoreline.

They also noticed movement, but it wasn't until later as they slowed down considerably, that they saw it was a large navy vessel painted grey and signed with Chinese characters. Uniformed men were also parading around its quite sturdy deck and one of them was binocularing them on their much smaller craft.

"Fuck it," said one of the crewmen. "It's Chinese navy."

With that, he raced somewhat sluggishly to the wheel where his mate was unsighted and their craft suddenly did a sharp counter turn away from its direct line to the bigger ship. Canlas was also shouting something in Tagalog, which Ruby couldn't quite pick up, because the engines were straining considerably louder than they had since the first morning of their escape.

Quite quickly they were idling alongside the coastline of the small isle, sort of sheltered in a semi-circle bay, away from the presumably Chinese ship – which at this stage didn't seem to be heading their way.

Canlas was very obviously totally pissed off as he told them all about, "the fucking Chinese patrolling our shoals and preventing us from accessing the deep coves where all the big fish are." Apparently it was a rather long-standing territorial dispute between P.R. China and Philippines, which was totally unbalanced with regard to numbers and equipment, in favour of the former.

"What will we do?" asked Norton, genuinely interested in this latest development, which had at least broken him from his self-analysis and ego introspection.

"We will wait a while," muttered Canlas, not daring to mention – just yet anyway –

his rather large cache of heavy-duty guns stored down below. "Maybe we will use our kayak to sneak in to the lagoon after dark to get some decent sized fish. They never see us when we do this."

The two rather grizzled crewmen nodded in agreement. It seemed that they were well-experienced at having to sneak into the cove – "our cove," as one of them reiterated – and having to fish at night, with a big net dragged behind the small skiff that was lashed to the cabin side. It seemed that of late this was the only way to make a decent catch and indeed many Palawan fishermen had stopped even trying to make ends meet and had given up fishing and started *sari sari* stores or something similar and safer.

So they sat and waited and Canlas shut down the engines completely. They ate tasteless bananas and drank some lukewarm bottled water, while Enrico – one of the crewmen – smoked deeply on some questionable cigars. Enrico was actually Romeo's father, which is why Ruby started chatting to him in quick Kapampangan. After she finally recognized him after having squinted at him for the last few days, puzzled as to why she could not put a name or an identity to him.

Norton smiled. A bit of action might just be what he needed. A bit more action actually.

76/2.

Woo had to stand on his brake pedal and swerve right across the highway, almost knocking down a gaggle of cardboard box collectors, who had been rummaging amongst the night bins for any signs of empty cartons and who were – despite the thin trickling rain – endeavouring to snatch a few dollars from their catch. Sadly, their only way to be even able to exist in the financial-free-for-all that was Hong Kong.

It hadn't been this elderly gaggle however that had made Woo nearly shit his own dirty pants, but the sight of the PLA troops in thick marching order, coming straight down the centre of the same road, without any vestige of them altering their route. Woo was amazed, for he had never seen so many P.R. China troops in his life before – at least not in the flesh, so to speak, and certainly never in these rain-speckled streets of suburban Hong Kong, at 5.00 in the morning.

Even the gerontion box brigade was almost standing upright and none of them was even making an effort to scramble for scraps. They were as flummoxed as he. The troops merely marched onwards and scarcely even glanced at the van or the toothy balding driver, who was sweating whether or not this might finally be his big showdown. But, no – they certainly weren't interested in him – something or someone else was their prey.

As they curved around the bend behind and as the box pensioners started gobbling up their clumps of cardboard, Woo did notice one thing – all the PLA soldiers were armed. This was no training exercise. They were intent on capturing? Killing? Cornering? Controlling? Who?

He went about the rest of the mornings' deliveries very quietly and made sure that he did not raise his eyes up too much, except when he really had to. No eye contact with strangers, only mumbled replies to greetings. Always head down when picking up goods.

Woo just didn't like the heavy vibes around. Even if he didn't seem to be a quarry anymore – or so he prayed anyway - Hong Kong had quickly changed. And he didn't like it much, even if he could now sleep lying down and without getting wet.

It was only while he was having his mid-morning noodles, when he glanced up at the local news channel lambasting the canteen TV screen, he learned more. The scenes of mayhem and crowd eruption being streamed through stole his eyes and made them stare. There was on the one hand a massive protest at something, and also – worryingly – a thick phalanx of policemen and women and PLA army ranks staring it down. And beating it down into small clusters, whenever the two groupings had somehow gotten too close. Woo could hear background screams and see baton shadows, while the commentator was speaking with a pitch that was far too charged. The rain had also arrived in force and the next shots were of people sprawling all over the greasy streets of downtown Central and then the sound of what could only have been gunfire, from not so far away.

Then the screen suddenly went all dumb and advertisements rumbled in to disturb the flow.

Soon after, Woo headed back further up and away, back up north towards Tin Shui Wai, where he hoped that there, at least, was some vestige of peace. It was nearly his finish time anyway, since he'd been driving since the dull early hours.

And Woo hated anything complicated, troubling, violent. *Ho ma fan. Ho ho ma fan.*

Maybe by tomorrow everything would be settled again, he hoped, although deep down, he knew that was not going to be the case.

Suddenly he was very tired. More fatigued than he had ever been in his entire shifty, shitty later life so far.

And just as his brain hit the sleep button he heard the *buzz buzz buzz* of the helicopters flying low and fast above him.

POLICE
警察

77/4.

It was quite a clear evening and Canlas could seemingly sense everywhere. Even in the dusk. The tepid moon shared no solace, but Canlas could see that the Chinese navy vessel was all quiet and that no one was even looking in their direction. He whispered to the *mestizo*, Norton, that they would keep on paddling silently past this vessel and for him to keep an eye on any possible sightings. Norton had nodded in agreement and they slid on, well past the hull of the ship and deeper into the lagoon.

Enrico was the first to dive into the quiet and delve for fish, grasping in one hand a massive interwoven net and in the other a hosepipe, without any mouthpiece, through which he would breathe, via the tenuous connection to the rusty diesel compressor skulking on the thin prow of the kayak.

Canlas followed and told Norton to, "just stay there and wait for a while." Nothing more, as he then also plunged like an invisible man over the side and down to help his older *kaibigan*.

The compressor churned awkwardly onwards and Norton sat back and burped away all the dry sea biscuits and green banana compote he had earlier ingested, hoping that the dull chug chug sound would not arouse the Chinese vessel..

Norton began to think all over again, while he waited for the two Filipinos to resurface sometime. He knew that Canlas wouldn't be a long time under the surface, as there was only one breathing hose. He reflected just how crazy his life had become in the last couple of months and all the deaths he had witnessed, heard about and caused. For some reason he wondered who had killed Euris all those days ago and why her supposed boyfriend had never even mentioned this to him or even seemed very affected by it, except for his one outburst of tears back in J. Pintella. What was that all about, he wondered? These Filipinos never seemed to get over-emotional, he guessed. He did not reflect on his own rather stoic acceptance of Makere's demise, however.

Norton knew who had killed James Monaghan and why.

He wasn't absolutely 100% sure about the murderer of his ex-wife and her brother however, but was reasonably certain about Hemara's instincts. "Too late now anyway, eh," he reflected.

Just then Canlas did resurface and – spitting out seawater – smiled widely. "Man, we've struck gold down there," he spluttered. "Enrico will stay down and push in more fish and then let us know when to haul up the net."

Quite how they would be even be able to pull up a net teeming with fish, let alone drag it anywhere with such a small skiff, which they had trouble enough all sitting in, totally escaped Norton. But he said nothing and smiled at Canlas' smile. However, he did ask, as innocently as he could, about Tuazon, and where he was now going to go, as they waited.

All Canlas would offer was a further smile and a shrug. Something to the effect that Tuazon was, "a survivor who knew a lot of people." And when Norton was going to push him a bit more, he felt the entire craft shudder suddenly and shakily. Enrico was shoving a fairly full net of shiny fish under the keel of their skiff and – it seemed – then lashing it to the prow with some twine. It was only when Enrico chucked the breathing pipe back on board, shook off his ancient rubber goggles and clambered back and said, "row," when Norton realised that was how they were going back to their fishing boat snaked away from the lagoon entrance. They were going to have to heave their hearts out to get any momentum whatsoever, yet also to keep as quiet as possible as they approached the lurking Chinese craft loping across the entrance. And the moon wasn't that dim.

So the three of them stroked hard and – slowly, infinitely slowly, as it seemed to Norton the New Zealander, so far from his native land – their thin canoe sputtered into some sort of crawl. The compressor had long since been turned off and all was pretty still – except for the occasional flopping of netted fish trying to get their lives back in order under the base of the boat.

78/2.

Although and because brothers Lok Mai Chun and Lok Yi Yi had been murdered, their local online buddies were by now really ramming home the message that the Americans had quintessentially ransacked the entire international online and telephonic worlds. And that – more worryingly for them, as Chinese citizens - that the P.R. Chinese authorities had also ramped up all efforts to thwart anyone promulgating this awareness. There was a sort of double bind at play here: the buddies wished to let people know online what initially was called the Snowden-Manning effect, yet were hampered by the resultant chronic restrictions on the web in their own territories. None of this was made any easier by the rather uneasy alliance of the Americans with the Hong Kong administration, and the equally unsteady collusion between the Mainland and the SAR, itself hell-bent on restricting freedom of any genre.

So all these counter-forces were countering throughout Hong Kong, while Ho Fat was an integral part of all this, as he took backhanders from anyone who chose to utilize his and his rather large in-terms-of-numbers triad.

Woo was indeed no longer his number one priority, although he would still have been a nice residual catch in the now larger trawling operation Ho Fat was organizing, through Kowloon and Central Hong Kong in particular.

79/4.

"This is fucking madness," was the main thought that kept crossing Norton's mind as he heaved on the oars/paddles and tried to keep the thin skiff balanced. "These fucking fish must weigh a ton," he spluttered to no one in particular. He slunk a spy at the other two men, who seemed fully oblivious of anything other than the need to row their respective guts out, which was what they were doing right then. There was a slight grimace on Enrico's unshaven face, while Canlas was straining and sweating to the extent that his whole face was like a grim liquid.

And yet, slowly they were making some sort of progress – they were by now astern the Chinese boat, which had only dim mooring lights on and absolutely no sign of anyone patrolling anywhere.

The next time Norton looked up, they were out in the open sea and the waves were pressing them closer to the mother fishing boat, making it easier for them all. It was then that he realised that these guys were veterans at doing this; ludicrous as it all had seemed to him.

Later, as he lay flat panting on a coir mat full out on the deck, with a limpid moon lazily lolling directly above, he could hear the other crew member congratulating Enrico and their skipper, Canlas, as they drew in the net steadily, turned on the hoist mechanism and finally stowed their catch in the chiller.

Ruby stood, hands-on-hips, a bemused smile on her lips; shaking her head in recognition of the madness of her life recently. This was just more filler.

It was then that the lights went on all over the Chinese boat, even though it was not yet in their direct line of sight, and they heard its big engine being fired up.

Canlas quite literally sprang into further action, yelling out quick fire to get his own boat underway and to stow their recent kayak chariot behind them more firmly. He then seemed to duck down beneath the deck and within minutes – as his boat chugged increasingly fast further down the coastline – sprang back into sight clutching some huge firearm, the likes of which Norton had never seen before.

Then the Chinese boat was there too and someone was yelling through a microphone to them, which didn't alter their escape plan one iota, primarily as no one could understand what the Chinese were actually going on about – only that they now had a mighty spotlight thrust directly onto them and that both boats were going faster and faster.

80/1.

Not everyone knew about what was going down, down in Aotearoa – or as the Caucasian majority population still called it, New Zealand. But that majority was actually in the minority in the clichéd wider scheme of things – for let's face it half the world had never heard of the country or had no idea where it was. While many of the remainder of the world's inhabitants had no access to finding out anyway, as they were too busy just trying to eat and survive. Or just didn't think it was particularly important.

But systems in that skinny country were in chaotic upheaval and this had been building up for quite some time. The Māori rebels had fired up a rebellion, starting in the Urewera high country, where they were almost untraceable, due to the rigours of the geography there and due also to their own skill at evasion. Several government troops and so-called special agents had vanished into what seemed thin air, except for the couple of headless corpses of unilaterally despised policemen who had first been dispatched to quell the initial skirmish – and dispatched they had literally been. Decapitated latterly by Hemara and by several of his cousins, the latter of who had been strongly fulminating against a Pākehā, rotten, Americanized government for decades.

Including Te Matekairoa and *Ngā Wahine Toa* who had developed an enviable ability to strike and then scatter amongst the hinterlands of central Aotearoa – helped by the fact that their numbers were rather rapidly increasing: including now also, women from other countries, who had reasons of their own to join.

But theirs' was only a part of a nationwide and speedy upheaval. Protestors of various ilk and ethnicity – and the country now had ethnicities to burn – had marched against Parliament in Wellington, and in various other scattered locales in both of the two main islands. Others had settled either into work-to-rule patterns or mounted simple strikes as a protest against what they saw as New Zealand – or Aotearoa – selling out to Americans. For it had been revealed only that month, that their country, which they had prided in being fiercely independent, was merely a cattle dog of a much more potent, belligerent and quite nasty superpower across the other side of the Pacific Ocean.

For New Zealand had been spying on its own citizens as well as Pacific neighbours and abetting espionage on millions of supposed non-allies of the Anglo-American hegemony – that is quite literally what it was – for years, via a scurvy network of satellite stations and supposedly secret information caches sprinkled around its vastly under-populated rural regions. Except that right now – as an ignorant-of-all-this Norton was trying to escape not only his own put-upon-him past and soon quite literally gunfire from a Chinese naval vessel somewhere in Philippine national waters - several of these suspected spy stations were burning or at least under siege.

Not much news of this basic people's revolution was being transported into other nation's homes however: perhaps their own administrations didn't want to give their own populations any silly notions about fairness and justice and independence. But some countries did their utmost to expose just what was going on, albeit their news commentaries were in Spanish or Portuguese. Or Arabic.

And, of course, rebels everywhere always somehow managed to inveigle the latest global news and then put out the word.

And as the conflagrations went on, the USA was sending rapid response teams straight down to their southern ally, to suppress as much as they could as quickly as they could, all in their declared *Assisting an Ally* programme.

Trouble was, several of their supposed New Zealand allies had already deserted and gone over to the other side, had discarded their government issue uniforms a while ago and were training wanna-be rebels high up and away in the Urewera foothills and forests.

That's where Jim Pelorus was right then, aiding and abetting many of the guys he had helped to put away in prison for the last few years – always as a last resort, mind you, in his own mind. Pelorus was a gun with guns too, which is why the rebel hierarchy accepted him. They needed his nous and anyway, he was related to most of them somewhere along the line.

Pelorus had also served in South East Asia with Monaghan – the late James – and Norton, who was back in that vicinity, and, as it happened, who would soon be fighting more Asians.

Pelorus yelled at one of the younger recruits, who had the rifle all arse-about-face and wondered if they would ever beat the bastards who had taken his own great, great grandmothers' land all those years before.

Utu – blood revenge – had a very funny way of lying dormant for donkeys' years and then – *whap/bang/wallop* – it suddenly struck back, like it had been running on a silent energizer bunny all that time and had never actually been gone.

Trouble was, with acne-scarred kids like this gun-wary one, these Māori weren't going to beat anyone for some time yet. Pelorus grabbed the rifle away from the skinny teen and told him to, "Fuck off and boil some *kai* for our dinner tonight."

Pelorus looked around and smiled a little, because one or three did have some ideas about how to fight. He also glanced across at some of the newly arrived women guerillas. They had come in only last week from Asia somewhere and they sure did know how to handle firearms. They looked ready to battle.

And fight is exactly what they would soon have to be doing a lot of.

81/4.

The first shot must have been a mere warning shot, because to Norton's ears it came nowhere near any of them on the fishing boat, as they also shot off now on full throttle deep into the coves and crannies of the coastline of that particular low-lying shoal. He had soon realized that Canlas was canny and was fully aware that the draft of the much bigger Chinese patrol boat was never going to allow it to come as close to the remaining shoreline.

But he also had quickly cottoned onto the fact that they would soon actually run out of any close-by land formation and that they would soon also be run down out at sea. He was also angry, because it had been made glaringly obvious to him that this was still Philippine national territory and that the Chinese were not only trespassing, they were belligerently and aggressively enforcing 'rights' they did not actually have.

So Norton, who was about the only one on the boat with insufficient duties and therefore was well able to look around and across at the bigger vessel, decided he had better try and even up the odds. It wasn't merely because he reckoned he owed Canlas, for his earlier safe delivery, but because he just didn't like unfairness and indeed, he never had. It had always been Norton, who sided with the underdog. Every time. So nothing was about to suddenly change for him right then.

That is why he seized the firearm from the base of the steering column and checked it out. "O.K," he said to himself, "I can fire this fucker…but what with?"

Canlas must have been telepathic, for as he was steering his boat he was also indicating to Norton that the gun was already loaded and was making trigger pulling motions with his intermittently free hand. The others were tying up and down anything that even looked like coming loose, while Enrico had disappeared into the engine bay to tend its sometime hiccupping sickness.

The first shot from Norton's usually steady hands nearly blew him over the side of their craft. The firearm certainly had some potency. He had never used an elephant gun before, and this wasn't one either, but it whacked him backwards pretty much as he imagined such a big game gun would have.

He then heard all of the others yelling excitedly and he stood back up from the side, still clutching his gun like he was suckling his own mother's breast for the first time. The firearm had blown a huge hole in the side of the other vessel's main cabin and men over on the other boat were screaming and yelling at each other and at the Filipino craft.

'Jesus,' Norton thought, 'these cartridges must be metal piercing,' - and with that thought firmly in mind, he pumped out two more shots, a bit lower this time.

This time also he had managed to remain on his own two feet and this time also he noticed that the much grander Chinese craft was on fire somewhere and that there was a lot of running around going on over there. Although pretty soon he could only see smoke on the horizon, as Canlas had persuaded his boat to get the hell out of there.

The moon was merely smiling at all this from directly above and after another half an hour they were back inside another cove, this one deep and hidden enough to avoid any potential foreign eyes and – again – obviously well-known by the crew. Who were now scampering around covering as much of their boat as they could with canvas and coaxing it – and the still buoyant kayak behind – to gently scrape the rocks on the gently lapping shoreline.

They waited and waited and said very little one to another. There was by this time no sign of smoke anywhere; no sound of engines; no distress lights; nothing all in fact.

"We sleep here," was just about all Canlas would say, tiredly, yet sort of still jubilant.

Although just before full-on night came down and squashed them all, he did add quietly to himself, "We won't be going to Taiwan now."

Norton looked at Ruby for perhaps the first time since he had left on the skiff earlier that evening, and shrugged his shoulders. She smiled back, hands on hips, rather pleased that her new man was O.K. and that they had somehow thwarted their immediate confrontation with the Chinese intruders.

Ruby crossed to Norton and hugged him. "C'mon," she said, "Let's try and get some sleep."

They went down stairs beneath the steerage and crashed onto their thin wooden bunk. The mattress – if you could call it that – hardly maintained their combined weight, and it was too hot for any linen – but they couldn't have cared less right then. Up top, Enrico was assigned the task of watchman, as the night slumbered on.

82/1.
Hemara and his merry men had not really counted on being strafed by stealth jet fighters.

Which is what happened after Fatso and a few others had been decapitated and violence had broken out quite spontaneously in several locales sprinkled throughout the skinny country. Suddenly there were streams of tracer shells exploding around the Urewera terrain and more than a couple of the bro's lay dying in their wake. It had all been totally unexpected by all but a few of the ringleaders, who had had some idea that the Americans would not be taking lightly to having their assumed world dominion threatened, let alone usurped in any way, shape or form. Especially by a motley group of warriors who had mettle, but limited firepower and machinery.

And of course also the inept and feeble, dickey-licking New Zealand government had invited their superior-firepower allies into their own domain, so as to assist the global clamp down on this terrorist insurgency, which seemed to have spontaneously erupted like a festering carbuncle in many, many zones internationally.

It was going to become a long, unsettled and unsettling guerilla skirmish or, rather, a series of such, and Hemara, for one, had been more attuned to this possibility. Which is why he and a few other cognoscenti had retreated way into the *manawa* of the territory almost to the point of being unlocatable, invisible, untraceable. From there they would launch their own retaliatory and unexpected strategic raids at odd intervals and continue to bolster their support from others who had not been as clued up as them, who had been among the first wave to be surfed on by the fighter planes and who were surely in sore need of leadership, organization, solace.

And the Americans in their usual misguided fashion, by invading the territory of another supposedly sovereign land, actually boosted support for those dissatisfied with the way things are. Because their silly aggression merely augmented the warrior ranks, turned away the so-called neutrals and made even the staunchest

New Zealand grovellers in Wellington pause to ruminate a bit more than they ever had. Ethnicity no longer divided the nation; rage had reduced the rifts. Hemara shook Pelorus' hand for the first time in their lives: such an unusual alliance was now becoming the norm. There was now a concretized enemy for both of them.

They would be better prepared for the next air attacks, eh.

He also listened closely, a few days later on – when Pelorus shared with him the name of whom the New Zealand Police had finally determined was the true killer of Trevor King and Makere. James Clement Monaghan. Who had almost convinced all and sundry that Norton was the killer.

But as Pelorus lamented, "We couldn't touch that bastard Monaghan. Orders were to let him go. All high-up political shit, apparently."

Hemara turned away and uttered a silent prayer to himself and for his brothers.

> *Kororia me te Pata,*
> *Ranei tu,*
> *Ranei to,*
> *Riiko e!*
>
> *Te wai te pikine,*
> *Huoro Pata*
> *Hema ta pi*
> *Wai wi rau te,*
> *Rire, rire, hau!*

[Glory to the Father and to the Son and to the Holy Ghost, as it was in the beginning and ever shall be, world without end, Rire, rire, hau hau!]

83/4.

When the sun hit them square on sometime the following mid-morning, the first thing they noticed – each in their rambling sequence of wakefulness – was just how quiet and calm everything was. No clouds above and no swell below. Certainly no Chinese frigate anywhere near in sight – primarily because it had burned to the baseline and had sunk with a considerable loss of life.

No one realized that fact, until a few hours later, when they spotted the first of several spotter plane sorties, zooming around the vague area where they were ploughing along, en route now to Hong Kong.

A couple of them soon quite literally put two and two together and counted up the probability that they had caused write-off damage to the Chinese vessel and that the aeroplanes up above were circling in a seeking mission. Mind you, no planes really came near them or showed much interest in them: they were, after all, a small rickety looking wooden fishing tramp plugging along slowly and somewhat arcane, well away by now from the previous evening's infringements.

This meant Canlas gradually relaxed and set his ship towards the Chinese subsidiary territory of Hong Kong. He didn't tell his cousin, Ruby, this until well into the next day either, mainly as he didn't think that it would matter so much to her and her tawny boyfriend, covered as he was in tattoos. That fellow seemed fairly oblivious to most events actually - for he seemed to dwell inside himself, to be self-supportive, to be able to create his own agenda and follow it without too much – if any – need for much outside co-operation. "Christ," and here Canlas crossed himself for he too was a pious Catholic, even Ruby seemed a bit unnecessary to this New Zealand guy. He was a different one, that was for certain. Canlas shrugged and turned away from the pair, who were canoodling at the stern. He had far more important practical things to worry about right then.

And who would purchase their fish now, he wondered?

None of them knew that sometime the previous evening out back of Puerto Princessa, Rustico Tuazon had been snaffled by the MILF Islamic movement, albeit that being quite accidentally for him. These Moro separatists had mistaken him for a rich ransom-able dude and had not any idea whatsoever that the riches Tuazon bore were far more esoteric and weighty than a few *peso*. Still, it did mean that Tuazon was out of the immediate plot for a while, deep down in Basilan Island. Probably much safer there, given all the shit happening in the World right now. And he had invested all his information bank material with relations in Puerto Galera some time ago already. *Swerte*.

And the vessel plundered on through the swells and small storms that broke out over the next few days.

Norton and Ruby by now knew where they were headed and both had ample time to reflect what may happen after they arrived in Hong Kong. Ruby was pleased that she would catch up with her own kids and their kid – for she was now a youngish grandmother - while Norton had been thinking more than he had done for years previously.

He was concerned that the Chinese authorities would inevitably put two and two together and catch up with them either before the boat slunk into some oblique New Territory port overnight, or soon after when they landed and – as Ruby had explained, "moved in for a while with my daughter". She was O.K., for she was a Hong Kong permanent resident anyway and had actually left there without going through any airport channels in the first place: it was like she had never gone away. But Norton was worried.

He also ruminated that even if the Philippines authorities might have no idea where he was, their Americano counterparts would be more enthused about tracking him down precisely. As fuelled by their own as well as their partner New Zealand government's insistence in wanting to know how Monaghan had been slaughtered, and why the killer was yet to be incarcerated, let alone found. Given that the latter had no idea yet that he – as a convenient 'wanted killer' in New Zealand – was anywhere near the Philippines. Interpol was mixed into the morass as well.

Norton knew the Kiwis would not let up until they had someone to blame for the deaths, while the USA agencies would further be very concerned by the recent wildfire spread of supposedly closet information about their multifarious and supposedly clandestine espionage activities, which had now gone global, despite their best efforts to shut up the sources. Such as to assassinate rogues like Tuazon.

And he didn't even begin to consider what their espionage peers in P.R. China would be doing, primarily because he didn't know much about the leaks regarding their very own sleight of hand double-dealings with their own peoples across their own massive territorial zones.

So, he was rather quiet much of the remaining trip and even Canlas' rather jovial mood couldn't cajole him much. At least not until Canlas announced that they would be near Hong Kong in the, "next couple of days," as he broke out the big bottle of Fundador and started to sing *High*, by The Speaks, at the top of his voice in celebration. Only then did Norton forget briefly that Los Americanos had at least 16 separate spy agencies and unlimited members on the payroll, as he sipped on a few shots of the rum. In unison with a happy Ruby, who was thankful that the boat voyage would soon be over. She just shrugged when Canlas asked what was wrong with the *putih*?

Ruby had enough stuff of her own to contemplate.

She wanted to have far more control of her own life for once. And to simplify it.

And she knew the only way that could happen, would be to stop relationships with riven men.

Which probably meant all of them.

84/1.

Some time later, Hemara had news from some of his cronies overseas. Seemed like a contingent of Australian-based Māori were going to come over – closeted of course – to join up with the so-called rebels in the Urewera ranges, but they would need a lot of assistance to be able to do so. Hemara then had to think up more stratagems to get them to him. One piece of news he did savour, was that the Australians had ample weaponry, but – again, of course – needed help to get it there without being sprung. It seemed that they were going to travel to the East Coast via fishing boat and would need to be unloaded there, as quietly as possible and them and their armaments trucked down the Coast and across the ranges as quickly and cunningly as could be accomplished.

"Bloody difficult," is what Hemara said to his mates as they cooked stray sheep on the open fire that evening and drank down the cool clear spring water. They all knew that the roads were blocked off and that spies were in the airspace around them everywhere. It would have to be a mission-and-a-half, way across the rural back-blocks and hills, where security was nowhere near as rampant.

Still, there was nothing they could do right then and there, but sleep and listen to see if any enemy aircraft were on the near horizons, or if the rumoured SAS troops were in fact coming in stealthily to nab them. Personally, Hemara doubted the latter, as he knew many of these elite troops were his own *whanaunga* anyway and had already deserted to join them. All good, as was the news about the Australians.

Just before he went to sleep himself that evening, Hemara had a quick flicker of a thought about his old mate Norton. He wondered – quickly as he was about to doze deep – where Norton could possibly be right then and what he was doing and who would be after him. Hemara knew naught about the death of Monaghan at this stage of proceedings. He had absolutely no inkling where Norton might be either.

Next morning early, he was woken up by Hobo Kingi, with the news that some others also wanted to cross the Tasman and join up with them in their good struggle. Hemara wasn't so sure that this group were the sort of allies they needed, but it would not be his decision, for he would have to run it past their Council of War first. Would they want Arabs to join them?

Hobo was Trevor King's younger brother. He had been with the group as long as Trevor King and he had made especially certain that his nieces, Makere's daughters, were well looked after, when they came over from Ruatahuna a few weeks back.

As well as their mates, especially that young Filipina, who could load and fire a rifle quicker than any of them.

"Where did you learn that?' he had asked her in some awe yesterday, as they sat next to each other by the fire.

Euris only laughed and said nothing.

85/2.

Not far from Lau Fau Shan, Canlas stopped the fishing boat completely. Indeed, they were actually closer to Shenzhen than Hong Kong. Shenzhen was where he was going to dump the load of chilled fish, for the good money he knew he could get there from Chinese middlemen who would on-sell that delectable deep sea catch. Much of it illegal in the sense of being banned, as it was theoretically nearly depleted. Canlas knew better, but wasn't going to tell anyone about that.

Canlas called over Ruby and told his cousin that he would get one of his small crew, "to take them"– her and Norton – "that night, when, it was really dark," on the skiff, which they had actually caught much of the catch from. They would be dropped off just up from the Lau Fau Shan jetties. "Don't worry," he added, because he had been through this sort of procedure many times in many countries. Ruby wasn't so concerned as she knew the area well and in fact one of her own children lived in Tin Yan Estate, which was within a reasonable walking distance of the small, often shadily utilized, harbour point of Lau Fau Shan.

Norton was far more anxious when he heard this news. He had sort of gotten used to Canlas' company and – besides – he was pretty worried about being in Hong Kong, where he knew the authorities had a legalistic infrastructure second to none. In other words, if the New Zealand authorities had sent out a notice about him being a person of interest internationally, here would be as good a place as any for him to be snaffled. And he also knew from experience that the bloody Americans would be closely involved with any capture, for whatever reason any one of their multifold clandestine agencies chose to muster.

As for the Philippine authorities he sighed inwardly, because he had soon learned in his recent escapades there, that they would get no empathy from their Hong Kong counterparts. Sighed because although he was eminently culpable after killing Monaghan, he knew that Hong Kong had a doubly weird relationship with the Philippines Republic. They had slapped a black travel ban on going to the Philippines some years previously, yet continued to employ on shit wage rates, thousands and thousands of Filipino OFWs or overseas foreign workers. To do all their shit work. If anything – depending on the mood at the time – Hong Kong SAR may even disregard any such Philippine request to extradite him. Once again, his sense of fair play had been aroused.

Norton also shook his head when he saw the skiff being dragged over to the side of the larger vessel and Enrico jumping down and aboard with a massive torch, which lit up the immediate environs. Not so far away Norton could see the silhouettes of Shenzhen's many towers beckoning Canlas, while a little more distant on the other side were the dim lights of Hong Kong's more isolated North West.

"C'mon," yelled Enrico and Norton glanced back down at the skiff a few metres below, where Ruby, clad in a coat too big for her, had already scaled the rope ladder down to and was now sitting looking up expectantly at him.

Just as Norton stopped sighing, outwardly this time, and was clambering over the side, a hand seized his shoulder.

It was Canlas wishing him luck, with his usual smile spread across his face.

Next minute he was safely in the skiff, which had already picked up speed and was shooting towards the Special Administrative Region that was Hong Kong. Enrico was really powering it along, for he knew that he had to get back to Canlas soon, so as to shoot right up against Shenzhen and unload their catch as fast as possible, before it got too light.

Ruby was merely mulling over what she would say to her daughter and her young boyfriend, who wouldn't be expecting visitors or guests in their small public housing apartment on the 23rd floor of Yan Chung House.

Norton, on the other hand, had a brain churning and turning about what the hell was going on now. He was a man on the run from two murders he didn't commit and from one killing he did complete, partly so as to save another's life. He was a marked man wherever he went of late. He was going to have to rely on Ruby again here, that was certain - for he didn't know a soul in Hong Kong that he could remember and couldn't utter a word of Cantonese.

Then it hit him. Les Wereta may still be around. Yet another old army buddy from what seemed another quite distinct lifetime. Didn't he marry a Kowloon girl and settle somewhere in Hong Kong?

Before he could get his brain into a higher gear, he sensed that the skiff was slowing down and that Enrico was *shhhing* them. No torch now. Only a dead-moon-dark sky and the quiet lap of the waves against the hull and – not too distant now – the concrete plinth of somewhere near Lau Fau Shan.

After they had been quickly and wetly dispatched to the harsh concrete ramp by Enrico - who had immediately swung around the prow and zoomed back to his mother ship - Ruby and Norton were left to trudge through the slush and mud and stench up toward the small settlement of Lau Fau Shan itself. Dogs were baying and barking and the lighting was at best pallid in places - or else totally non-existent.

Then it started to rain and Norton's inner turmoil vastated into an outer struggle to keep as dry as possible under the thin protective eaves of some of the winding alleyway that led toward the other side of this fishing village. There were no people around at this time of the early morning and they slopped onwards as best they could, tripping once or twice on the corrugated concrete and banging into unseen-in-the-dark obstacles.

It took about another hour to reach Ruby's daughter's apartment building, by which time dawn was visiting and – thankfully – the rain had dwindled into a pathetic rumour. Then Ruby had to punch in a some code on the outside board, so as to even get into the block and – fortunately yet again - her code numbers still worked, given all the time she had been absent from Tin Yan. They crept up in the rather creaky lift, after first smiling at the sleepy looking security guard, who smiled back when she realized she had seen Ruby before.

Up on the 23rd floor it took a while for anyone to come and answer the door after

Ruby had rung the bell twice already.

Po Lam was there, bewildered at seeing her bedraggled mother for the first time in months and – more – by the tall, dusky, whiskered man standing next to her with tattoos all over his brawny arms. Norton smiled at her a little inanely and soon they were ushered in and Ruby showed him where to shower and dry himself.

Po Lam and her mother were chatting in rapid Cantonese when he had finished in the rather bare bathroom and put on a pair of dry track pants that Po Lam's boyfriend had thrown his way - after the boyfriend himself had gotten out of his bed and started to get ready to go to his job as a cook. Po Lam was half Hong Kong Chinese, for her father was that Chinese guy, namely Godfrey Woo, who had done the big runner several years previously and generated for himself an alternative family up near Shenzhen itself, with his Mandarin speaking mistress. Before she got the colds for him and he had headed back down to Kwun Tong.

Ruby had had to cultivate several talents, not least of them being able to speak several languages more than competently. She was a true survivor, something Norton was coming to appreciate more and more – a thought that smashed across his forebrain just before he crashed onto the sole big bed – the marital one – and had fallen horrendously asleep.

Ruby had explained that she and her new man – while Po Lam wondered what had happened to the last one, the American doctor – would stay for a while to sort out a few things. Ruby also enquired about Po Lam's bother, her son Jeremy, whom she had named after an Australian jockey, who had been a winner back in the day when her son was born. Then she too, succumbed to showering and sleeping, laying beside the snoring Norton, while Po Lam went out early to buy some extra provisions to feed this unexpected pair.

Later that day, Ruby woke to see Norton on the sole computer; basically trawling through the Internet in an effort to see any news about himself. There was very little there that actually mentioned him by name, but there were huge news bursts about the ongoing insurrection in Aotearoa and the riots pummeling central Hong

Kong itself. Ruby naturally asked him what was happening in Pampanga, but all seemed relatively quiet on that front, except for a bit about Subic Bay suddenly re-opening for an expectedly large contingent of American marines and mariners. Oh, and something about large protests in Manila. Norton then went back to browsing about all this new topsy-turvy world upset and upheaval that he had not known about, specifically because he had been so busy running away from his own issues and hassles and imminent arrests. For far too long now.

Po Lam had come back with that day's *South China Morning Post* – among other things – and soon Norton was also devouring all the updates to the disjunctions and dysfunctions he had only just learned of. Soon he was also devouring the noodles Ruby had quickly prepared out in the small kitchen over the gas stove; he peered up once only to see Po Lam staring at him with rather worried looking eyes, as he gobbled away.

The world indeed seemed to have gone quite mad in his absence from it and he was now wondering what would happen next. Maybe all the revolutions and upheavals popping up here and there across the globe might take the heat off him and Ruby. Maybe.

Norton swallowed the can of ice lemon tea, blinked a couple of times and went back to the paper.

Meanwhile Ruby was fast on the phone via Viber, *chika chika*'ing to her sister Ivy who had joined in the quite massive street demonstrations swamping metro Manila. No one – it also seemed – wanted the return of Los Americanos military. And several demonstrators – their cousin Grace included – were ramping up the scale of their protest by calling for complete transparency and of course solutions as regards the recent, as well as historical, disappearances of family members. Grace had not received a solitary *peso* in compensation for the disastrous loss of her daughter, let alone an explanation, let alone a culprit. All she had received was innumerable visits and questionings – and an invite for a date of all things – from Almodevar, the so-called whiz-bang police inspector in charge. 'No wonder she joined in,' she had said to Ivy about her daughter, in a still angry voice.

Ivy had merely replied in sympathy, "Bloody men."

Ruby, in turn, mentioned this and that about now being in Hong Kong, omitting various details about how exactly they got there and not mentioning anything about Norton's manslaughter/murder of Monaghan. Ivy – however - knew all about this occurrence anyway, having their entire family in Pampanga, living just around the scene of the death.

Later, it was Grace, not Ruby's youngest sister, who brought up the subject, after Ruby next contacted her. Grace basically confided in Ruby that no one had any real idea about what went down in the market, but that Norton, the *tsokolate putih* as everyone called him, was responsible. It was also Grace who asked what they – meaning Ruby and Norton – would do now.

"I'm not too sure," replied Ruby in Kapampangan, "I know I will stay here for a while. As for him, he's trouble!"

Grace sniggered and replied, "Aren't they all!"

Ruby did not yet want to share with Grace that she had a fair idea who had killed Euris. That could wait until she thought about it a bit more.

So it went that unsettled afternoon. Still, both protagonists, made quite wild and passionate love in the solitary bedroom, when Po Lam went out to Mongkok to be with her boyfriend late in the sun-declining afternoon. For now, that was sufficient.

Sometimes, fucking was all that made sense.

Po Lam did tell them, when she came home late with her husband - a tired Isaac Wong - that there had been a lot of activity on the streets of Mongkok. She had even heard that tanks were about the area, although she and the rather quiet Isaac never actually saw any. But they did see a couple of bloodied young people sprawl their itinerant ways past them.

And several bedraggled looking young PLA foot soldiers trying to march as a unit...

86/2.

Norton knew very little – if anything – about any of this weirdness, but was intelligent and experienced enough to know that if he went outside, he would have to keep a very low profile, if possible. Here he was sitting in Ruby's daughter's Tin Yan flat, musing about his next option. Ruby had gone out with her daughter to visit her son and Po Lam's brother, Jeremy, who had recently moved back to Tin Shui Wai with his young family. All this meant leaving the somewhat weary-with-all-this-shit Norton alone, an alien in Hong Kong. An outsider in the World. But thoughts of Colin Wilson were the last thing on his mind right then, given that he had read that seminal book many years ago; when he was bright and idealistic. And naïve.

He tried to ring back to Aotearoa to speak to Hemara, to see if there was any update from him, but no one picked up Hemara's telephone. He scanned the latest New Zealand web site news items, only to discern the fairly obvious chaos there. The riots were continuing. He googled his own name, only to still learn very little. If the relevant authorities were after him, they certainly were not letting on, on the Internet. The only references to him were a couple of nibbles about his writing a bit about Existentialism thirty years earlier, when he had a brief flirt with academia, before dropping out and becoming a meat worker.

Norton also tried to find a Hong Kong telephone number for Les Wereta, but no luck there either.

Next, he decided to go outside and see what he could see. Po Lam had reconfirmed with her mother the door code for the building and she in turn had passed it on to Norton.

After going down in the deserted lift to the ground floor and nodding to the uniformed security woman, sitting by the front desk television screens, Norton found himself in a wide nondescript square, with a few scurrying citizens and the odd school kid who was off on some truant mission somewhere. He stood out like the proverbial sore thumb. Keeping quite close to the covered walkways, he found a smallish shopping centre and traveled the slow escalator up to the first floor to see what he could see. Not a lot at first, but later – as he strolled into a larger building with more shops and more people - he did see quite a contingent of policemen and women patrolling and looking as if they were searching for someone or something. He dropped back into a nearby 7/11 as some of the *ging chat* strode past at pace. The vibes were there all right. Something was going on.

Norton went and sat outside in the wan sun and drank another can of iced lemon tea.

87/1.

Hobo Kingi had turned towards Islam several years previously and had become pretty adamant in his strong beliefs that Māori Muslim would be the strongest and most faithful components of this rebel corpus. They could all fire weapons at will and accurately. They showed no fear. They had been training in the Australian outback for what seemed like aeons, spoiling for a chance to overthrow the infidel and his wantonly wicked ways.

Hemara was by no means sure, however and said little that day. Besides, he had just a bit more on his mind right then.

Norton had sent him an encrypted email apparently – a message relayed from a brother who actually had an Internet connection – and was alive and seemed well. Norton had wanted contact details of a shared mate, Hemara's own cousin, Les, who had long since vanished into South East Asia somewhere.

Hemara smiled a bit wanly and thought to himself that Norton had always been a strange bastard. No, actually, a particularly strange bastard. He lived inside himself and seemed fuelled by some non-sequential time sequence, for he acted only according to his own weird subterranean drive. Which was as he had once confided to Hemara after too many Lion Red beers, was, "my Māori ontology". Whatever the hell that had meant.

Hemara went ahead and replied via the shared-mate-in-Ōpōtiki's computer, all the cogent details of Les Wereta that he could rustle together.

He also let Norton in on what Pelorus had shared with him about Monaghan.

Not that it made any difference now.

Besides which Norton had rationalized away that killing, into his own peculiar system of living.

Hemara remained fairly silent after this online exchange. He prayed to himself however. Unlike Hobo Kingi, Hemi Hemara was also a staunch Ratana church follower and he intoned a mantra taught him years previously, "Kei te tu te rākau, a, ko tēnā mōrehu tōna tāna rākau. Ko te papa ngākau te oneone, ko ngā whakaaro ngā puāwai, a hei te whakatutukitanga i aua whakaaro ka kitea ai ngā hua, he pai rānei, he kina rānei. "

[People are like trees. Even as the trees stand, each survivor is his or her own tree. Your heart is the Earth in which it grows, your thoughts are the flowers, and when your thoughts are put into practice, you will see the fruits of your tree, and know whether they are good or bad.]

88/3.
Grace was very angry, naturally. Captain Almodevar and his cronies had basically
been absolutely useless in uncovering the murderer of her daughter, even after
she had scrimped several thousand *peso* to free up their tongues. No such luck.
Walang swerte

It had all come down to the wife of one of the few remaining American – albeit
retired – servicemen still looning around Angeles City, who hadn't deserted his
Filipina wife or girlfriend and the kids he had left her with. Judith was also another
cousin anyway. It had been her who had dropped the very strong hint to Grace that
the killer of Euris had been some Americano up in Manila.

Which was the strongest possible reason for Grace to have joined with the others
in the burgeoning street marches against the rumoured return of those *putih*
bastards and their army of indiscriminate penises under their stacks of dollars. So
she had gone to Manila on the slow bus, over-stacked with all manner of chattels,
and joined in the fray down there. Her cousin Ivy met her as arranged, and off they
set in the furnace sun.

Besides which, from what she gathered from Ivy, such street protests had spread
like petrol-fuelled wildfire right across the globe.

Why not here too? Not, 'only in the Philippines' anymore.

The very significant thing that Grace soon learned, was that she was by no means
the only mother who had somehow had their child murdered or disappeared. She
soon met up with tales of rogue police squads and vigilante cops. But the stories
that really hit home to her were about the special trained-by-the-USA police units
who had been instructed in and around Subic, to ensnare NLA guerillas, MILF
bandits in Mindanao, and anyone else deemed a threat to the nation. Which would
be millions of people if the powers-that-be interpreted it any way that they wished
to. They had already imposed a curfew in several cities.

All of which merely served to make Grace angrier and full of desire for revenge on these manipulative bastards from abroad, as well, of course on the dirty local politicos.

It hadn't helped either that Euris' own father had been Daniel Demmett Junior, who had not only been a master sergeant in the U.S. Infantry stationed in Clark Airforce base on a security detail, and even though he had kept up some very intermittent connection, had also buggered off back to Missouri some years before.

It just made Grace yell louder at her own fellow countrymen security forces as she brushed past their barricades on EDSA. And to want to stab the next *putih* she saw – not that there were too many around after the entire Metro Manila area had been declared a danger zone by the new President of the Philippines, under pressure from certain overseas foreign governments, who wished to keep the zone as uncluttered as possible for their huge new casino construction there. Dirty tricks indeed.

As she bent down to pick up another sizeable piece of concrete to chuck at anyone looking in need of it, the helicopters just kept on whirring up above the mass procession and the onboard uniformed clones just stared at them all, down their long rifle scopes.

For the life of these young Americano troops, many of whom didn't seem to have begun shaving yet, this was all an irritant and they just wanted to go back up to the Clark-Mimosa restricted zone and to loll by the swimming pool at the Holiday Inn there. Where they were comfortably lodging at the expense of the USA - Philippine governmental coffers.

This confrontation thing wasn't why they had signed up to serve their Empire at all.

All this time, Ivy was acting as a sort of chaperone to Grace, to ensure the latter firebrand wasn't extinguished in any way. Besides, she had taken this day off her overwork, partly to give vent to her own inner tensions about men. American soldiers were a most convenient scapegoat right then and there, even if Ivy still was not convinced Euris was actually dead.

GET OUT!!
Americano

89/2.

Walter Wyshnowski was now back in Hong Kong, foaming at the mouth, in his tight air conditioned room in the American Consulate in Central. He was clutching in his rather greasy mitt, a typed statement of interest about one Ngahiwi Mac Norton, a New Zealand Māori who was a person of interest beyond the shores of that faraway nation and who was a prime suspect in the murder of James Clement Monaghan in – of all places – the Philippines. It seemed that – finally – the various cogs that were internationally disparate espionage and policing agencies, had begun to mesh together, for on the page were references to the New Zealand S.I.S service and the NSA and a photograph – bleary at best – of this Norton chap, as well as a truncated history.

Seemed that this late-middle-aged male, Norton, was once a bit of an author and had written quite impressively about B.Traven, of all people. And here Wyshnowski reflected that the latter was also a person of interest, as he scanned his computer files to double check up on his suspicions. He also gleaned that Norton had become a bit of a protestor after – of all things – serving in an Asian war some long time before. Seems then that he had dropped away completely from any surveillance from the authorities, primarily because he hadn't actually done anything of import for decades.

Wyshnowski sweated, despite the chill air blasting his toupee, and sat back a bit. 'So what?' was his prime thought, for this guy could be anywhere. And if, by any chance he was here in Hong Kong too, it wouldn't be quite so easy to redact him away, for of late especially even the usually placid and passive Hong Kong administration had become much more markedly antagonistic towards American suggestions, hints, requests and outright demands. They loved the U.S. navy bringing with them their ample dollars to Wan Chai to fuck Asian girls and to spend up large, but they nowadays kowtowed and bowed to bigger bosses from much nearer proximities.

Wyshnowski sat back even further and closed his eyes and thought a bit more about what to do next.

Three minutes later he was on his special encoded telephone to Comrade Da Zei, whom he felt owed him a favour or two. Especially after he – Wyshnowski – had been instrumental in the recent swap of Dr. Cross and those two most wanted counter-revolutionaries, resembling defrocked monks with hoods cowled over their heads, when they were brought back from the mainland USA, to the other Mainland north of Hong Kong.

But the good Comrade was in no mood to cooperate at all. He had too many more important things to look after; than some person who might be in Hong Kong and who seemed to have done zilch against the best interests of the Chinese state apparatus.

Indeed, '*T'iu lei gweilo,*' was about all he could muster in broken Cantonese, as he slammed down the handset on the white man.

Wyshnowski remained seated, somewhat stunned. What to do next? He was very wary of contacting anyone with any nous back in the States. Mainly because there did not seem to be any such staff serving there anymore. The current presidential regime, in fact, had become way more zany than any reality television show could ever conjure up. He could get completely contradictory directives, depending on the day.

He flicked through the pages of his thick notebook, which listed Chinese rent boys.

90/2.

On the other side of Hong Kong, Woo maintained his low profile, even from high up in the driver's seat of his trusty and rather rusty van, as supplied to him by Ho Tai Chung. He drove well within the speed limits, sometimes overly cautiously, so that he got horned from several irate speedsters, who wanted to flash off somewhere.

This particular morning, Woo was reasonably content and the sun was bearing down, if you could actually see it behind the dense grey wall that was Hong Kong's usual sky. He would have whistled if he could, but instead chose to hum a few incessantly repeated bars of an old Canto-Pop song, sung by the late Leslie Cheung. Woo had already ducked in to a nearby *dai pai dong* and wolfed back somewhat greedily on a plate or two of beef noodles, followed by a pineapple bun. *Ho mai.* Yummy.

So all was as good as it was going to get for a man of little means, such as he. Yet, because he seemed to have been born under a bad sign, trouble was waiting just up at the next intersection, out back of Hang Shui Kui. He braked the obedient van to a stop, as the traffic light shunted from amber to red and sat there as the engine dawdled and he drummed his nail bitten paws on the splintered yellowed dashboard.

He wasn't prepared for the mighty whack on the side panels of the van - and then as he startled his head around toward the impact - nor for the sight unfolding just in front of his wing mirror. Some kid was being pummelled to the ground by about six identikit thugs, all seemingly dressed in the same T-shirt from a 1950's American high school movie, and all wearing similar black trousers and black belts and shoes. One of the gang was hitting the kid – who looked to be no more than 16 years old – fair across the scalp with a baton-like piece of wood and another was kicking at him with these shiny clodhoppers.

No one was taking any notice of Woo, who took off as soon as he could when the lights blinked into green, although when he looked back via his rear view mirror, he was almost certain that he could see someone who looked remarkably like Ho Fat Kit. Seemingly as a passenger in the swift car that had just shot past, going the other way entirely.

Woo sank even lower than Chubby Checker could ever have done and his humming became a worried frown.

Up above the sun had also hurriedly become a scowl.

91/2.

Norton wandered quite aimlessly around the large shopping centre, attracting few stares from any of the increasing number of citizens. He wasn't really thinking much about anything, merely being satisfied to be on land again after all the time on Canlas' boat. He didn't speak a word of Cantonese and the English language of many of the shoppers, workers and itinerant school children was rudimentary, at best.

Eventually he slumped down on one of the several benches and sat there like the lost *gweilo* he was.

Norton was pretty sick of running, given that he had had to escape two countries' jurisdiction very recently. He had no clear-cut path when he fled Aotearoa New Zealand and was even further into miasma when he departed Philippines, what now seemed aeons ago. He put his shaggy and unshaven head into his hands and sank low into the bench, while next to him several old men dressed in somewhat ragged singlets, were chattering away, totally oblivious to him and were smoking resurrected cigarette butts.

Norton decided that he would have to somehow find where Les Wereta was nowadays - and he then hoped that the latter would be able to guide him to somewhere in Hong Kong that could provide some measure of sanctity and sanity. For he felt sure that he would soon wear out his welcome at Ruby's daughter's small apartment. He already felt Isaac Wong's opprobrium whenever he glanced in that direction.

How, though, to discover where Wereta might be? They hadn't been in touch for years now. For all Norton knew, his old drinking army mate might be dead, had absconded with another woman – again – or had even returned to Tauranga. Norton glanced around – these old bastards weren't going to let him in on any secrets, that was for sure.

He stood up and stretched his legs. Only then did he hear the sirens sounding, not so far away. He stretched his neck to see if he could sight anything over the first floor fence line, itself stretching around the benches, but there was nothing evidently amiss anywhere out there: just a millstream of traffic and buses spewing away fumes. None of the old men seemed to be giving a shit either. Yet the sirens continued and maybe – just maybe – Norton thought he heard what sounded like gunshots in the near distance.

The nearest singlet to him looked up at him as Norton passed back into the entrails of the shopping centre. He waved his half-empty can of beer as if in an abstruse signal about something.

Trouble was, Norton didn't see a thing, as he wove his way around the queue loitering and lingering hungrily outside a Yoshinoya restaurant. Must have been a special set meal on sale there that day.

The sirens seemed to have wound away by now and Norton took the escalator back to the ground floor, to roughly where he had entered the building. A few gulls and a few Tai Chi enthusiasts were speckling the square he had rambled through earlier that day and there were a couple of carton collectors at the far end, arguing about something.

Nothing spectacular to report on at all. Norton felt very fatigued at that moment. He just wanted to crash and sublimate all his worries, doubts and insecurities into sleep. He pressed in the building code, languished outside the lift as it took five minutes to descend and let him inside, and then jerked on back up to the apartment, to slumber away the rest of the day.

Which was where Ruby and Po Lam found him a few hours later: fast asleep and in need of a close shave.

That evening Norton woke to the sound of food being prepared, so he stumbled out into the naked light of the dining room to see what was going on. Ruby was dishing up a large sprawl of noodles dressed in chili and Poh Lam was twirling around - in a bowl filled with some sort of sauce - a pile of chicken wings, with a pair of chopsticks. The rice was already ready, just waiting to be eaten.

No one said much as they dined steadily through the meal and guzzled on diet Coke and lemon tea in cartons. Poh Lam did say – in English – that Isaac was working overtime and Ruby mumbled something about having sighted her older child – her son Jeremy Ka Lun – briefly before he went back onto his basketed bicycle, as a delivery man/boy for a fast food restaurant.

Just another day in Tin Yan.

It couldn't last.

92/2.
Part of Norton's manifold problem was that he had still never actually grieved for Makere; despite their later fallings-out. Never broken down and bawled no-holds-barred, except on that first day. Something about having had insufficient time to latch onto all the shit that had gone down in Aotearoa New Zealand and the concomitant continued fleeing this way and that way ever since. But here in Tin Yan, Tin Shui Wai, Norton was finding some sanctity and – probably naively – wasn't going about looking over his shoulder, quite so literally.

He found himself sobbing the next day when sitting out in the stronger sun, just beyond the nullah and watching the barber trim a few clients' hair for a few dollars each. Something just clicked a gear inside him and he began to swell up with emotion and then to – quite quietly – cry gut-wrenchingly. No one seemed to notice him do this and it didn't last a long time, so by the time Ruby came downstairs after hanging out the laundry, she didn't really pick up on Norton's red eyes, partly because he was wearing the usual shades.

Maybe his grief had been triggered by the amateur, yet proficient musicians who were performing under the trees. A woman was warbling a wailing song and the *erhu* player was quite expert. The sounds were alien to his ears and worked on him deeply.

Another part of Norton's manifold problem was that – true to his form – he hadn't ever told Ruby much about anything – and especially not about Makere and Monaghan and the rest of the gang. More, he had never mentioned that he was the father of two rather estranged daughters either. Here and then was as good a time as any, so he rambled on for a bit disassociatively, about his dead ex-wife and a bit about his dead ex-infantry buddy, whom he had killed back in Pampanga. Then he spoke lovingly of his kids.

Norton had found his voice again.

Ruby listened fairly intently, at least until she sensed that someone else was around them and seemingly, also listening in. She quickly looked around and noticed only a couple of old men, dressed in holed singlets and Bermuda shorts, that had elongated themselves after too many days spent out on the clothesline and the rain and wind torment that meant. It wasn't them then.

Norton was still in his spiel – sort of – for he too now looked up to see his lady friend looking away from him, out into the near distance. He snatched off his dark shades and scanned also. Didn't seem to be anyone much over there. He shrugged at Ruby who sort of returned the compliment and smiled. If there had been anyone there, they must have been Lightning Jacks and sped off already.

"C'mon," said Ruby kindly, "let's go and eat."

Yet, as they strolled toward the shopping centre and the Ngan Long diner, both felt the vibes distinctly: someone or something was spying on them, from somewhere close by.

The diner wasn't overly crowded at that stage of the morning, so they ambled in and sat down across from one another and ordered – or rather Ruby did as she was the only one proficient in oral Cantonese, while all the many items on the menu were written only in Chinese script.

They scoffed down their assorted meals and sank the *tong ling cha*, without too much chatter at all and then sat back to digest their meals and the morning thus far.

"So, what's next?" enquired Norton, who continued with his passivity.

"Well, I think we will have to stay here for a bit. You cannot go back to Philippines and from what you've just told me, you cannot go back to New Zealand either," was her reply. "Trouble is, someone is bound to come looking for you here too – especially after what happened out at sea…"

Norton nodded. He had no real idea what to do next, let alone where to go. He hadn't taken much ownership of himself of late; had lapsed well into *mauvaise foi*, if that was the correct term he had remembered from his near-year at university, what seemed like two thousand years ago.

"Anyway," continued Ruby, "I want to stay here for a bit. My kids need a bit of support from me. Po Lam has no job and is pregnant and Jeremy Ka Lun is in trouble again with the law, for driving a car without a licence. And his kid is only a few months old too."

Norton sort of felt that the corner he was painted into was steadily becoming a patch barely big enough to stand in on one leg.

Then the tumult started – real loud. Some woman began screaming at full volume and another joined in. They started at one another and one was yanking hard on the others' dyed hair. Plates rattled from the bench they had shared onto the floor, and their drinks were soon swimming independently across the floor. Waiters were running here and there, with amazement scrawled over their faces and other guests – not all by any means – were staring open-eyed and open-mouthed. By now the bigger woman had the other on the floor and was literally pummeling her with a bag she had grabbed from her side of the bench. The waiters were attempting to separate them, but weren't having a lot of luck.

Outside the diner doors, quite a crowd had gathered to witness the chaos inside.

When the two young policemen finally arrived, they had to grab the more aggressive party, to stop her whacking the other now-bleeding-one again and again. The audience seemed to have quadrupled by now and few dinners were being served, as the cooks in the nearby kitchen, having free front row seats, were quite enjoying this distraction.

The women were still screaming at each other even then.

 When the police boys grappled the two termagants out into the thoroughfare, telling the assembly to go away, the waiters commenced cleaning up. Ruby and Norton had by this time completely forgotten what they were talking about earlier and it was only when they walked back out into the gathering sunlight that they sort of blinked back into sequence after this break in their stories.

Indeed, it was Ivy's sudden telephone call from Manila that soon rerouted them back to an approach to their potential futures, for Ivy had quite simply said that pictures of Norton as a wanted man were all over the newspapers and the television news. Captain De Leon had also appeared smilingly on GMA News and pointed out that the man, a foreign national, was a wanted suspect in the recent murder of another man in Santo Tomas market some weeks previously.

It also appeared that someone had placed a quite significant reward on this wanted villain.

When Ruby relayed all this to her newfound bedmate, he flinched a bit. He was, by now, on a very steadily shrinking floor space indeed.

They strolled back to the apartment, to find Po Lam unhappy that there weren't sufficient funds available to feed them all for much longer. Reassuringly, however, Norton flicked her a few American dollars; part of the trove he had, prior to crewing with Canlas and which he had easily earlier exchanged in SM Mall, San Fernando.

Po Lam was soon smiling and off to the market with her mother, leaving Norton to worry over the latest news headlines yelling at him across the wide frontage of the *South China Morning Post* he had just bought at the 7/11, and from the Internet news sites from across the globe. Arabs were killing Arabs - Syrians were skewering Syrians; USA trained marksmen in several locales were wiping out their fellow countrymen via a fusillade of fire with a glissade of guns bought easily online from Wal Mart. And Russia had invaded Ukraine – yet again.

The World had - somehow - gotten even nuttier than yesterday.

Way crazier than any of those clever dick scriptwriters in Hollywood and Bollywood could ever conjure up, eh.

93/2.
Po Lam came back the next day in the mid-morning, sweating and upset.

She claimed that someone had been fairly obviously following her from Chung Fu shopping centre, after she had visited the market to buy fresh vegetables and fish. She described them – for there had apparently been more than one of them – as Mainland Chinese, because they wore identical black formal trousers, black shoes and T-shirts in a fashion style that had been deleted from more up-market locales thirty years ago.

Inevitably, both were smoking and one had attempted some vestige of anonymity by wearing dark sunglasses.

Po Lam was adamant that they had settled on her tail, because every time she looked around they had been the same distance behind her and pretty much in full view the whole time.

"So how did you get away from them?" asked her mother.

"I didn't really," replied a calmer-by-now Po Lam, "I just pressed the access code for this building, got to the lift and came up. They were hanging around outside the front doors when I last saw them. Scary!"

Norton, of course, had no idea what was being said in this dialogue, but Ruby soon told him about the incident. Po Lam believed that they had tailed her because they knew Norton was in the building somewhere, after he had probably been seen with Po Lam and Ruby over the last few days.

Norton, however, wasn't convinced. Why would Mainland Chinese – if indeed they were – possibly be interested in him anyway? He discounted the fact that he had helped destroy one of their sea craft not so long ago, on the grounds that no one could possibly have known that he had been on board. Instead he asked Po Lam – in English – whether her husband, Isaac Wong had any debts?

The young woman nodded affirmatively and then fell quite silent for most of the rest of the day.

Ruby, however, wasn't so sure - and kept her doubts to herself completely. She had had experience of enforcers from beyond Hong Kong, when she had to deal with them searching for her then useless husband, Godfrey Woo. These latest guys did not sound like them. So, she just silently shook her head and went about making some lunch for them all.

Isaac Wong, when he came back much later, to find these visitors and his wife sitting around the dining table, immediately sensed the unease. When they had some space further into the evening, he enquired of Po Lam what was wrong and she too told him all about her earlier experience and asked if he had failed to pay back the racing bets, as he said he had done, to her a couple of days previously.

Isaac nodded, for he had paid up in full and felt quite confident these men weren't looking for him. After all, they would have known exactly where he lived anyway.

Po Lam didn't mention any of this to her mother.

Instead, she quietly lit the incense sticks next to the smiling Buddha figurines and bowed three times; praying for harmony. Just as she had been taught by Woo's own mother, all those years ago. She stroked the pomelo as a sort of afterthought, remembering its propensity for abundance and good fortune.

94/2.

When checking on her emails that evening, while Norton lay snoring and snorting intermittently on the sofa, Ruby learned that Eric Canlas had scored a job supplying fresh fish to the base at Diego Garcia in the Indian Ocean. Ruby didn't know very much about that place – only what Rustico Tuazon had said some time previously - but she did wonder how Canlas would have managed the very high security clearance to enable his employment down and around that very secure and secretive American base. Hadn't he been up their way only a week ago, or something like that? She smiled to herself and again shook her head silently.

Later still, in the quiet of the apartment - as Ruby had herself gone to sleep and the young couple had gone over to Kingswood Ginza to see a new movie - Norton was a little alarmed. For when again google-searching for his own name on the Internet, he found he was now definitely a wanted suspect in Pampanga province of the Philippines. While – as he already did know – the New Zealand authorities had placed an all-points bulletin on him and that Interpol was most definitely on alert about him.

At the same time he also saw evidence of fresh so-called terrorist activity in his homeland and even wider splashes of the retributive reprisals that the New Zealand special armed forces had mounted in the central North Island region. Still, his cousin Hemara had come online a few nights earlier and stated that he was, "fine"…

Just before he went to join Ruby, now snoozing on the thin mattress spread-eagled over the hard tiled floor of the apartment, Norton was reading some news item. About American military might being shifted in stages from Okinawa to Guam and that the soon-to-be man in charge there was vaguely familiar to him, for he was sure that he had seen him somewhere recently. He just couldn't quite rejig his memory sufficiently to remember whom it was glaring at him from the photograph.

One thing was paramount right then though. Norton knew that he had to escape Hong Kong very soon. It was only a matter of time before he was captured and probably sent elsewhere. He gave no credence to any Chinese agencies being on his tail – but then again he didn't realize that Mainland security wouldn't be chasing Isaac Wong for mere gambling debts either.

Where to next? Norton did have a pretty good idea, for he had learned via a series of emails to mates back home, that Les Wereta was now in Luang Prabang with a newish Laotian wife.

The irony wasn't lost on him at all. Laos was where he and Monaghan had spent quite a lot of time many years before.

He would have to talk to Ruby about all this very soon.

But, before he could bring up any such ideas the next day, and indeed before she could tell him what was on her own mind, the shit started to hit the fan in rather a big way - the very next morning. Indeed, it had already started flying around in downtown Hong Kong some hours before they awoke.

Seems that the latest big protest seeking universal suffrage and freedom of speech in the Special Administrative Region had turned very violent. Local television services were replete with close-ups of bleeding skulls and shouting people. Helicopters were on the rampage and in one shot, the gathered residents in the apartment were unified in saying that it looked like a troop of PLA soldiers were right there in the mix also.

Norton was tempted to go into town to see a bit more, but Ruby was having none of that. Too dangerous *per se*, let alone him being a wanted man and all. "No," she responded, while Isaac Wong and Po Lam said nothing of note at all.

"Well, let's at least go for a walk out of here," shot back a-becoming-more-disgruntled and steadily-more-rattled Norton. "Let's get a bit of fresh air."

Po Lam was quite happy to hear this and spoke encouragingly to her mother to go. Isaac Wong also had a bit of radiance plastered to his normally rather dour visage.

"O.K." said Ruby, relenting, "We'll go down by the nullah, where it's not too crowded."

As they went down all the floors in the somewhat rickety elevator, Norton flashed that he had seen that American administrator, in the Philippines somewhere recently; maybe in the pages of a *Philippine Star*, left cursorily at Ivy's apartment. He had no way of knowing that Wayne Wyshnowski was actually still in Hong Kong, looking for him, among others.

Nor would he ever, ever have imagined that one of Wyshnowski's veteran henchmen, Dr. Cross, was soon to be delivered back to Asia by one of the myriad secret agencies, ostensibly to assist with the mass marine transit to Guam.

And Ruby had never told him the name of her former American lover either.

Or that she too had close family in Guam.

Strolling in the warm sun alongside the relatively uncrowded nullah, Norton began to unwind just a bit. He at one stage grabbed Ruby's hand and was about to tell her about his immediate plans, but stopped when he saw the pair of policemen strolling their way. He did however feel the tension in Ruby's own palm, when she also sighted the junior cops.

It seemed that the police were in no way interested in Norton or Ruby, however, for they also lankily walked past, one of them talking on his small receiver.

So – after another fifty or so paces when he was ready to broach with Ruby yet again the subject of their immediate future – Norton stopped and gestured toward an empty bench, under a couple of sprawling and shady trees.

As they were about to sit down and relax even more, Norton heard the gunshots not so far away. He knew they were gunshots because he knew guns.

Ruby appeared quizzical, but Norton was beyond that stage. Something was seriously amiss if there were gunshots out here in the remote New Territories, which he had soon clicked onto. This was, after all, a Saturday mid-morning, when traditionally most people were working or at the market somewhere. If not doing that, at a Café de Coral or a Fairwood food chain restaurant, chewing on their breakfast. No rowdy demonstrations ever happened out here, they would have bet on it.

No, these shots were loud, clear and close.

The few people on the walkway were running now, away from the gunfire, which had only just abated. The two young policemen reappeared too, looking harassed and haggard and one had lost his cap.

Then Ruby and Norton saw what the fuss was all about – as they looked back.

Their discussion was going to have to wait a bit longer.

95/2.
Woo also heard the commotion coming his way.

He had slept-in these last few days, if sleeping-in wrapped in a soiled blanket on a pile of cardboard boxes, stashed well under the nullah tree canopy, is the correct term.

The van he had been driving was in a garage for repairs - something Woo could once have done himself and could have again, had he a workshop anymore. So his boss had told him to take some time off. Woo was luxuriating in two solid meals a day and had even had access to a shower or two of late. He was feeling quite good about things for once and had not sensed any recent Ho Fat vibrations either.

Hell, he had even seen his ex-wife strolling hand-in-hand across Tin Yan Estate with a tall brown-skinned and tattooed guy. Woo had followed them for a bit too. Hell again, his ex-wife looked pretty good after all these years of his not seeing her. But he didn't want them to spy him, so he had slunk back to his rabbit hole and snoozed for most of that day.

Still, all this approaching noise must mean something significant was erupting in the normally quiet district. Woo stood up, spat out some dry snot from his gangly lips and scratched his arse for a bit. He slipped his feet into his sandals and started across to where the din was headed. Looked like quite a few others were of an equal like. Quite a crowd was building up, when the two young policemen hastened their way and told them all to disperse. When somebody asked, "Why," they were told in no uncertain terms to "*Lei hoi igar...*You go now". Ordered to, in fact.

But the command was just a bit too late to prevent the spectators seeing the brawl that by now had mushroomed into their immediate environs. Two crowds of young and not so young triad members were whacking the shit out of one another and chasing each other further and further toward the Chung Fu shopping centre, obviously not caring about who might be there: they all being that locked into their battle.

One of them had a pistol and was firing somewhat indiscriminately and erratically, although Woo didn't initially see anyone who seemed to have been hit by the bullets. He did soon see, however, several bloodied gangsters, by now almost immediately in front of him, and a couple of prone bodies further back. Then the sirens started to reverberate around the entire zone. The police were on their way, in force.

Yet the two bands of brawlers didn't cease – if anything they went even more full-on in their rampage against each other.

Then, right then and there, Norton and Ruby saw someone crash onto the harsh cement environs, that made up the floor plan of the entire estate. He seemed to be a middle-aged member of one faction, of what must have been an internecine triad war – or else a very well-staged action movie set performance. Blood was flowing profusely from his head wound and such was the significance of his demise, that several younger members of his tributary immediately ran over, picked him up and bustled him away as fast as they could, thus leaving only a couple of brawlers still engaging in the free-for-all show.

It was all a bit late, however, for their leader, Ho Fat Kit, was mortally wounded by the shooting and was dead on arrival at the clinic they rushed him to, just around the corner. Someone had a gun, all right.

Police were by now swarming everywhere and their presence quelled the screams of the audience somewhat.

The melee was over as quickly as it had begun. Several triad members were immediately arraigned – primarily the walking and downed wounded factions - while other policemen and women were hurriedly swishing away the broken bands of spectators from what was now a major crime scene. Ruby and Norton merely stared at one another.

Woo, meanwhile, had slunk into a corner out of eyesight and earshot of almost everyone still on the scene. He had noticed his ex-wife on the other side of the square, but felt that she could not possibly have seen him in the chaos of that afternoon's episode. He also felt sure that he had again sighted his own son, whom he had deserted all those years ago, ride his bicycle past the site, intent on delivering the pizzas he was employed by Pizza Box to do. Apparently totally oblivious to what had just transpired. Jeremy Ka Lun didn't seem to have any idea about the pitched triad skirmish; indeed he was more intent on weaving his wobbly way across the shopping centre carpark, on his way to wherever. And he was listening to and much more focused on the music streaming into his earphones. He had only that day transferred back to the Tin Shui Wai store, after a stint at management training near Sha Tin. Hadn't been for him.

When Woo looked up again across the stage, his ex-wife and her presumably new lover, were long gone.

Ruby and Norton were lucky to find a seat in the Ngan Long diner, given the weekend sprawl, but find one they did. They didn't say much about what they had both just seen, basically because they were still processing it all in their respective brains. To Norton it was eerily reminiscent of his front line infantry days; for Ruby it was more like the cowboy films she used to go and see with her sister and brother back in the dusty, outdoor, standing-room-only movie theatre in Pampanga.

It wasn't until much later, when night had started to take advantage of the day and when Po Lam switched on the news and Ruby translated it for Norton, they understood. They learned that the rationale for the fighting may well have been over which triad was going to capture suspects behind the so-called steady Internet campaign to supposedly overthrow the Chinese government. It seemed that the Mainland powers-that-be had called for the immediate rounding up of anti-state revolutionaries. In other words, the exponentially expanding band of Internet savvy persons who were spreading the word about what their government was covering up and restricting, as well as the word about an international band of similar-minded people who were also disseminating the information about global American surveillance activities.

The Chinese and the puppet Hong Kong administration were very paranoid about too much exposure and encouragement to rebel and to reveal the truth behind their and other governments' use of technology to keep their citizens in place. Freedom fighters everywhere – it seemed – were now serious enemies of several states. Thus, the lucrative contracts the triads were now lethally squabbling over.

What started out as an incentive to capture suspects quietly and clandestinely had instead ruptured into a mighty newsworthy publicity campaign for the very people who were supposed to have been disposed of. Lok Mai Chun – had he still been alive – would have been smiling widely, while Rustico Tuazon – had he ever heard down on Basilan Island, where he remained safe in primitive captivity – would have been his equally mirthful doppelganger. Lok Yi Yi would know, in a dead kind of fashion, that his files were now far more widely open to view, for far more than the knowing few.

As the riots also spread through Canberra, Vancouver and Cardiff.

Part Six: Marianas

96/6.
Walter Wyshnowski, meanwhile, now stationed resolutely in a Faraday cage in
Agana, Guam, also smiled as he realized – when he had news of that afternoon's
activities in Hong Kong relayed to him very soon after – that his own espionage
agency was also heavily meshed into the saga. For he had been the one who had
leaked Norton's name to the Chinese in the first place, as a major Internet
revolutionary and had further intimated that he – Norton – was very possibly
somewhere in Hong Kong. No mention of his being a murderer.

All the more need to nab him too, as American software sales had plummeted to
an all time low. No one trusted their spy-ridden merchandise anymore. So, it would
be great to pinpoint such a new scapegoat.

Indeed, Norton was by now a wanted man in several places, almost everywhere in
fact, for crimes he hadn't actually committed or even thought about. In his rather
unperturbed – at least on the outside – way, he didn't seem to show the slightest
awareness of just how perilous his position was becoming, although he was no
fool.

It was by now all a matter of time.

Part Seven: Okinawa

97/7.

Dr. Cross, now in Naha in Okinawa, learned a little later about the Chung Fu Affair, as the *South China Morning Post* dubbed it, and shrugged his shoulders, as he sunk back on another Orion beer at the strip joint, just outside of the airbase. Being a chameleon at the best of times, he slashed out his tongue to snatch back a few drops of the brew that had cascaded onto his chin and then turned to ogle the pretty little, pretty slim Japanese bar girls behind the counter, his penis caught somewhere between a rock and a hard place.

Part Eight: Laos

98/8.

Les Wereta meanwhile, had been in touch from Luang Prabang – all via a stubborn Internet bypass that was not easily traceable. He had told Norton that he was welcome to somehow get into Laos and he – Wereta, being a computer savvy and very adaptable man with manifold connections worldwide – would find him a job.

Wereta did warn Norton however, that the Chinese were building a behemoth railway system throughout Laos and that he – Norton – had better be, "bloody careful," in his movements there. Because of this and, "because of course," said Wereta, "of the bloody undisposed-of-American-ordnance," which was still festering the Laotian countryside in massive droves and constantly blowing all and sundry innocent indigenous people to erratic smithereens.

"Bloody Americans," echoed Norton, when he heard this further piece of information, "still killing, even if they're not there."

99/2.

Ruby had crashed on her daughter's thin floor mattress. She too was so very tired of all this shit. Had had more than enough of being the glue holding all the bits and pieces of everyone's life tale together.

Perhaps a serene dream or two was in order.

<u>Ruby's panaginip</u>

Euris was smiling at her Ate.

Beckoning Ruby to come and join her.

The waves looked serene and the sand seemed so joyous as they touched base on the beach, in a form of tropical lovemaking.

Ruby placed her foot into the water. Oh! So warm, so she started to paddle deeper and deeper.

She melted into the tranquility.

Ruby put her head under and saw Euris, still smiling, as she reached out to hold her hands.

All would be well.

100/5.

Comrade Da Zie couldn't have given a shit what Wyshnowski wanted, or whom.
For him, Americans were all vapid prattling buffoons who had absolutely no
comprehension about other cultures, particularly Chinese. Still, this supposed
wanted man, whom Wyshnowski had pin-pointed as an Internet-savvy terrorist
manqué would be better eliminated, if only for the bad example he would set for
Mainland Chinese youth. Who were already infiltrating the great firewalls of China
and whom were now themselves rattling on about such stupid dictums as freedom,
democracy, universal suffrage and their ilk.

Da Zie snorted and spat voluminously onto the flower garden on the ledge of his
34th floor security building in Shanghai. This New Zealand citizen, Norton, would
have to be apprehended and brought in soon, if only to be invited over a cup of tea,
to impart some Western state security secrets that he supposedly knew all about.

Da Zie picked up the landline telephone, for he hated these trendy modern cell
phones and all their concomitant paraphernalia. He wanted to see if any of his men
in Hong Kong had any information about this man – was he in fact even there?

And while he was waiting for someone to actually answer the phone, he spat again
at the annoying thought that two triads had been reported as fighting over the
money and kudos they would get by dragging in these Internet vagabonds who
were besmirching the good name of Peoples Republic of China: all very bad
publicity.

"*Tā mā de,*" he yelled loudly, after ringing another unanswered number. It was time
to go down to the nearest *cha chaang tang* for a special brew. It also helped to
have a nice young mistress, who worked there ostensibly as a tea lady, but more
obviously as his own pride and sexual joy.

Just as he was about to catch the lift down to the podium floor, he caught a
glimpse of his dyed jet-black hair and the party pin stabbed through his lapel in the
mandatory mirror. He smiled and farted and smiled at the fart.

101/3.

Captain de Leon felt that he had done his very near best to find out the killer of the *putih* in Pampanga, but the leads had dwindled into nothingness. Who was he to discern exactly why two foreigners had a fight in a wet market in the middle of Santo Tomas? He filled out the appropriate forms and flicked his cigar ash onto the floor. De Leon avoided its fetid vapour and strode off across the road to the cockpit to see who was there. A small bet or two would inevitably make him feel better anyway. "When in doubt, go to the cock-fighting. Works a charm", was his mantra. He adjusted his shades a millimeter or two and brushed his sweaty hands through his thinning hair. He patted down the revolver further into his groin and went inside.

One of Grace's cousins was adjusting the blades on the spindly legs of his killer rooster, nicknamed Mr. Clavio.

More blood would soon be spilled.

Especially since tomorrow de Leon would have to travel to Manila to help smash the burgeoning infractions down there; something he had been dreading doing. Seemed the movement was just getting too hard to handle.

"When can a man have a goddam rest in this bloody country?" he was heard muttering not too silently, as he watched the Mr Clavio eviscerate the bird he had just bet thousands of *peso* on.

Hemara looked at the large assorted group sitting around him way out back of Ruatahuna. There were certainly many young people in this mix. By no means all Māori anymore either. For example, thousands of Pasifika had also joined this legion in similar remote spots throughout the skinny country.

There were also several examples of up-to-date weaponry – some stolen from an early hour break in of the armoury near the capital city last month. There was a palpable air of expectation, especially since this was a *hui*, a meeting called to discuss the next steps in the rebellion against the entrenched and oppressive regime in the Dominion. There was complete silence as an older, staunchly bearded Māori male stood and read a *whiti* or poem – firstly in his own tongue and then in English, mainly for the newcomers – most from within Aotearoa, some now also from offshore locales.

Hemara noticed that at every pause there were loud yells and applause, until the momentum built well beyond individuals decrying what they felt were the injustices of New Zealand's administration, historical and contemporary. Because toward the end of the passionate reading, it was though this group had become bonded into something harder, resilient, unbreakable – and maybe even invincible. He spoke to Jim Pelorus, who was a few steps away, somewhat wide-eyed and beaming.

"Well, what's next?" asked Hemara.

Pelorus just looked at him briefly and spurted out, "More of the same *e hoa*. More of the same." By which he meant a continuation of their guerilla warfare; tight quick snapping raids here and there across the land, until something busted for good, far beyond repair.

Hemi Hemara said no more. He was prepared to wait, despite some misgivings about how much longer they could successfully continue their fight in the face of the superior firepower and resources of what had become their mutual enemy. Namely the cohort that was being forced to quench and attempt to quell other worldwide uprisings against their respective regimes – in this case Anglo-American in genesis and enforcement. He prayed within himself as the poem ended in acclamation. Nothing was clear.

The future was indeed uncertain, yet the end was drawing near.

During the hui Hobo Kingi had sought out Sheila Raumoko, when he found her smoking over by the trees. He wanted to learn something about the pretty Filipina he had seen again today.

"Who is that *wahine Piripaina*?" he enquired.

"Why?"

"Oh, I am just interested how come she is here," lied Hobo.

"She came to join us, of course," said Sheila, rather irritated by the questioning.

"I mean, how did she get here?"

"You will have to ask her *e hoa*." Sheila Ruamoko was getting up to stroll over to *kōrero* with Te Matekairoa, "You ask her eh."

Hobo Kingi tried one more question, fired at the back of the departing Sheila Raumoko. "Well, what's her name, then?"

Sheila stopped, turned and stared back at her fellow foot soldier. "Man, you are persistent. Look, all I know is that she keeps to herself and does not want anyone to learn that she is here," she turned away again.

"And before you nag me again with another why, I'll tell you. She knows if people back in Philippines find out she escaped to Aotearoa, well...then her family back there will suffer big time." Sheila threw this information over her shoulder at Hobo, in the form of snappy bits of information as she walked away from him, back into the crowd.

Kingi said no more.

103/2.

Norton was back to stabbing. Quite frenetically too.

Only this time he had no weapon to speak of, merely his fingers and fists as he –
voice raised – was trying to make the point to Ruby that they had better get out of
there soon. He was saying, "I don't like the vibes, man", or some such, which was
what she gleaned from his rising rage. Too many people knew he was there and
he was feeling trapped.

"It's time to move on," he stressed, which, for Norton, at least, was always his way.
He never succumbed to lineal time, but rather felt within his very bones that
everything was connected space wise, time wise, distance wise: all in one holistic
pattern. Which – if he had ever been pressed to articulate more firmly – he would
call, unflinchingly, Māori time. In other words, he was telling himself somehow, that
now was a good occasion to go somewhere else, because now was always
present.

"So, where do you think we can go to?" asked Ruby, quietly, having already made
up her mind to stay in Tin Shui Wai for a little longer, even if this was to see her
kids for a bit more. Especially as her itinerant son was back in the vicinity again,
riding around and around the identical-towers fortress.

Norton had Luang Prabang fully on his brain, because that morning Wereta had
sent him an encrypted email pointing out that because the Chinese were building a
massive railway curving crosswise through Laos, there would be plenty of positions
for explosives experts – which Norton had actually been in a past life. He tried to
cajole Ruby into coming along with him, but it was the farthest thing from her own
already long-ago-made-up-mind. In her sights also was Guam, because her cousin
Nicole Cruz, had suggested she come on over there and work for the family
business, selling all manner of pasta products and eggs. As sourced from the small
farm Nicole's parents had put together and nurtured some years before, when they
had escaped Manila for better fields. Only Ruby didn't tell Norton any of this.

Impasse. Stalemate.

Isaac Wong had long since headed off to his job driving delivery vans in Kwun Tong and Po Lam was left on her lonesome having to try and decipher what this semi-argument was all about. Po Lam busied herself playing with the cold-water washing machine and attempted to stifle her own eardrums from the politely raised voices emanating next door in her own living room, although she did overhear her own mother stressing the plain fact that Laos was full of bombs anyway....

Yes – you guessed it. "American bombs," she was stating matter-of-factly. "I'm sick and tired of Americans."

104/2.

Johnny Tramadol spat deeply onto the scant grey pavement outside the 7/11. It was raining, so the pavement had other things to worry about than this thin spittle from the pursed lips of an albino American, alone and way out of his comfort zone in Tin Shui Wai, Hong Kong.

Tramadol inhaled fully on the last rites of his Marlborough stub and threw it to accompany his sputum. He clasped the pistol more firmly into his waistband and – shuddering just a little with a sudden chill wind drift – moved under the shop verandah to where he had been told to wait for the hit.

Johnny Tramadol was one of Wyshnowski's very best assassins – one of the few remaining of the old clique actually. He had been yet another compatriot of Monaghan and Norton at one stage and he thought it a little ironic that he had been ordered here to kill Norton, who – it seemed certain now – had in turn wasted Monaghan. Tramadol didn't even question quite why Norton needed to be expunged: it was beyond his brief and anyway he had learned many years previously to never doubt an order, especially if the concomitant remuneration was so damned excellent. He never once paused to reflect that his purported clever bosses all-too-often sent out their own agents very inappropriately – to places they had never ever visited before. Compartmentalisation was king.

Tramadol eyed the many high-rise apartment buildings, towering like beached masts all over the immediate zone. Somewhere in one of them Norton was supposed to be living nowadays. Wyshnowski had it on good authority that apparently, Norton came to this 7/11 every day to buy the latest *South China Morning Post*. Tramadol just had to be patient, chose the exact moment, shoot with the silenced gun, and slink merging into the nearest mass of passersby, before quietly going back to the hotel and wait to be escorted to the airport.

He spat again and the rain responded somewhat by increasing its own drive downwards. Tramadol had to be careful that he wasn't hit by these soaking projectiles - which had by now surpassed mere drizzle. He stood silent, as the limp sun vanished completely, far too early in the day and a choir of elongated umbrellas took over the immediate horizon. No one looked much at him, if at all, for Tin Shui Wai these days had become somewhat of a melting pot of all and sundry ethnicities, including, of course, Wo Sha Ni triad members. They had been told by their immediate boss Ho Fat – not long before he had been slaughtered himself – to also keep an eye out for the ex-American ally Norton, because he was purportedly an IT maven, so he might know a lot about espionage networks. He was some renegade guy who may therefore be of use to P.R. China itself. Alive rather than dead.

Especially as it seemed he – Norton - may also have had recent dealings in the Philippines with some of these annoying and very dangerous anonymous hackers and young Internet whizzes, who were infiltrating the entire electronic realm and feeding back absurd ideas about freedoms and imposed restrictions and espionages, to an equally captive peer audience.

Then there was also the very distinct possibility that this guy Norton may have an ability to sink into the Deep Web, from whence – somewhat ironically - Tramadol himself had been summoned. A nexus, more ironically, which had initially been instigated by paranoid American espionage interests anyway. Sets of Babushka dolls and Chinese boxes prevailed.

Norton, of course, knew nothing of such concerns and had been largely passive about Rustico Tuazon's rants about American and Chinese (and their respective allies) infiltrations into cyberspace and the concomitant need to fight back, via these selfsame mechanisms. Norton was Māori and intrinsically felt that the entire Internet medium was a form of imperialistic bullshit, regardless of any potential positive uses.

For him cyberspace was a small part of a much wider battle against the autocratic forces of (neo) colonialism and suppression of Indigenous people per se. Indeed, the entire English language was for him – and indeed several others he knew – a form of deliberate suppression of Māori realities about how time and space were all conjoint. That the past was always here in the permanent now and how everything in the physical realm was interconnected and animate. For him, civilization and lineal time were sham or 'humbug', as his great uncle Hopiki Piripi was wont to say and spray, when he vehemently spat out that word.

"Remember, son, their progress is our regress," was yet another of Piripi's rants to the very young Norton, who had already at his age, queried the complete lack of teaching of his own indigenous language, namely *te reo* Māori, in his South Auckland school. Where the white faces were predominately those of the teaching staff only.

Which is why also Norton very rarely read anything in sequential English language formats, like the so-called novel, which to him increasingly became a Pākehā or European/Western stamp of their linguistic and thus, cultural dominion. Rather, he picked and chose - and rambled round and through any manuscripts and comics in any language and rarely went near libraries or bookshops either.

Which is also why right now he was going to return to Laos, as if he had never actually left – even if approximately 40 years had passed in the interim. No one much bothered with Pākehā culture there, he reckoned. And there also the English language was a mere flibbertigibbet.

However, somewhere within the synapses of his brain, the thought had arrived. He might just try to write a book himself one day.

105/2.

Woo was back driving around the North-Western New Territories, delivering and picking up as discreetly as possible his many and varied – well actually not so varied – packages. In such crazy times as the current, more and more were smoking, some chain-like, and Woo's immediate bosses had the handle on the bootleg *El Cheapo* cigarette trade in that particular zone. Over this last revolutionary week, business was quite literally booming and fuming for them all. Cartons and barrels of rancid smelling and sometimes filter-less reefers were piled in the back of Woo's van, as he stopped here and there to drop off some and to load up other packages in return for them - with bundles of crisp new Standard Chartered banknotes among them.

He came around the corner as dusk was being delivered that Tuesday, to see pretty much the usual sights at that time of day: a bustle of men and women, as burnt out as all hell breaking loose, trudging back home after a far too long day, at wherever they had to work.

Plus the general ragged melee of bedraggled-by-overloaded-schoolbag school kids, who had been kicked off the school premises by the janitorial staff. These students all being reluctant to return to their claustrophobic, all-too-narrow living quarters in high rise apartments, where they would have to merge in crammed and cramped with dead-tired parents, brothers and sisters – as well as some assorted aunts and grandfathers. Exactly the same as the Lok twins' home environment had been for that departed duo.

Yet this particular time there was a couple who stood out a little from the norm. Over by the rather stooped looking 7/11, were his ex-wife and her obvious current new boyfriend, who was quite tanned looking and tall and both of whom Woo had seen nearby a few times over the past week already. They were walking rather languidly, hand-in-hand, believe it or not, as if they had only just met up on a date, while the male was jabbering away somewhat animatedly about something.

Woo watched for a while from the high front seat of his repaired van, himself a little worn out by the events of the strenuous last couple of days and the frenetic sights that he had encountered during this time. Something came into the corner of his field of vision right then and he slowly turned to see another, very white *gweilo,* dressed in a dark top and trousers and hiding his stark white hair under a dark cap. He was seemingly pointing something at the darker-skinned man parading with his ex-wife.

Peering closer, Woo made out an outline of a really long gun, and what he immediately gleaned then was that this guy with the orange beard and sunglasses, perched on his forehead like a pigeon, was about to fire the weapon at Ruby and her man.

Without any conscious awareness, Woo found himself steering the still throbbing van straight at the hired killer, Johnny Tramadol, who looked up in chronic alarm as the old lumbering vehicle lurched all too swiftly at him in heavy menace. While on the rear vision mirror, the hanging row of prayer bells rattled more rapidly across Woo's synapses, the faster he drove.

106/2.

Norton and Ruby had no idea that Ruby's ex-husband, the vagabond Woo, was going to become instantaneously authentic, an accolade no one would ever have plastered him with, given his life up until right then. But authentic he was about to become, as he drove the van right at Tramadol, pinning the American mercenary fairly directly to the hard concrete back wall of an unsuspecting Jockey Club and maintaining him there, like the rare specimen he was.

Tramadol didn't, 'need this shit,' as his forebrain was drumming through to him, so he fired at the windscreen of the behemoth van, which was now slowly sucking the life from him. Godfrey Woo took a direct hit in the chest and, while slumping over his steering wheel, his foot trod more firmly on the accelerator, and his brain and heart ceased functioning altogether. Just as Tramadol was squashed quite flat and lifeless, like an awesome example of an extinct beetle, at the recent Hong Kong Convention Centre exhibit of nasty creatures.

It was only then that Norton shut up, when the crashing sounds vibrated through to them and both he and Ruby looked across the quadrangle and tried to discern exactly what had happened. However, in the dying light and with the strong throng of twisted heads and necks between them, they really could not work out exactly what had just occurred over there. So, soon enough Norton was shrugging and finishing his news about how he would get into Laos with the Malaysian passport he had earlier bought in a back street boudoir in Manila and sent to Laos, now replete with a Laotian visa all ready. The latter of which his old war buddy Les Wereta had supplied and sent to him: probably from Wereta's own very shady dealings on the Deep Web.

It seemed Norton had arranged a passport-less flight from Hong Kong, on a shady cargo plane service to Viet Nam, as extra cargo. And that once landed in his old former haunt of Ho Chi Minh City, then he would be picked up and transported directly to the Laotian border. Norton was quite excited by all of this cleverness, mostly done on his behalf, and was slightly annoyed by his Filipina girlfriend's steadfast refusal to join him, even, as he pushed her, "to come later, if you want to…"

As they heard the sirens wailing closer and closer to them, Norton clutched the day's version of the *South China Morning Post* firmly under his arm and – launching themselves back toward Tin Yan Estate – tried yet again to convince Ruby of the benefits of leaving Hong Kong.

It was all a waste of time however, as her mind was set on staying there – for a while. Besides, Ruby was sufficiently self-sufficient not to need any man right now – and perhaps for a considerable period of time into the future…

"No," she said firmly.

"And," she reflected quietly, "I'm 53 years old soon. I'll take care of myself from now on."

107/2.

As abruptly as their short story had started and just as amicably, it was about all over too.

Norton wanted to get out of Hong Kong as soon as he could. He didn't know that he had nearly been assassinated only a day earlier and he hadn't really minded the general ambience of the place – not that they had ventured much beyond Tin Shui Wai and only once to nearby Yuen Long town. He did sense however that his time there was running out and that there were likely all sorts of weird agencies very saucily on his tail. Call it a gut reaction spreading exponentially from the news about him, which he had searched for and gleaned openly on the web.

No; it was more because he wanted open spaces and greenery and more familiar terrain to roam. Somewhere he had been before and liked, albeit many years ago. With people he felt more comfortable around too. He very much wanted Ruby to come with him. Indeed he expected that she would accompany him, so he was pretty pissed off when she gave him an outright no. This was something that he hadn't really considered at all, actually. Sexism seemed as much a part of his DNA as any other man.

Still, he had been on his own for considerable periods plenty of times before in his rather circuitous non-linear pastiche of a life, and he knew he could and would cope.

"Are you sure you won't come with me – maybe a few weeks later, Ruby?" He called her by name, which was unusual for him, but here seemed to make his invitation more formal and by association more effective. He waited for her to react to this latest entreaty.

"No," was again about all she mustered in response. Followed about a minute later by, "It is not safe there and I don't know anyone there and I reckon they would soon see me there and send me back home, wherever that is right now."

Ruby knew that her being a Filipino, a pretty Filipina in particular, was tantamount.

to being hassled and harangued about visas and paperwork wherever she went. Which is why she felt secure as a Hong Kong permanent resident (although she had not felt as secure before she received this preferred status) and as a Philippine passport holder. She just wasn't going to chance going somewhere with a man she probably loved, to a place she knew only as primitive, away from her own families. No way.

Ruby was concerned enough to add – again after another minute.

"Will you be O.K in Laos, though? Doesn't seem such a great country to go to, although I guess no one much will be after you there... for a while, anyway..."

It was Norton's turn to be mute.

Someone had just come to the door and was speaking in typical machine gun Cantonese to Po Lam, who came away from the encounter in something resembling full-on shock. She spilled out the gist of the door encounter to her mother, who later – much later – translated it back to Norton.

Right then wasn't the most suitable time to speak about what was the death only yesterday of a man who may well have been her ex-husband and Po Lam's father, Godfrey Woo – for the caller had not been 100% certain.

"What was that all about? "asked Norton, none the wiser.

Ruby spluttered that she would tell him later and made eyes in the direction of Po Lam.

"Well, anyway, I'm supposed to be going to the cargo depot tomorrow afternoon," was just about all there was left to say: so Norton spluttered that message right back.

The only one who made much of any noise at the late evening dinner, was a happier Isaac Wong, because he had been told by his wife Po Lam that one of the.

visitors was going to depart the tiny flat as early as the next morning.
Norton later reflected, that it had been the sole occasion when he had seen
anything like a smile on Isaac Wong's usually stoic face.

Alone on the living room floor mattress later that night, Ruby asked her beau once
again if he would be O.K and how he would survive. What would he do to ensure
he had an easier existence than he had recently over-experienced?

It was Norton's own turn to smile – not that anyone could see it in the dank dark of
the apartment. Right then and there, he stated, "I'll just have to keep away from
fucking nutters." This was about all he could muster.

108/2

The next morning, Ruby and Norton made love for the last time. Norton may not have known it, but Ruby sure did.

They got up, showered and after a paltry breakfast at the nearest McDonalds, where they had to wait in a monstrous line for far too long, they boarded first the light rail and then the *zappy* West Rail to Tsim Sha Tsui, where Norton was to meet another crony of Les Wereta - one Lance Rehu. Who was a priest of long-standing at the Catholic parish there. He was to escort Norton safely to his cargo plane transport away from the SAR and – hopefully – onwards to Laos.

They embraced for a long time and Norton kissed Ruby full on the lips, until she broke away saying, "You had better go. Father Rehu is waiting."

Rehu was rather impatient, as he had a funeral to run at 11 am, so he made his feelings known by tapping his fingers against the flash billboard advertising lingerie, in a less-crowded back street. A location where it had been decided for them to meet up, "just in case someone sees you in Nathan Road," as Ruby had put it. Which was why they had chosen the most obscure MTR exit available.

Ruby didn't cry, but would later reflect that she could see Norton was blinking back his own tears.

For her, Norton was all on his own now. She had quite an agenda of things to do. She and her children would go to the quiet ceremony for Woo the next day. Her neighbours, on seeing her around Tin Yan again, had confirmed that it was indeed he, after one of their policeman sons had mentioned it to them. The police had had to scan the dead man's fingerprints to certify his identity. Ruby felt that it was the least she could do, even if he had turned out to be a real waste of time. He was, after all, the father of Jeremy Ka Lun and Po Lam.

She had also never told Norton that Dr. Cross had been emailing her again in the last few days and wanted to meet up with her in Saipan, where he reckoned he was on a 'special mission'. He had apologized about his lack of contact, because of so-called business reasons, which Ruby felt was a pile of shit, as well as being fairly typical of that individual. She wondered why he had really taken so long to contact her: Ruby did not know that Cross had initially left Philippines for Hong Kong, until much later, and couldn't fathom why he had not even let her know about that. She also wondered why he never questioned what she was doing in Hong Kong SAR now herself.

Still, she had never been to Saipan and it also meant she would be well on her way to Guam at his expense, for he had promised to pay return tickets to and from Hong Kong for her.

And one other thing she kept tight to herself was the further news from cousin Grace online. Grace was certain that it had been this Doctor, in fact, who had murdered Euris, quite some time beforehand now. For not only had Cross been in Manila during the occasion of Euris' disappearance – a fact further vouched for by one or two Pampanga residents who had seen him there – but he was also known to have been in the vicinity of the death, by others. Since Grace had joined in with the supposed insurgents protesting with their vast vista of grievances, some of them had confided in her that they knew a few specially trained Americans had been working in Manila for some time - and that Cross was one of them.

Interestingly enough, only yesterday her cousin, Ivy, had once more asked why the coffin had been so firmly sealed? "Did anyone of us actually see Euris inside?" she pestered Ruby, who had no answers.

Ruby went home to sleep in the afternoon. There was too much on her mind and she needed to sort out how to deal with it all.

This time, no dreams introduced themselves to her, as she scrolled the rosary beads linked around her wrist and sunk into sleep.

Dear Ruby.

I really am missing you.

But, you know that I really did have to get away from Hong Kong and everyone trying to find me there. And just about everywhere else actually!

Over here in Laos, I feel a bit safer: no one knows anything about me and Les has found me a job. I'm also pretending to be someone else.

It is more peaceful and there are not too many signs of revolution here, although I do know there have been several major protests in Vientiane against both Chinese and American interests in this country. I reckon all these protests around the world will continue to grow, but I also know just how determined America – and its allies, whoever they are – will not back down. I see this going on for a long time in Philippines, New Zealand – everywhere. In my tongue, this is *he whawhai tonu mātou.* Our struggle without end.

It is best for me to merge and then emerge again one day. So - I am just going to stay well hidden in these back jungles, blowing up trees and rocks for the railway north – and yes, I do see the irony here. China is behind the railroad expansion and we come across unexploded American ordnance every so often too. It's a nutty world, eh.

When will I come to see you again? I do not know. Could be a long time. I know that right now, you don't want to come here, but I live in hope…

Take care and please do keep in touch when you can. And I do love you. *Mahal kita* – like you taught me.

Mac Norton.

He never sent it.

109/7

Dr. Cross was glad that he would be departing Okinawa tomorrow. The protests against American military bases there had grown bigger and noisier and more aggressive, even in the relatively brief time he had been sent to reconnoiter and liaise.

The fact that he had a pronounced drawl, which instantly identified him as an American citizen, didn't help him either, because he was subjected to quite a bit of abuse in Nada, when he was downtown looking for some sleazy bar to roost in.

He was also happy, because Ruby had said she would meet up with him in Saipan on vacation for a few days and he was pretty sure he could connive to patch up their relationship via gifts and money.

Then again, Cross never really had been able to understand women of any ethnicity. Which was one good reason why his Chinese wife had left him years beforehand.

He spent his final afternoon in Okinawa, drinking with some fresh-faced recruits newly-arrived from mainland Stateside, who told him all about their curfews. As imposed on the American forces after their many years of inappropriate behaviour toward local women on the island.

Cross didn't blink an eye and shook his head in sympathy with these kids. He couldn't see the logic of any curfew, because he was defiantly old school in attitude when it came to behaving towards women.

A bit of a dinosaur really.

Not yet extinct, though.

110/6

Stepping off the aeroplane into the palpitating heatwave, Ruby wondered if she had made the correct decision to come to Saipan.

She didn't really want to see Cross, but she did want to eradicate him from her life once and for all, rather badly. This would be a chance to do so.

Yes, it seemed pretty likely that he had been involved in the killing of her niece Euris, and probably other young Filipino, so-called agitators. But there was more. He had let her down far too many times, admittedly after being good fun and a decent provider earlier on. "But weren't they all?" she mused to herself out loud, as she crossed the tarmac into Immigration and beyond.

After showing her easily-obtained American visa - which she had organised earlier when she made her decision to go to Guam - she went through to the Arrival arena; only to see no sign whatsoever of Cross.

Her sour mood turned downright nasty, a stage she rarely ever entered. She waited, tapping her feet in annoyance and frustration, noticing some of the other passengers noticing her. Maybe fifteen minutes passed, only adding to her anger.

"Excuse, me, Mam, are you Ms. Ruby?" came a voice, seemingly from nowhere.

Ruby turned right around to see a slim young Filipina, with a large smile. At least Ruby took her to be a Filipina.

"Yes," she answered, cooling down a little at the same time.

"Hi. I am Delia. Dr. Cross asked me to meet up with you and take you to the hotel."

"Where is he?" asked Ruby, still not completely calm.

"He is busy working and sends his apologies. He said to give you this," as Delia proffered a small package, wrapped in brown paper.

Delia grabbed Ruby's solitary suitcase and escorted her to the carpark, where a sultry limousine waited for them.

"Have you been to Saipan before, Mam?" asked the younger woman.

"No, this is the first time," replied Ruby, letting escape a wisp of a smile.

They chatted a little on the short journey up the west coast of Saipan, in the car with driver included, to the hotel room that Cross had booked. Seemed Delia was a student at the Northern Marianas College. How she had ever encountered Cross, Ruby just did not want to ask, even although the young woman somehow reminded her of him.

The room was quite pleasant inside and outside, for, after overlooking a large blue-water swimming pool, it revealed a fine shady beach, replete with a few Japanese and/or Chinese tourists. Ruby was relieved to see that there was no double bed there and that in fact there was a smaller enclave bedroom separate from the main room. That's where she placed her luggage.

"Would you like me to take you around Saipan a bit, Mam? It is not a big island..."

"How long will Dr. Cross be? Did he say?"

Delia frowned. "I think he will be several hours."

"Let's get a drink first. And something to eat. That airline was miserly with their food."

The two went down to the restaurant.

Ruby wondered why her young acquaintance did not speak a word of Tagalog, but didn't want to raise the issue. Her thoughts were first and foremost on eating and drinking; then about that useless Cross man. Where was he?

She had remembered the package and had quickly opened it in the hotel room.

Another gold bracelet. She sighed inwardly and reminded herself to give this one to someone in the family who could sell it somewhere. Just like most of the other gifts that he had bestowed her.

After their lunch – for it was about midday – Delia again suggested she have the driver take Ruby around the island for a tour. "It is only a small place, after all – and you might like to see the sights here?"

Ruby shrugged. "Why not. But, let's do that later on – after I have a swim." Ruby loved the blessed waves, the blissful beaches of Philippines - and the beaches there in Saipan looked just as inviting.

So, she went for a relaxed bathe, given that the tide was out and the beach populated by only a sprinkle of fellow Asian swimmers, most of who appeared to be sleeping under the coruscating sun.

Delia and the driver, meanwhile, had had to depart to a class. "We will come back and pick you up at 3.00 o'clock," were the youngster's words directed at Ruby's back, when Ruby trod quite firmly down to the sand, answering the statement with a wave.

Under the water, Ruby found some semblance of freedom to think clearly, unhindered by others. As she careened to the sand under the warm, gentle swell, holding her breath for as long as she could without feeling uncomfortable, she reflected on Woo's sparse funeral and on her own kids during the last week she had stayed there with them in Tin Shui Wai. Fleetingly, she touched on what Norton might now be doing.

On coming up for air, those thoughts settled and filed away in her tidy mind as finished with, she took another long breath and dove back down. The warmth of the ocean was wonderful; a caress, a balm. But her attention was on something tempestuous, annoying, unsettling – Cross.

Ruby had resolved to dispose of the doctor as stealthily as she could, but only after extracting some money off him first. She had no qualms whatsoever about this. The man was likely an assassin. The man was rich. The man was an African American agent. The man was humbug. She felt used. She was so over being treated as disposable by men. Filipino men. White men. Mixed race men. Mixed up men.

She resolved to find the soonest and most expedient and most unassuming way to get rid of him, as she could. It would have to be quick and to not cast her as in any way involved. "Difficult," she agreed with herself, just as she ran out of air. "But there must be something I can do to avenge Euris, to support Grace and Rustico and Ivy."

She didn't want to admit it, but the way Norton talked about killing that *putih* in the market in Pampanga, had been so nonchalant; that he had made it all sound like an necessary everyday event. The Māori man's mien had rubbed off on her.

When Ruby strolled back onto the beach, she was somewhat surprised to see no other tourist swimmers around. Odd, because it was still hot: a pleasant afternoon to loll, swim, sunbathe.

Back in her hotel room, under the always-on aircon, she showered, dressed and waited. It was only when she was looking down at the beach and the pool from her second-floor balcony, she saw the uniformed men herding some people towards what looked like tourist buses.

Just then the telephone rang and the receptionist announced that Ms. Delia was downstairs.

Ruby went down on the elevator to find Delia was about the only non-staff member in the spacious vestibule.

"Where is everyone?" enquired Ruby.

From Delia's somewhat vague explanation, Ruby gleaned that most tourists had been escorted away from the hotel zone around Garapan, because of the fear of further riots. It appeared that the Marianas had also not been spared some recent quite savage protests against impending and further American military presence there and the theory was that tourists would be safer elsewhere. Especially since it seemed these hotels housed American soldiers too, as a sort of luxury barracks.

None of which made much sense to Ruby, especially as she had not been consulted or informed about any of this. Mind you, she had not been in any organized tour party either, so perhaps that was why. She couldn't be bothered to ask where the tourists were now; it all was giving her a migraine, something that she rarely encountered.

She blamed Cross and cursed him again.

The driver slowly cruised past the obligatory and somewhat faded shopping plaza, the golf course, the numerous high-rise hotels lining the sand. There wasn't much traffic around and it was the obligatory hot, despite full-force air conditioning in the car. Delia was raving on about, "some recent protests, so tourists were happier to stay for a while at the convention centre," which made increasingly less sense, if Ruby could be bothered to even ponder this. She was more interested in the drive north into a far more rural and very verdant area and then to sight what seemed like several tombs, shrines or something similar, solemnly lining a lengthy cliff face.

The two women got out of the vehicle while Lando, the Filipino driver of the car, remained seated inside.

A little further over, there appeared to be something like a police or army cordoned-off area. Ruby was aware of armed men standing guard around a roped-off zone. Some of the men were looking in their direction.

"So, where are we?" was her immediate question, although she felt like asking, 'Why the hell are we here?'

"Punta Sabaneta," said Delia evenly. "It's called Banzai Cliff. Thousands of Japanese jumped off here in 1944, because they didn't want to be captured by the Americans…"

"So that's why all these shrines are here. I see."

They strolled a little closer to the cliff face. It was a long way down and the waves seemed savage in intent: breaker mayhem. Down at the base, on what appeared to be rocks, Ruby could swear she saw a rubber boat and more military types, very intent on something only they could see. She drew back a little, as the sheer precipice was menacing.

A stern voice captured them. They turned to see an American officer eyeing them up and down. "Excuse me ladies, but I think it best if you leave this area, please. There has been an incident and we suggest you go back home."

He didn't seem the type to argue with at all. But Delia was naïve. "What happened, sir?" she asked.

The best they could get was that someone had fallen off the cliff and that, "security were investigating, so, please leave."

Saipan was one very odd place. The ambience there had suddenly become sinister. Ruby wanted out. Right away.

"I think it best that I leave, please," she put it to her hostess as they clambered back into the car and as Lando steered them around the rest of the island, past several seemingly military installations. And definitely with airfields reclining amongst the trees.

"O.K. We will take you back to the hotel."

"No. I mean, take me to the airport after I gather my things, please. I cannot wait for Dr. Cross any longer - and besides I have to go on to Guam to see family. I had already arranged this, before the Doctor contacted me."

Delia said nothing. Only looked surprised. She had been trying to ring Cross all afternoon, only to receive nothing but a voicemail message. She could not nag this Filipina woman to wait when she did not have any idea where he was.

Delia instructed Lando to take Ms. Ruby to the airline office to arrange her onward flight - which she intended to finance by cashing in her Hong Kong return ticket - and then to take Ms. Ruby back to the hotel to gather her belongings. All in preparation for the 10.00 pm flight to Agana, Guam.

Delia did not accompany Ruby after being dropped off in Garapan herself, after the flight was confirmed.

"Salamat po," said Ruby to her.

As she got out of the vehicle, Delia turned, with a frown. "Sorry, Mam," she stated matter-of-factly, her manner by now decidedly cool, "I do not speak your language. I am not from Philippines. In fact, my mother was Chinese."

And with that abrupt goodbye, she went into a set of apartments and Lando drove a relieved Ruby away.

It would be good to get away from here, she sighed. The sooner the better.

"Too many fucking nutters," as Norton would have put it perfectly.

111/6

Dr Cross had followed Da Zei's instructions to the letter. The translation, as given to him by his internet-savvy encryption team, via his cellphone was, something like this:

Namely: GO TO BANZAI CLIFF AND WAIT FOR ME. WE CAN NEGOTIATE MORE.

Of course, he was not going to go there alone. He had attempted to enlist Walter Wyshnowski to come along too, given that the latter wasn't actually on Saipan at that time. Wyshnowski knew better, especially after the earlier embarrassing incarceration of Cross in China.

American secret service protocols when dealing with potential suspect allies, were fraught with ambiguity, secrecy, danger at the best of times. This rendezvous would be no different; no less absurd; something similar to an encounter from a Le Carre espionage thriller, in fact. Even although it was now well into the 21st century. All par for the course for Cross and his perambulations throughout Asia.

The staff car had taken him and an offsider to the cliff, where they parked beside the largest shrine and waited for the Chinese delegation to arrive. All of them would pose as tourists.

Quite what Dr Cross expected from the very same man who earlier had him conveyed so swiftly to Xi'an remains unclear, primarily because no Chinamen were sighted within the next 15 minutes, at this rather remote spot in northern Saipan.

And Cross himself never came back from his excursion north. His offsider, in fact, was yet another in the rather long line of assassins provided by the reputedly clandestine U.S. security service. She pushed Cross over the edge of Banzai Cliff, after first ensuring no one was around and that Cross was no longer conscious, by whacking him across the skull with a tyre iron.

The Americans – well, at least some portion of a segment of them – had wanted Cross out of the way. He had, it would seem, become a liability. Was no longer a secure operative. Whatever that meant.

Of course no one informed his daughter, Delia, of his demise, his tragic accident. Or ever told the security forces in charge of military bases in Micronesia. And none of these deep undercover agents even knew Ruby had ever encountered him.

Everything was expendable in and for America.

And in their many domains.

112/3

Mrs. Tuazon rarely went to the huge white church on the corner anymore. It was not that she had ceased believing, but more because she was becoming increasingly tired and frail, even if the place of worship was just down the street.

This afternoon, however, she had made a special effort to call out for a tricycle to take her there again. She had a profound sense that she had to pray for her own family and to take the Eucharist offered to her by the sole old priest, dressed in his white vestments and the serious spectacles framing his wrinkled face.

As soon as she slowly walked inside it was another world. The choir was in full force singing to Jesus – their voices a miracle of harmony. The young children were resplendent in their pristine ironed white smocks and the candles already lit and fluttering on the altar like angels' wings under the massive crucifix mounted at the front, as the voices ascended ever higher. The many bunches of multicoloured flowers added more to the vibrancy of it all and Mrs. Tuazon immediately felt better, especially as one of the church elders, whom she had known for years, smiled at her and escorted her to a seat under the lectern.

She glanced upwards just then as the brilliant sunlight refracted itself through the kaleidoscopic stained glass panels high on the wall above her and she prayed for her daughters, her entire family, for the whole wide world, as the choir sang on proudly in rapture at it all.

"*Salamat panginoon sa pagbabantay mo sa aking mga anak, lalung-lalu na si Ruby nitong maa nakaraang buwan. Ipinagdarasal ko rin ang kaluluwa ni Euris makapahinganawa ng mapaya pa sa iyong mapagmahal na bisig.*"

["Thank you Lord, for looking after my children, especially Ruby these past few months. I also pray for the soul of Euris; may she rest in peace in your loving arms."]

Later, as she strolled outside into the sultry Sunday heat, she received a greeting from one of the younger fathers, who had arrived tardily during her prayers. He greeted her with, "*Magandang hapon Apu. Kumusta po ngayon araw?*'

She smiled even more and replied, *"Mabuti father, mabuti po,"* as she kissed his hand and he blessed her. *"Mano po,* father."

On days like this Acquilina Tuazon forgot any bad things and forgave everyone. She felt a warm surge of serene happiness well through her, as the tricycle pedalled by Romeo returned her to J. Pinitella in peace.

Prologue: Laos

Out back – way out back – of Luang Prabang – Norton was laughing his head off, or more appropriately he was laughing off his head, because the smoking dope there, 'was pretty damned strong stuff, eh,' as his frequent scouting and supply companion James Monaghan was murmuring contentedly from the other side of the canvas cabin. They shared this space with a couple of other New Zealand troops, who were never going to be affirmed as serving in Laos by their very own government.

Outside, Les Wereta was scoring a tribal tattoo – not from another member of his own tribe – but from an Hmoung hill man, who was steadily digging away at Wereta's upper arm. Wereta was eyes-glazed and grinning dopily and not merely because the early afternoon sun was so unbearably hot, but because there was no anesthetic up there, beyond the heavy duty stuff they were puffing their brains out on.

They hadn't actually done too much in the short months they had been assigned to act as relief and supply relievers for an undercover American troupe of always whispering, shade-wearing troops, who weren't inclined to share much of anything with these wild-looking New Zealanders. Who were not supposed to even be there anyway. Especially since the nearby real war was officially over.

Lassitude had set in and other than making rudimentary patrols every early morning and evening, these half dozen Kiwis basically sat back, ate spicy local food, drank, played cards and continued to smoke their combined brains out. Vietnam seemed a million miles away, although of course it was," just over there somewhere, maaan," as Monaghan also muttered all too frequently.

All too easy for a gaggle of Māori and a lone Pākehā, who had nowhere much else to go after leaving school all too early, except to prison or into the army. Well most of the Māori anyway - as Norton had stayed studying beyond his peers. Given that he soon forgot much of that stuff anyway.

Which is why they were all there and why Norton was ostensibly their highest-ranking officer, after Monaghan. Except that he knew sweet fuck all as to why they had furtively been placed outside of Luang Prabang, with a plethora of rockets, mortars, grenades and rapid fire semi-automatic weaponry – as well as the latest in radio-telephone technology. And the supply helicopter – like the Americans – only came by at staccato intervals too. Which only added to their gradual dawn of apathy, fuelled by the best smoking dope ever. It was better here than anywhere. Sure as hell beat their trepidatious few months back in Viet Nam.

Their next day started as any other, clichéd, hackneyed, banal.

Norton and his different *iwi* comrades in arms, having been transported to this non-battlefront, kilometres from any active war ground, were loitering about the strewn camp of canvas cabins, after having made their increasingly rudimentary patrol of the perimeter, as dawn had bred itself upon the day. As per usual nothing untoward had occurred and no Viet Cong had been sighted, nor any allies encountered. Indeed all they had noted that particular morning was a herd of wild and wild looking water buffalo, which stared them out morosely as they passed by. No villagers, because they were a way away from even a hint of a village, and with no helicopters sidewinding above them as yet either.

Norton, for one, was devilishly bored and reduced to trying to remember the six months he had spent studying literature at the University of Auckland, a couple of years before he had volunteered somewhat lethargically to serve in the New Zealand armed forces. As he lay back on the creaking air mattress in the sweltering early morning furnace, all that really came to mind was something about the structure of the 'English novel' – rising action, falling action, denouement; protagonists and antagonists; theme, plot, setting, style and something else that his weary mind couldn't recall.

Norton spat as much in irritation as anything and laughed to himself. Any novel he was in right there in the boondocks of Laos wasn't written to any prescribed and proscribed English format at all. That was all bullshit. Lineal progression and climax were severe misnomers in relation to his own personal circumstances, as far he was concerned. And as for any fictive message: it escaped him.

Just then a steady rummage of helicopter blades made itself heard above the regnant waves of silence. Norton opened his eyes and snatched a glimpse out of the wide-open flaps of his tent house. A couple of the other guys were slowly plodding towards the door of the chopper, where another couple in reasonably respectable uniforms was awaiting them.

Norton stood up, stretched and went out to see this interruption to the usual general nothingness of the last few months.

A dark lieutenant was saying something to Wereta and handing him a sheaf of paperwork; which Norton later read as orders for them to get ready to move out and move on. The guy had a funny accent as compared to his usual Americano buddies, which Norton later decided might relate to his name as signed on the bottom of the final sheet: Napoles Castillo Santos. Which Monaghan confirmed as being a Filipino name, "because I asked him where he was from originally, eh."

Norton's final thought about what all the visit meant was that he – like the Filipino officer, and like most of his tent mates – was on a sort of weird reverse migration. Back from Oceania, through the Philippines – where he had been on a fairly recent R 'n' R in Manila and Subic in particular – and into the heartland of South East Asia, backtracking on bloodlines, language and thousands of years of migration.

That was the last time he had any chance of reflecting on anything much, for his leisure time after that particular day was overrun by several returns to the real jungle, in attempts to snare any ally stragglers for survival.

What then ensued not too long after, for all of them, was their *hokinga ki te kainga* or return to the homeland, with its concomitant bifurcations and trifurcations into marriages, kids, so-called career path freefalls and pitfalls. And the million complications these ensured and they all endured, for the next thirty or so years. Norton ultimately went from infantryman to mutton butcher and could no longer sense the difference, let alone articulate it. A sort of febrile numbness soon set in and he became passive, played upon, reflexive. Any reasonably intelligent thoughts he might have had in later years, became as rare as his having an easy day.

Which is where Trevor King first slunk into the frame.

And much later, into Norton's locker, busting it open with his steel...

Stage One - The English Novel

There are several factors which will ensure an author has written a successful – that is money making – novel. Following these simple suggestions will place them well on the road to Hollywood. Because a good novel should automatically lead to a film version made there.

A successful novel must –
1. Have a storyline that is believable and not full of coincidences and lucky breaks that will turn readers into disbelievers. Therefore, the plotlines should be clear and follow through a sequence of introduction, development, contrasts, climax and denouement.
2. Similarly, characters should be differentiated, so that a reader can at least identify with some of them.
3. Dialogue is vital and maintains forward momentum. Long sections of boring and/or repetitive material are a definite no. Readers are generally not buffoons and should be able to sort out things for themselves if a novel gives them ample clues, without being an information dump.
4. An author should not try to be too clever with aspects of so-called postmodernist tricks; flashbacks, disordered time sequences and so on. Vocabulary needs to be simple too.
5. If an author must introduce more languages into the mix, other than the dominant English tongue, the author must at least grant the readers a glossary.
6. There should not be too much depiction of sexual activity or display of bodily functions. There is no space in modern fiction for another Tobias Smollet.
7. Cliche and strained and/or elaborate and flowery expressions and phrases are also a major no no.
8. Finally, and importantly, there should remain no loose ends in a plotline. Readers want a tidy ending and expect everything to be neatly resolved.

GLOSSARY:

Word or Phrase	Translation	Original Language
e hoa	friend	Māori
he matakite	a seer/prophet	
he poaka momona, nē rā.	a fat pig, eh	
he tangata ngaro	a lost people	

he utu reka, nē rā.	sweet revenge, eh	
he whawhai tonu mātou	our struggle without end	
hokinga ki te kāinga	return home	
hōhā	hassle/nuisance/bother	
hongi	rubbing of noses/greeting	
hui	meeting/gathering	
hūpē	snot	
iwi	people/tribe(s)	
kai	food	
karakia	prayer	
kia ora	be well/hello [greeting]	
kihi	kiss	
kina	sea urchin	
kōrero	talk, speak	
kuia	older women	
mahi āpōpō	work tomorrow	
manawa	heart	
moko	tattoo	
mokopuna	grandchildren	
Ngā Wahine Toa	the women warriors	
ngutu	beak-like	
Pākehā	Caucasian/European	
Piripaina	Philippines	
tāngata whenua	indigenous	
tangi	funeral	
te reo	the language	
tika	true	
tino rangatiratanga	self-determination/independence	
toa	warrior	
tūrangawaewae	place of origin	
urupā	burial ground/cemetery	
utu	recompense/revenge	
wahine	woman/women	
whānau	family	
whāngai	adopted	
whare	house	
whare moe	sleeping quarters	
whiti	poem	
adobo	Philippine dish	Tagalog
asuwang	Philippine monster	
ate	aunt/older woman	

babae maganda	beautiful woman	
bading	queer/gay	
barangay	district	
basura	rubbish	
bifstek	Philippine dish	
bola bola	bullshit	
caldereta	Philippine dish	
chika chika	gossip	
Eat Bulaga	popular GMA TV show	
halo halo	Philippine dessert	
hindi ko alam	I don't know	
hindi kona problema iyan	not our problem	
jeepney(s)	bus-like form of transport	
kaibigan	friend	
kailan balik	when [will you] return	
lelaki	man/boy	
longanisa	type of sausage	
maganda hapon apu. kumusta po ngayon araw?	good afternoon mother. How are you today?	
mahal kita	I love you	
mano po	bless me	
masarap	delicious	
menudo	Philippine dish	
mestizo	mixed ethnicity	
mimi	piss	
minum	drink	
palagi	always	
panaginip	dream	
peso	Philippine currency	
putih	Caucasian/European	
pulis	police	
salamat po	thank you	
sari sari	small store	
sinigang	Philippine dish	
sino	who	
tambay	standby i.e. not working	
tsokolate	chocolate (coloured)	
walang problema	no problem(s)	
walang swerte	no luck	
cha chaan teng	cheap restaurant	Cantonese
dai pai dong	open-air food stall	
gaylo	gay/queer	
ging chat	police	
gweilo	Caucasian/European	

ho ma fan	troublesome	
ho nan	difficulty/problem	
ho mei	delicious	
lei hoi igar	you go now	
leng loi	beautiful girl	
ngo ng zi	don't know	
pak choi	Chinese cabbage	
pak fan	cooked rice	
tong ling cha	ice lemon tea	
t'iu lei gweilo	fuck you white man	
erhu	stringed instrument	Mandarin
jing cha	police	
peng-you	friend	
ta ma de	fucking!	
wo bu zhidao	I don't know	
yuan	Chinese currency	

About the author.

Vaughan Rapatahana is widely published internationally across several genre and in more than one language. He won the inaugural Proverse Poetry prize in 2016. *Novel,* is his second novel. His New Zealand Book Council Writers File can be accessed here - http://www.bookcouncil.org.nz/writer/rapatahana-vaughan/

An earlier version of *Novel* was long listed for the inaugural Michael Gifkins Prize.

9 780099 510466 2